Stardogs-Book 2
Redemption

by
Herbert Grosshans

Published by
Melange Books, LLC
White Bear Lake, MN 55110
www.melange-books.com

Stardogs-book 2, *Copyright © 2008, 2011* Herbert Grosshans
ISBN 978-1-61235-020-2

Credits

Editor: Taylor Evans
Copy Editor: Mae Powers
Format Editors: Mae Powers
Cover Layout: A Bratt

Stardogs-Book 2
Redemption
by
Herbert Grosshans

On the trail of slave traders Major Dan Griffin travels to Isram to rescue his aid and lover Meadow and to investigate rumors of a looming Holy War. He finds himself on a sexual journey and discovers a menace that could destroy a whole planet.

Stardogs-Book 2
Redemption
by
Herbert Grosshans

Herbert Grosshans lives in Winnipeg, Canada. If he's not busy with some other project, he writes stories. He loves creating new worlds on alien planets; that's why most of his stories are either Fantasy or Science Fiction. For him, writing a story is like reading a new book. He doesn't always know where the characters will lead him and what kind of adventures are waiting. Sometimes they go their own way, and the story doesn't end as planned. That's what happened with 'Stardogs,' which he wrote a few years ago. He left it sitting for a while and then re-wrote most of the story. Did it turn out the way it was planned? Yes and no. The characters will always try to go somewhere else. That is the excitement and pleasure of writing. He hopes you'll enjoy the book you're holding in your hands and want to come back for more.

You can visit Herbert at his blog
http://www.hegro.blogspot.com

The Xandra Trilogy
Seeds of Chaos Book 1 Eden's Gate
Seeds Of Chaos Book 2 Hell's Gate

Plus you'll find Herbert in numerous short story digest compilations.

Stardogs-Book 2
Redemption
by
Herbert Grosshans

Prologue

My name is Dan Griffin. I was born on Redsky, or Chantra, as the native population calls this planet. My home until ten years ago, when I was falsely accused of my brother-in-law's murder and sentenced to spend the rest of my life on the prison planets of the Terran Empire.

After spending five years on the most hostile planets in existence, my innocence was established, and the scientists of the Empire turned me into a super-soldier.

When the government of Redsky complained about problems with the indigenous population and imminent war with Isram, an independent country on Redsky, they sent me and four other soldiers to investigate.

Killic, big and bulky, his blue eyes as cold as a mountain lake.

Cherryh, tall, wide-shouldered, dark-skinned and good-looking.

Kelsey was short and stocky but as strong and fast as a desert-dragon.

Wu, one hundred centimeters tall, stocky, nearly fat with a round, smiling face. Harmless in appearance, until one looked into his cold black, slanted eyes.

Those men had joined me on this mission. Men I could trust with my life. They all had undergone the same treatment as I.

Lieutenant Meadow Rainseeker, my aide and lover, also accompanied me on this mission. Meadow, incidentally, is not human but a beautiful alien woman. Beautiful and deadly. She is also an Empath, which means she can read emotions as easily as others understand spoken words.

Solving the problems on Redsky was not the only thing on my agenda. I was determined to find the people responsible for taking away ten years of my life and bring them to justice.

The first thing I discovered was the fact that my wife, Lane, was married to another man. A man I hated. A man named Castor Margin, the mayor of Old Town, and a good friend of the Prime Minister, Sir Charles DePratt.

I met with the Prime Minister in Capital City where I confronted some of the people who sent me to prison. I found out I was not a welcome guest, but Lady Evana, the Prime Minister's wife, welcomed me with open arms and took me into her bedroom.

On the way back to Old Town, an attempt was made on my life, but Meadow and I managed to overcome the assassins and took the only survivor to the police station in Old Town, hoping to find out who was behind the assassination. However, Chief Slovinsky, another *old friend* of mine, set the man free.

It wasn't hard to see that nobody was happy about my presence back on Redsky and about what I might discover during my investigation. Inspector McClaren of Spaceport Security tried to intimidate me and asked me to close an eye and not look too closely if his name should pop up. A favor from one professional to another, as he called it.

I was not intimidated. I knew the man was deep into something and feared discovery. I didn't trust him, and neither did I trust his partner Sergeant Marc Cleaver. Something about that man didn't smell right.

I went to visit another old friend San Deloose. He and I, we went back a long time. He had been a friend of my father's and, after my parents were killed, he more or less took care of me until I could look after myself. He owned a small shop in the run-down part of Old Town buying and selling anything he could get his hands on, and he was not too concerned where it came from or who bought it. His ancestors had been among the first settlers a thousand years ago.

Many times he took me into the mountains to deal with the mountain-tribes, and when he went to jail for a year, he left me with the Stag-clan, whose young chief Threehorn took a liking to me.

Yet unknown assailants killed Threehorn and Garth, my brother-in-law. I was convicted of Garth's murder, after they found me lying across his dead body, the knife that killed him in my hand.

My troops and I came to Redsky in a small battle cruiser and brought with us Professor Goldblat, who introduced us to his brainchild D.I.D.A., Digital Intelligence Data Analyzer.

After they hooked me up to Dida, as the professor called it, I met the Artificial Intelligence inside and found out it was more than just a mass of computer chips and wires. Much more. The AI took on the persona of a beautiful woman, and I called her *Angel*.

Meadow and I decided to travel north to the Strathon Mountains. Our goal was to find out why thousands of native warriors were gathering there. My good friend Darl Mitas, now a member of the police force, and Lieutenant Niels DePratt, the son of the Prime Minister, accompanied us.

I didn't care for the man. Unfortunately, we had no choice but to let him come along.

We stopped at a ranch to buy Harsa, strong scaly beasts, bred for the harsh country we were about to enter.

The ranch belonged to an old friend, Ben Dar, who had died since I had last seen him. His daughter, Aleethy, ran the ranch now. She had been a little girl when I used to visit her father, but now she had grown into a beautiful young woman.

I have never been able to resist the allures of a beautiful woman. When Aleethy confessed that she had always been in love with me and invited me into her bed, I did not deny her request.

This did not lie well with Meadow. You can't hide anything from an Empath.

Meadow, out of necessity, had become a Windsister. A married woman without at least a couple of handmaidens traveling in the company of three men was unthinkable. A lone unattached woman wouldn't travel with three men...unless she was a prostitute, which would make her available to anyone who offered her money. So she became a holy woman.

This did create a small problem when we spent some time in a local bar in Tangai, where we joined the caravan that would take us across the desert of Dangar. The innkeeper asked Meadow to take his daughter, Aika, to her aunt in Neh-mar, the first city north of Dangar.

Meadow had no choice but to accept this responsibility.

The caravan master assigned her a space on one of the sleds; covered platforms, carried on the backs of four beasts of burden. There was a group of eight young girls on the same sled, brides on their way to join their eagerly awaiting future husbands. They traveled under the protection of an agent. Somehow I suspected they were slaves on their way to a slave market, and their so-called protector nothing but a slimy slave trader.

During our journey through the desert, we encountered a fierce sand storm. Meadow was forced to kill the slave trader, which left us with the company of eight more girls.

Among the travelers was a group of Yellow Horns, who took us prisoner after the storm. They were on their way to join their fellow warriors for the Holy War to liberate Shantra.

Deep in the mountains, we discovered a base of the Stardogs and came face to face with the aliens. We also discovered that they were Shape Shifters and were using human women as breeders to create a race of hybrids.

With the help of my teammates, we managed to destroy the alien base. I signed a peace treaty with Calawhan, the Great Wir, and I promised him better weapons to even the balance of power between the settlers and the native tribes.

After we got back to Old Town, my ex-wife Lane visited me in my hotel room. So did Aleethy, who came to town on business.

My teammates and I went back to the airport, where we had set up our headquarters. The airport was considered a small piece of the Terran Empire, not governed by the laws and restriction of Redsky, a Class D planet.

The technical personnel there had detected an alien spacecraft, a huge alien ship, hiding on one of the moons.

We knew it belonged to the Stardogs.

Slave traders kidnapped Meadow, Aleethy, Aika and the other girls. The kidnappers demanded we leave Redsky immediately.

That, of course, was not an option. I would not leave Meadow behind, and we could not condemn the other girls to a life of slavery.

Killic had taken a liking to one of the girls, Ninca. He would tear the planet apart to find her again.

We decided to pretend we were giving in to the demands of the kidnappers to insure the safety of the girls. Then we made plans to rescue them.

Chapter One

San Deloose seemed surprised to see me again. He looked up at Killic, who accompanied me, and grinned. "Another one like you, Dan? His eyes are even colder than yours."

"Killic is okay, old friend. You can trust him."

He nodded, filling two large mugs with black liquid from his forever-boiling pot. "Here," he said, handing one to me, the other to Killic. "Drink this, and then we talk."

I felt myself sliding back in time, as we performed the ritual we had gone through many times, so long ago. Accepting the hot mug, I held it against my lips, inhaled the pungent aroma, let it sting my nostrils. It left a bitter taste in my throat when I sipped from it.

Killic coughed beside me. "What the hell is this?" he croaked.

I chuckled. San grinned toothlessly. "It's an ancient drink brewed from *tekka-leaves*. It soothes the nerves, makes you calm, but sharpens your wit." He drank noisily, and then he set down his mug and wiped his thick mustache. "Now, Dan, what's on your mind?"

"Slaves," I said.

"Slaves?" San repeated. "You're buying or selling?"

"Neither, San." I smiled. "You know what I think about the slave trade."

"I know. But ten years is a long time to change a man's views."

"I am a Lawman, San. I'm supposed to keep law and order." I smiled as his bushy eyebrows danced in his wrinkled face.

"Just testing," he said, but he didn't smile.

I felt his unease, when I mentioned law and order. San Deloose was not a criminal, but he was not your upright model law-abiding citizen, either. He treaded the fine line between law and crime very carefully, the odd times leaning a little too far to the wrong side of the law.

"Don't worry, old friend," I said, making the truth-sign and touching his blue-veined hand. "We didn't come for you. I just want some confidential information. You have eyes and ears in places I can never get to."

9

I told him about the girls, about Meadow and Aleethy.

San Deloose twirled the ends of his bushy mustache. "I did hear about a bunch of young girls. They're destined for the east, that's all I know."

"The east? What a coincidence! I had plans to travel there myself," I said. "By the way, what do your eyes and ears tell you about weapons?"

The old man took a long time refilling his mug. His wrinkled face showed no expression when he answered. "There are times when it isn't healthy to know too much. Curiosity can be fatal." He glanced at Killic. "Your friend here is awfully quiet. He's a good listener."

Killic's lips smiled, but his eyes stayed cold. "Like the Major said, we have no interest in you."

San Deloose sighed, chuckled. "The Major, eh? Well, well. You never told me."

I shrugged. "I don't have to impress an old friend, do I? So...how about an answer to my question? Who is bringing in all these illegal weapons?"

"Rumor has it the man behind it is a powerful puller of strings. Nobody knows who it is, just some big wheel. A respected citizen by all outward appearances, a man with great influence." He chuckled again, his bushy eyebrows performing their merry dance.

I sighed and touched the old man's shoulder. "Thanks, San. You've been helpful in some way."

He shrugged. "Sorry, son, if I couldn't give you anything specific. I'm not as informed as I used to be. Getting too old for that kind of stuff."

I smiled. "I understand. However, there are still things you can help me with. We need to get into Isram without attracting too much attention. I know there isn't much communication anymore between Newland and Isram, but trade-caravans must still travel between the countries. You carry certain exotic spices which are produced in Isram."

He nodded, his small eyes studying me curiously. "You want to join one of the caravans, I assume?"

"If it's possible."

"Anything is possible. It'll take money."

"No problem."

His fingers were busy with his mustache. "None of these people are above committing crimes. They'll cut your throat without mercy if they find out who you are. You can't just join them...even with money."

"So what does it take?" Killic asked. I knew he was getting impatient, but his voice didn't betray him.

"Connections," San said. "It takes connections."

"I know you still have them, old friend," I said.

He stood there behind his ancient counter, trying to light his big pipe. I knew he was holding back, and I couldn't really blame him. He was scared. Scared for his life if he talked too much to the wrong people. We were the wrong people.

I pressed on because I needed his assistance. "Nobody needs to know about your involvement, San. All we need is information and some names."

He had managed to light his pipe and took a few long drags, puffing blue clouds of smoke. Searching under his counter for paper and a pencil, he put it on to the counter, began writing. He handed it to me. "For old times sake, son. Be careful."

Killic and I walked the short distance to where Kelsey waited for us with the skimmer. Last time I walked this way it had been night. The streets had been deserted, except for the scum who attacked me. Now the sidewalks were busy with people. Merchants stood behind their open counters, displaying their wares to wary shoppers.

Children were dodging in and out of doorways and alleys, playing games only they understood. Beggars stood on street corners, holding out their hands, hoping for a few meager coins.

This was the heart of Old Town, the part where the poor and hopeless dwelled. And the criminals, who preyed on rich and poor alike.

I stopped, waiting for Killic, who had stopped to look at something that seemed to interest him at one of the counters. A hand touched my arm, and I turned to look into a young girl's smiling face. "Would you be interested in an afternoon of great delight," she whispered, opening her cape for a quick moment to give me a fleeting glimpse of her naked white body.

Her breasts were large and sagging, her body thin, almost bony. She was not as young as she appeared and had seen better days.

"Thank you," I said, gently disengaging myself from her grip.

"I am very good," she insisted. "You won't be sorry. And I am clean."

"No," I said firmly, "maybe another time."

Her dark eyes clouded, her face screwed up into an almost ugly mask. "What's the matter? Am I not good enough for you?" she shouted. Ripping her cape off her shoulders, she stood naked in front of me...screaming.

Damn! I cursed and fumbled in my pocket for some money. People stopped to stare at us. On the other side of the street, two men started to cross, their faces ugly. I clamped a hand over the woman's mouth and put my lips to her ear. "Shut up!" I said sharply, "or I'll shut you up for good." I waved the money in front of her eyes, and she stopped her screaming. Her hand shot out to rip the money from my hand. I let go of her. She bent down to pick up her cape, giving me a nice view of her rump. For a thin woman she had surprisingly fleshy buttocks and long, slim legs.

Staring at her white body, gave me a sudden hard-on.

Damn the Stardogs and their potent aphrodisiacs. How long would this still last? I had assumed that Angel removed all the traces of the venom from my system.

The woman must have seen the bulge in my tight-fitting pants. "Changed your mind, huh?" she said, smiling sweetly. "You just bought yourself more than an afternoon. Hell! For this kind of money, you can fuck me for three days." She reached for my hand. "Come on, let's go."

There were gasps and rude remarks from some of the watchers, as they walked by, but most didn't care one way or the other. They stopped only to watch the entertainment.

I felt extremely tempted to follow her invitation, that's how painful my erection had become. She pulled me into an alley and put her hand on the bulge in my pants. "My," she giggled. "Is that all for me?"

As her hand reached inside my pants to encircle my hard rod, I heard a faint noise behind me. Turning aside, a descending club missed my head, bounced off my right shoulder and smashed into the woman's neck. I felt her go limp, her hand still inside my pants, her fingers tightly curled around my member. I wasn't in the best position to defend myself.

"Damn it!" a man cursed. "You've killed Londie."

The club came down again. I reached for it, but hampered by the woman, I almost tripped. Prying the woman's fingers loose with my left hand, I grabbed the club with my right, absorbing the jarring impact with my shoulder. Freed of the woman, I jabbed my left into my attacker's abdomen. With a loud 'oomph', he collapsed. My right foot shot out, caught the second man under the chin. There was a loud crack as his neck broke.

Too bad for him. His knife clattered to the ground, bounced across the stones. The one with the club lay gasping, halfway across the woman's still body.

I looked up to see Killic coming around the corner.

"Major?" he called. "What the hell happened here?"

Curiously, nobody else seemed interested. That was the problem in Old Town. A guy could get mugged, even killed. Nobody wanted to get involved. Everybody was scared. *Better him than me*. It was a haven for cutthroats and thieves.

"A little argument." I grinned, closing up my pants. "Nothing serious."

"Nothing serious?" Killic shook his head. "A dead woman, one dead guy and one who may be dying...and it's nothing serious? I beg to differ, sir. This is serious business. They're civilians, not soldiers."

"They're thieves, Killic."

I bent over the woman, checked her pulse and probed her shoulder. Her collarbone was broken, but she was alive. So was her friend, a tall, lanky youth with wide, bony shoulders. Probably her brother. He looked a lot like her.

He was barely conscious.

The second guy was dead, as I suspected. He lay in a crumpled heap, his head bent in a funny angle. I had broken his jaw and his neck. He seemed a little older than the other one, not quite as tall.

I didn't feel sorry for him. He attacked me with a knife, maybe not with the intention to kill, but how could I know? He took a chance, and now he was dead.

Killic looked at the dead man and then at the woman. Her cape had opened, exposing her white legs and her pubic area.

"How do you do it, Major?" Killic asked.

"What do you mean?" I said, fully understanding what he meant.

"You attract trouble like the flame attracts a moth." He shook his head.

"I've been a sucker for trouble from the day I was born." I shrugged. "You get used to it. Let's get out of here."

"What about them?"

"Don't worry about them. One is dead, two live, that's all."

"That's all?"

"Right, Killic, and that's all there is to it. Now...let's move."

As tough and hard as Killic was, he was a civilized man and a gentleman. He had not grown up in the gutter the way I had. He bent down to cover the woman's exposed body and pulled the cape over her bare bottom.

He moved at the same time I did and rolled on the ground into the darkness of a niche in the building to his left. I heard the rat-tat-tat of a sub-machine gun echoing from the stone walls and the whine of the ricocheting bullets as I dove to an entrance in the building across from Killic.

Damn it! Neither one of us carried any weapons.

"Did you get them?" One of our attackers called out. There were at least five of them. I'd only caught a glimpse of their shadowy appearance when they stepped around the corner into the alley.

They had been careless. When I had heard the click of a magazine being pushed into its place, my built-in defense system took over, and before I realized what was happening, my body moved away from the immediate danger zone.

Their eyes must have adjusted to the level of the light in the alley. "Where the hell are they?" the same voice asked.

I heard their slow footsteps as they came closer.

"That's Karp over there on the ground. Looks like he is dead!"

"You killed Karp, you stupid *Urk*!" another one cursed loudly. "And Londie, too."

"Something must have gone wrong. They weren't supposed to be here. Only Londie."

"Then why did you shoot at all?"

"I didn't know she was here, honest. I didn't see her, just the two guys."

They were close now. Only three of them, the others were probably still back at the entrance to the alley. Waiting. Watching.

The man, who had attacked me with the club, stirred. He saw the approaching men and sat up abruptly.

"What the hell are you doing here, Lenny? What happened?" One of the newcomers asked.

The tall youth held his midriff and coughed. His gaze fell on the dead man on the ground. "Karp!" he groaned. "That bastard killed him."

"There were two of them. Where are they?"

The one called Lenny looked around. He looked straight at me where I stood in the darkness. His eyes widened, and he lifted a hand.

I moved before he could utter a sound.

Lenny was no threat, but the one with the sub-machine gun was. I kicked it from his hands, grabbed the guy and lifted him high into the air, and then I threw him into the other two. They toppled over like a couple of bowling pins. A machine gun began to hammer behind me.

Killic!

One of the men at the alley entrance screamed and fell to the ground. The other three, I had been wrong, there were seven not five, ducked back around the corner.

The three on the ground cursed. The one I had thrown lay still, the other two pushed him off and rose to their feet. They looked at Killic who was watching the end of the alley, but they didn't make any moves toward him. Lenny helped the woman get up. She held her left arm, which hung limply in front of her.

"I'm hurting," she whined. Her eyes fell on the dead man, and then she saw the other unmoving form on the ground. "Darkness!" she cursed softly. "Who did this?"

Lenny pointed. Her dark eyes looked at me, and then, for the first time, she noticed Killic. "Who are these guys?" she asked. "And what happened? Nobody was supposed to get hurt. They told me to keep this guy busy." She looked at me, again. "I'm sorry, I had no idea."

"Don't apologize to him!" Lenny snapped. "We thought you were in trouble. Besides, we figured we should get some of the action."

The two new arrivals stared at their friend, who was stirring on the ground. He rose and brushed off his pants. "An easy job!" he cursed, shooting an angry look at me. Then he glared at his companions. "They call this an easy job?" He spread his arms, facing me. "Look, why don't we pretend none of this ever happened? All I want to do now is get away from here...alive. Nobody gets hurt."

"A little too late for that, isn't it. Two dead men, so far, and your friend Lonnie injured. You tried to kill us," I said in a gentle voice.

"Yeah, I'm sorry. Nothing personal." He looked at me with a sly expression on his ugly mug. "How did you do it? I mean...there I was standing with my invincible weapon and next thing I know I'm flying through the air. What the hell are you?"

"I've never seen anyone moving so fast," one of the others added.

"Practice," I said. "Lots of practice. By the way, who put you up to this and why?"

"We don't know why. We were told to watch out for you and rough you up a little. Kill you, if necessary."

"Who told you?"

"Markell," the woman answered. "But it wasn't his idea. He gets orders from someplace else."

I nodded. "We'll deal with him later," I said. "For now I want you all to disappear…fast. And take your friend here with you."

They obeyed and we watched them hurry around the corner, back onto the street. When we came to the other end of the alley, we found the lifeless body of the one Killic shot. Nothing we could do for him. No sign of his accomplices.

Five minutes later, we joined Kelsey in the skimmer.

"What took you so long?" Kelsey grumbled. "I was beginning to get bored."

Chapter Two

According to the information I received from Sans, a caravan had passed through Old Town a couple of days before. Caravans moved slowly, so it would take this one a few days to reach the border of Isram. We could join it just before that happened.

The information proved correct. The tech-team located the caravan just past the mountains to the east of Old Town and calculated its progress. We didn't have much time to lose.

I decided to take Cherryh with me. Killic wasn't happy when I told him he couldn't come along, but he realized that Cherryh was the best choice, because of his skin color. He was dark-skinned, like the majority of Isramelites. The other men would be on standby, in case they had to come and rescue us. We would go in nearly weaponless. None of the men liked that idea, but they agreed to its necessity. We couldn't afford to take any advanced weapons with us.

Isram has its own language. Neither of us spoke it, so we took a crash course to learn the language and the customs and part of Isram's history.

Professor Goldblat and his team had been busy. They found a history professor living in the Terran Embassy, who had studied the Isramic culture and its people. They picked his brains and downloaded everything he knew into the Digital Intelligence Data Analizer, the machine Professor Goldblat named Dida, but I called Angel.

After that, it was Cherryh's and my turn to be joined with Dida. When we were done, both of us spoke fluent Isramic and were versed in the religion of that country. We could pass easily for stout believers in the Mislanic Faith.

I have never been much of a believer in anything and neither has Cherryh, so it wouldn't be hard for us to pretend. We didn't have to worry about comprising our own beliefs.

It took us two days to make our preparations, and then we were ready.

We needed someone who knew the backcountry of Newland to operate the airsled that would take us just outside a small settlement close to the Isram border. Someone I could trust and who would keep his mouth shut, and I happened to know someone who fit the description.

"You realize this is a secret mission, and not without dangers, son." I said to Anton, the young man I had come to like.

Anton nodded and made the truth sign. "You can trust me, Major Griffin. I appreciate what you've done for me. I can never repay you, sir. I'll be loyal to you for the rest of my life."

I smiled. "I wouldn't hold you to that. I'm just happy I could do something for you. Now you can do something for me, it's as simple as that. However, that is not the reason I've chosen you. I picked you because I know I can trust you, Anton."

"Thank you, Major. You won't be disappointed."

We left that same evening. It was a dark night, which made it easier to pass through Old Town without drawing too much attention to our airsled.

We made a quick stop in one of the stores to pick up a few things we still needed, and then we were on our way.

Before we left Old Town, I made one more attempt to contact Meadow, but to no avail. My men and I had surgically implanted communication devices in our bodies, but Meadow relied on external devices. Small they might be and not easily discovered, but should she be tied up or unconscious, she may not be able to operate them.

Airsleds didn't travel this road to Isram, only caravans and people on horseback. The border was about three hundred kilometers away, but we had to travel slowly, because of the many obstacles on the road and the endless turns. The road led through the mountains and became quite narrow at times.

Anton dimmed the lights of the sled. We had barely enough light to see the road, but we couldn't risk discovery.

Once we passed the mountains, traveling became easier. Unfortunately, our lights could also be seen from far away, so Anton shut them off completely. Only one of the moons was out. The smaller, the darker one, but it threw enough light for us to see ahead. This part of the country was quite desolate, mostly desert with small, stunted trees and lots of hard sand and many rocks. We were forced to crawl at a snail's pace, to avoid hitting the rocks.

We couldn't chance to catch up with the caravan, but we needed to get to the settlement before the caravan did, without being spotted. This meant we had to leave the road and travel across even rougher terrain. It was almost morning when we finally arrived at our destination, which lay a few kilometers outside the only settlement this close to the border.

Anton stopped the vehicle. "This is as close as I can take you, Major. Any closer and we might run into hunters or just someone taking a stroll."

I grinned at him. "Hunters, maybe, but no one in his right mind would be out for a stroll in this place, not at this time of night."

He chuckled. "You know what I mean, sir. Good luck." He held out a hand. I shook it. "Take care, Anton, and be careful driving back. Don't take any chances." I handed him the energy-pistol I had carried. "Here, take this, you know how to use it. I showed you back at the base. Just in case."

He took it and turned it around in his hand. "Thank you, Major," he said with a lopsided grin. "I hope I won't need it, but I haven't forgotten what you taught me."

We watched him turn the sled and start his way back home. I knew he'd be safe. He also carried a transmitter, in case he ran into trouble. Besides, the technicians on the base were tracking our movements on their screens through one of the spy-satellites they had launched. He'd be under surveillance until he got back to base.

Cherryh and I shouldered our backpacks and began walking toward the village we knew to be only about five kilometers ahead. In the east, we could see the red umbrella of the rising sun creeping up toward the distant mountaintops. Isram lay on the other side of those mountains.

The garb we wore was old and worn. And not very clean. We purchased it in Old Town in one of the stores in the poorer section, where they sold used clothing. The dirt we put in ourselves. I wasn't quite prepared to smell somebody else's sweat and grime.

Kelsey grinned at me, as we walked across the hard ground. "You look like a vagrant, sir, if you don't mind me saying so?"

I grinned back. "Speak for yourself, Kelsey. I can smell you from here. Did you roll in an animal pen?"

He wrinkled his nose. "The same one you rolled in, Major."

We walked on hard ground, but there were sections where the wind had built dunes of sand. Perfect hiding places for the ferocious beasts that made the desert their home. Very little vegetation grew here. What did manage to get a foothold in the infertile ground was stunted and brown, at least that's what it looked like from the outside. I had lived on Redsky long enough to know that the brown and hard exterior of the plants protected soft pulp and enough liquid to sustain a thirsty traveler, human or animal.

As we got closer to the settlement we saw a few cultivated fields, but whatever grew there, didn't look too healthy. Most people in this village lived off hunting and trapping. There were plenty of fur animals in the mountains and in the desert, and animal skins were highly prized in the cities.

We arrived at the edge of the village shortly after sunrise. This early in the morning, not many people were on the street. Our destination was the tavern, the only one in this place, where we knew we'd be able to get a room.

The old man behind the counter gave us an inquisitive look when we stumbled into the room. Kelsey made a show of slapping his hat against his thighs, creating a small cloud of dust around him.

"You have a room for us?" I asked.

The old man stared at me. "We didn't expect anyone yet," he said. "Besides, nobody ever stays here, unless they're wanted by the law."

I smiled at him. "Had a little run-in with exactly those kinds of people. They attacked our caravan."

"They attacked the caravan?" He shook his head in disbelief.

"It wasn't the regular one that comes through here. We decided to form our own group. Figured we could save some money." I gave him a gloomy laugh. "We were wrong."

"How many in your group?"

"Seven."

He shook his head again. "You were fools. The only way to travel safely is with the large caravans. Sure, Caravan Master Dragor charges a lot, but he is known and respected. And feared by the bandits who roam this desert. They'd never dare attack him." He looked at me with pity. "Where is the rest of your party?"

I shrugged. "Dead. We managed to flee, just the two of us. But they took our riding beasts."

"Where did all this happen?"

"A couple days south of here. On the old 'Tri-star trail'."

"Nobody uses that one anymore. Where'd you come from?"

"The Blacklands."

"That's a long way from here. You should have taken the 'South-trek' to Old Town, and then joined the caravan east." He studied me with interest. "Not many people live in the Blacklands. I hear it gets quite hot in the summer. Nothing but giant lizards and even larger rock-birds."

I grinned. "And *Sun Crystals*."

He nodded. "So that's what you fellers have been searching for. Maybe that's why you were attacked. *Sun Crystals* are precious."

I padded the small leather pouch I carried around my neck. "They didn't get what they were looking for."

"Shut up, Grif!" Cherryh put his face close to mine. ""Remember what I told you! Don't trust anyone!"

I chuckled. "Come one, Cherryh. This old man is no threat. He's an honest man, can't you see that?" I turned to the old man. "My partner is suspicious of everyone. Don't mind him. He also has a bad temper. But he's all right." I winked. "I'm sure you can keep a secret. We're on our way to Isram. I guess we'll have to join the regular caravan now."

"Why do you want to go to Isram? Why didn't you try to sell you crystals in Old Town, or in Capital City?"

I leaned on the counter, looked the old man in the eyes. "We had a bit of a run-in with the law, nothing serious, mind you, all a misunderstanding. So we figure Isram would be a better bet. Safer, you know."

He looked at me, his eyes calculating. "Caravan Master Dragor is quite a suspicious man. He won't let just anyone join his caravan. You need connections." He eyed the pouch around my neck. "For a tiny fee, let's say two per cent of what you got in there, I could put in a good word for you."

"Two percent?" Cherryh almost shouted. "Are you trying to rob us, old man?"

One look at Cherryh and the old man seemed to shrink into himself. "Don't blame me for trying!" He glanced at me. "He *does* have a temper. How about one percent? It'll be worth your trouble. You'll never get in without me."

"All right," I said.

"You're still robbing us!" Cherryh glared at him. "For that you'll have to throw in a room and some food."

The old man grinned. "Let's see the crystal, and you have a deal."

"Give him one of yours," I said to Cherryh. "You have more than me."

Cherryh grumbled and groped in his pocket. Pulling out a small pouch, he opened it and shook out the contents. The old man gasped when he saw the sparkling crystals. "So many," he said with awe. "I've never seen that many in one place. In fact, I've never seen any. Just heard about them."

Cherryh picked one and handed it to him. Then he grunted and gave him another one. "Here, I feel charitable."

The old man almost kissed his hands. "Thank you, sir. For this, you can have all the food and drinks you can manage to consume. You are most generous." He fondled the two small crystals. "To think it took millions of years to make these!"

"Remember to keep you mouth shut, old man! You didn't see anything. By the way, what is your name?"

"It's Tetrus, sir."

"All right, Tetrus, show us our room and a place where we can wash up. I need to get out of these clothes."

Tetrus rang a small bell, which he had on his counter. A young woman came out of one of the curtain-covered doors in the back. "Yes, Father?"

"Saskia, show these fine men our best suite and then fill the tub in the bathroom with warm water so they can relax and wash up."

She threw him a curious glance, shrugged and told us to follow her. We climbed up a set of stairs to the second floor, down a short hallway, where she opened the door to our room.

"This is our best suite," she said and stepped aside to let us enter. "I'll draw your water for you now. I will call when you can come down."

Cherryh shook his head in disbelief and looked around. "I'd like to see their regular rooms," he said and sat down on one of the beds. The mattress almost collapsed under his weight.

I laughed. "What did you expect in this forsaken place, Cherryh? We're lucky we have two beds. Aren't you glad you were so generous with those *Sun Crystals*?"

He grinned. "If the old man only knew it took our technicians just a couple of hours to make them."

"Nobody will ever know the difference." I said. "They're as real as the natural ones. We just shortened the time it took to create them."

The young woman called us an hour later. We followed her into the bathroom. There were actually two wooden tubs in there. "I only had enough hot water to fill them partially," she apologized.

"More than enough." I smiled at her.

"I'll scrub your back," she volunteered. Then she looked away. "If you want."

"That would be great," I said. "Maybe you can get us some clean robes and wash our clothes. They have seen better days."

She nodded. "I'll see what I can find."

She left the room to give us a chance to get undressed.

Cherryh and I stripped, put our backpacks within easy reach and sank gratefully into the tubs. Saskira came back a short time later. Her eyes grew large when she looked at us. I couldn't blame her. She'd probably never seen men with muscles like ours. I noticed her hesitation when her hands slid over my shoulders.

"You have hard bodies," she murmured.

I chuckled. "We work hard," I said. "Life in the Blacklands is not for the weak."

She put her lips close to my ear. "Maybe we could continue in private somewhere, tonight, without your friend," she whispered. "We have a couple of empty rooms."

"Your offer is tempting," I whispered back, "but not tonight, I made a vow to be celibate until the next moon-cycle."

"That is too bad," she said. "I could have given you a good time." She looked at Cherryh. "What about your friend?"

I shrugged and grinned. "Why don't you ask him?"

She left me and walked over to Cherryh to rub his back. I saw her whisper into his ear. He smiled and whispered something back. If I would have wanted to, I could have tuned in and listened to their conversation, but it wasn't my business how Cherryh spent his nights. As long as it didn't interfere with our mission.

I declined her proposition, not because she was ugly, or that I wasn't interested. She was actually quite pleasant to look at, and when she rubbed my back, I had reacted. It didn't take much to get me into the mood these days. My reason for not accepting her offer was almost noble. I had been thinking a lot about Lane, my daughter Kelly, Aleethy, who had grown into such a lovely young woman, and about Meadow. All the women I cared for, all of them in some kind of trouble.

To make matters worse, there was Aika, who I had promised to protect and to deliver safely to her aunt in Neh-mar, and the girls we inherited when Meadow killed their master.

In addition, above everything hung the threat of the Stardogs.

Damn it! Why did it have to be Redsky they had to pick? Why couldn't it have been any of the hundreds of other inhabited planets in the Terran Empire?

Saskia handed us a couple of towels. Then she left.

"Looks like I'll be busy tonight, Major," Cherryh grinned.

"Just be careful," I warned him.

Saskia came back with two robes. She smiled at me when she held out the robe. "Changed your mind, maybe?" she asked in a low voice.

I shook my head. She pouted a little, and then walked over to Cherryh. He took the robe from her, laughed at something she said, and then slapped her on the rump. She giggled, picked up our dirty clothes and walked out of the room.

Women! Seems they're always attracted to strangers. Had I accepted her invitation, she'd probably screw me first and still jump into Cherryh's bed.

"Come on, let's have something to eat. I'm starved."

The old man Tetrus himself took the order. There wasn't really much on the menu, just some boiled eggs and fried tubers. I didn't ask what creature had laid the eggs. On Redsky, you never knew, especially in these little towns. If you were lucky, an actual bird laid it.

Another girl came out of the kitchen in the back and cleaned our table. Younger than Saskia, but much prettier, most likely her younger sister. The resemblance was unmistakable.

"What's your name?" I asked.

She gave me a shy smile. "Cassia."

"Well, Cassia, how would you like to earn yourself one of these?" I asked, showing her a small Sun Crystal.

She blushed. "What would I have to do?" Her dark eyes riveted on the sparkling stone. I could see the desire in her face. Couldn't blame her. This little rock represented a fortune. It would buy her a way out of this place, away from her father, away from pawing customers.

Cherryh cleared his throat beside me. He gave me a questioning look. I ignored him. "We need a couple of riding animals. Where would I be able to buy them without getting robbed blind?"

"There is only one place. The Woodfield Ranch," Cassia said.

"Can you take me there this afternoon?"

She hesitated. "I'd have to get permission from my father."

I smiled at her and held up the crystal. "With this in your possession, you won't have to ask anybody ever again."

Her expressive dark eyes flickered to the counter where Tetrus stood, and then back to the Sun Crystal. "You are right," she said. I detected the rapid beating of her heart. "I'll take you there."

"Order is ready," called the old man.

Cassia smiled at me. "I have to go and get your food."

When Cassia came back with our food, I asked her, "When do you expect the caravan to arrive?"

She shrugged. "I don't know. Probably in a couple of days."

"Does it stop here?"

"Not all the time. But sometimes they stop for supplies, water mostly. There is nothing between here and the other side of the mountains."

"Thank you, Cassia. I think we better eat the food...before it gets cold."

Smiling, she walked away. She had a nice wiggle when she walked. I liked her better than her sister.

While we ate, I looked around the room. There were only three other customers sitting at another table. Two men and one older woman. Probably trappers, judging from the way they were dressed.

"I'll be going with Cassia to buy us some transportation this afternoon. Maybe you can pump the old man for more information about the caravan master, what he likes and so on. The more we know about him, the easier it will be to join up with the caravan. These people are very suspicious. They trust nobody. Make friends with Tetrus."

Cherryh's eyes were thoughtful when he looked at me. "And his daughter Saskia?"

I grinned. "It won't hurt to make friends with her also, but I think you've already made arrangements."

He grinned back. "Just checking, Major. I wouldn't want to go against regulations."

"You know better, Cherryh. How we accomplish our mission is our business. We pretty well make the rules, and sometimes we have to make sacrifices for the good of the Empire, if you know what I mean." I winked.

"I understand, sir. Collateral damage and all that."

"Correct. Just don't be too generous with the Sun Crystals."

We finished our meal and then went up to our room. We were still wearing the robes Saskia gave us, and I didn't feel like walking around in them, so we waited until she brought our clean clothes. I lay down on my bed to take a little nap, while Cherryh sat in the only chair, checking his backpack.

He got up when Saskia knocked on the door and let her in. She didn't have our clothes. "I'm afraid your clothes won't be dry until tomorrow. I hung them out into the wind and sun, but they don't dry that fast. Sorry." She looked apologetically first at Cherryh then at me.

"Is there a place where we can procure some clothes?" I asked, slipping from the bed.

She shook her head, looked up at me and smiled. "Not unless you want to rob someone."

"I'm almost tempted to do just that," I said. Damn it! I should have at least brought another pair of pants or a change of underwear. All this planning and we forgot the basics.

"I'm fine with this robe," Cherryh said. "I'll be hanging around the tavern anyway."

"But I won't," I said. "Saskia, go ask your father to lend me a pair of pants and a shirt."

She looked me over and laughed. "I don't think they'll fit you."

"There must be something we can do," I growled. Then I went to get my backpack. Groping around in it, I took out some coins. "Here, find me some clothes. I'm sure someone in this town is my size and will sell me his pants and a shirt."

She looked at the money, licking her lips. I could see the greed in her eyes. "Maybe I can help you, but it may take a few more coins."

I sighed and gave her more. She must have talked to her sister, because she gave me a sly look. "You know, it won't be easy to find something so fast. One of those Sun Crystals you carry could be of great help in my search. We are all poor people here, and I'll have a hard time persuading anyone to part with his clothing."

26

Sighing again, I pulled out the little pouch and searched for a tiny crystal. Handing it to her, I said, "I hope you'll remember our kindness. I'm giving you this only because my friend here has taken a fancy to you. Do me a favor, though. Keep this a secret. We don't want everyone in your town trying to rob us. We've lost too much already, and my good will is slowly coming to an end." Anger suddenly boiled up inside me, not at her, but at myself for being so sloppy. I smiled at her, the way a Mountain-skat would smile at its prey just before it launched itself at it.

She must have sensed the feral anger inside me, because she stepped back a little, but not before she snatched the crystal out of my hand. "I'll find you something," she murmured, her eyes averting mine. Before she left our room, she threw a glance at Cherryh and gave him a little smile.

"Problem?" Cherryh asked me after she'd left.

"It's nothing," I growled. "I think I miss Meadow. If she were around we wouldn't be in this predicament. She'd have made sure we had spare clothing."

Cherryh's teeth flashed white in his dark face. "Yeah, she can be a little mother sometimes." He became serious, looked at me gravely. "Don't worry, Major, we'll find her."

Chapter Three

Cassia hitched a *Raesca,* a small horse-like animal, to a wagon. *Rascas* had a bad temper, and they could inflict serious wounds with their long canines. That's why they usually wore a muzzle. It surprised me a little to see that this one didn't. It eyed me suspiciously, when I walked by it, keeping my distance.

Cassia laughed when she saw the way I skirted the animal. "He won't bite you," she said as she climbed onto the wagon. She took her place on the narrow seat and patted the spot beside her. "Climb on, we don't have much time."

She was right. It had taken her sister longer than I hoped to get me some clothing. The pants I wore had seen better days, but they weren't a bad fit. The shirt was a different story. Too small in the shoulders, one sleeve missing, but I fixed that by tearing off the other one. It left my arms bare, and that was fine. But it made me look like someone who had robbed his little brother's closet. It also gave me the appearance of being intimidating and ferocious, which I would have liked to avoid. I needed people to trust me and not be afraid of me.

"Is the Woodfield Ranch far from here?" I asked.

"Not very. We should be there in a little over an hour. But you might want some time looking over the animals and negotiating a deal."

She clucked her tongue and flicked a small whip, which she pulled out of a sheath beside the seat. The *Raesca* let out a shrill scream and began to trot away. These little animals weren't very tall, but they were strong and despite their bad temper usually quite dependable.

The trampled, packed soil of the road probably turned into a river of mud after a heavy downpour. However, now it was as hard as rock, and it could have been a smooth ride, had it not been for the deep crevices and small chunks of dried soil.

Cassia had put a blanket on the seat, but my buttocks were sore in a short time.

"How did you come in possession of those Sun Crystals?" Cassia asked me.

"I searched for them," I said. "In the Blacklands."

"This must seem to you like a comfortable place after spending all that time digging under a hot sun and living in primitive conditions," Cassia said. "It must have been rough. How long were you there?"

"Too long. It is a lonely life." I was hoping she wouldn't ask me too much about it. I'd never been there myself. All the information I had came from unreliable sources. We didn't have enough time to gather more facts.

"Were there any women?"

I chuckled. "What sane woman would want to spend time in a place like that, in the company of rough, unwashed men?"

She shuddered beside me. "Not me. I like civilized comfort."

"Civilized comfort?" I laughed. "That concept is relative. Some people find sleeping inside a tent made from animal skins comfortable, while others need houses with solid rock for walls and timbers on the ceiling to feel safe. And pillows stuffed with feathers to cuddle their soft bodies."

"Not you." She smiled. "Nobody develops muscles like yours by sleeping in soft beds." She threw me a sidelong glance. "When was the last time you've been with a woman?"

That question came a little unexpected. "It's been a while," I said. Actually, eight days since I had been with my ex-wife Lane. I didn't count the time I spent with Angel, since it had not been physical and she was not really a living entity but an intelligent machine.

"And you?" I asked.

She gave me a puzzled look, and then she laughed and blushed. "You mean with a *man*?"

"Of course with a man. You don't have to answer," I said. "It is not really my business."

"You're right, it isn't," she said, still blushing, and smiled. "A while. There are not many young men in our town."

She stayed silent for some time. I didn't mind it. I was too busy concentrating on my sore buttocks. "Is it far still?" I asked.

She shook her head and pointed. "See that smoke over there? That is the Woodfield Ranch."

I looked in the direction she pointed and adjusted the focus of my eyes. I could see a number of structures, one a residential building, one a bunkhouse, the others clearly barns. I also saw a few corrals, with animals moving inside them.

The road made a turn, and we began heading toward the ranch. As we came closer, I also saw men on horseback, trying to drive a small herd of animals into one of the corrals.

"It looks like a large operation," I commented.

Cassia nodded. "It is. If it weren't for the ranch, we wouldn't get many travelers coming to our town. The Woodfield Ranch is well known for its fine horses. There are not many breeders on Redsky."

"I didn't know," I said, truthfully. I'd never been in this part of Newland.

When we drove into the yard, one of the riders came to meet us. The man who jumped lithely off his horse wasn't young, but he moved with the powerful stride of a young man when he walked up to us.

"Greetings, young Cassia," he said, giving me a quick glance. "I see you brought a companion."

"He's not really a companion," Cassia smiled. "He is a guest at my father's tavern. He would like to buy two of your horses."

The man looked directly at me. His steely gray eyes took in my shabby pants and my sleeveless shirt. I could see that he wasn't inspired by my appearance. Add to this the fact that I hadn't shaved for a couple of days. Not really an arousing impression. "You're sure it's horses you're after?" he asked me.

"I'm sure." I treated him with a friendly smile.

He smiled back. If a Yak-bird had teeth, it would have looked friendlier. "I have no doubt that you would like to buy horses. The question is *can you pay for them*?"

"I only want to buy two," I said.

"You don't look like you could afford to pay for one, never mind two."

"He can pay for them, Mr. Woodfield," Cassia said, "I'll vouch for that."

Mr. Woodfield still didn't seem convinced. "I never caught your name," he said.

"Dan Griffin." I held out a hand, but he ignored it.

"Well, Mr. Griffin, climb down from that wagon and take a look at our horses."

He grabbed the reins of his horse and stalked away, toward one of the corrals. Cassia shrugged and chuckled. "He is not really the friendliest man on Redsky, but he breeds fine animals."

We followed Mr. Woodfield. He stopped at the corral and called something to one of his ranch hands who came running. Woodfield spoke to him in a low voice. The ranch hand nodded and took away the horse.

"That's a spirited stallion you're riding," I said, just to make some conversation.

"He's not for sale."

"Too bad. I like him."

He looked at me coldly. "We don't sell any stallions, only geldings and mares."

I shrugged. "I'm not going to breed them. All I want are two strong, healthy riding animals I can depend on."

"We have the healthiest and best horses you'll find anywhere, Mr. Griffin," he said impatiently. "Go, have a look around, but don't take all day. My time is valuable."

"So is mine, sir," I said coldly. This man was beginning to irritate me. I pointed at a large pinto I had been watching. "That one." The big piebald horse with the beautiful brown and white patches had caught my eye immediately.

He harrumphed. "Good choice. But let me warn you, he is strong-willed."

"Good," I said. "Then we'll get along fine." I pointed at another one. A big mare with a shiny black coat. Cherryh would look good on her.

Woodfield looked at me for a moment, and then he said. "You might want to reconsider. Let me choose one for you." He studied the small herd in the corral. "How about that one over there. She's very docile."

I shook my head. "I'm not looking for a docile horse. Besides, that one has seen better years. Too old. I'm sticking with my choice."

"It seems you know your horses," he rumbled, respect in his voice. "Unless you were just lucky picking them."

"Not luck," I said. "I spent much time catching mustangs in my youth."

"Only the Shantra-natives catch mustangs," he said, eying me with suspicion.

I looked into his gray eyes and said softly, "I know. Not only did I catch mustangs, I also spent much time with one of the tribes. I was brother to Threehorn of the Stagclan." I didn't give away anything that could jeopardize our mission or me.

He didn't speak for a few seconds, and then he took off his wide brimmed hat and slapped it against one of the posts. "I guess I read you wrong, Mr. Griffin. There is more to you than I figured. Let's talk business."

I looked at the sky and at the sun disappearing behind the mountains in the west. Pulling out my little pouch, which I had hanging around my neck on a leather thong, I removed one of the larger Sun Crystals and held it up for his inspection. "I think this will compensate you more than adequately, Mr. Woodfield," I said.

He didn't flinch, and his gray eyes were steady when he looked at the stone, but he couldn't hide the sudden increase in his heartbeat and the tiny beads of perspiration on his forehead. I knew what I offered him was worth the price of ten horses.

"I think it will suffice," he said, his voice cool and composed. Then he looked into my smiling face. "You don't strike my as a stupid man, Mr. Griffin," he said slowly, as if hating himself for what he was going to say. "That is a Sun Crystal you're offering me. You know its value."

"Of course I do, Mr. Woodfield. I'm not a complete idiot," I said, still smiling. "I'm willing to part with it, if you'll also sell me all the gear I need for the horses, like saddles, saddlebags, blankets. In short, get them ready for traveling." I glanced at Cassia, who hadn't said anything all this time, and added. "Throw in one more horse, one of your more docile ones." I grinned. "But not the old mare, please."

The man actually laughed and held out a hand, "We have a deal, Mr. Griffin. You drive a hard bargain."

Sure, I thought. *Now you really think I'm a sucker. If it makes you happy. It means nothing to me.* Strange, how money can change a man's attitude.

"How about coming in for a drink while my men get the horses ready?" Woodfield said amiably. "To seal the bargain."

"Sure, why not." I turned to look at Cassia who had been plucking on my shirt to get my attention. "Does this present a problem for you?" I asked.

"It will be dark shortly," she said. "We should get going soon." Her eyes bored into mine, as if trying to tell me something.

"You heard the lady," I said, "I think we'll just wait here. Maybe I'll be back another time." I handed him the Sun Crystal.

He didn't seem too happy with my decision, but he shrugged and turned away. He called to one of the men who were busy in the corral next to ours. Cassia pulled me away out of earshot of Mr. Woodfield.

"Let's get away as fast as we can," she whispered so low I could barely hear it.

"Why?" I asked.

"You should not have flashed your pouch so freely," she whispered fiercely.

"I see," I said and smiled. It seems Mr. Woodfield was not as honorable as he presented himself. "Don't worry," I said, "I can take care of myself. Go, get on your wagon and start driving away. I'll catch up with you."

She hesitated. "You'll have to handle three horses."

"I've handled more than that. I'll manage. Now...get going."

Reluctantly, she climbed onto her wagon and drove away, without looking back. I watched her until she was out of the yard then I turned my attention back to the two men who were getting my horses ready. They were taking their sweet old time. Looking around, I saw Mr. Woodfield talking to a group of men who were mingling around by the bunkhouse. They were throwing glances in my direction. They tried to be discreet about it, but I saw their smirking faces quite clearly.

Enhancing my hearing, I had no trouble making out the words my new business partner said to his anxiously listening audience. "...kill him, if you must, but make sure his body disappears without a trace. Strip him naked, bring his clothes and all his possessions to me, including the leather pouch he carries around his neck. Especially the pouch. You understand?" He looked in my direction, smiled and waved when he saw me watching. "It won't be long now, Mr. Griffin," he called loudly.

I waved back, smiling also. If he only knew the trouble he asked for, he wouldn't be smiling. And neither would his henchmen.

"What about the girl?" one of the men asked.

"Kill her. We can't leave any witnesses."

One of the men in the corral brought my gelding, saddled and ready to mount. The other one brought the black mare and a reddish-brown smaller horse. Both were saddled and tethered together. They even had thrown saddlebags onto their broad backs. *Talk about playing out a charade right to the end.*

I didn't wait until they were out of the corral. I entered the enclosure, swung myself into the saddle of the piebald horse and grabbed the reins of the big mare. "Thank you very much," I said and dug my heels into the pinto's soft belly. He neighed loudly, protesting the sudden pressure and shook his head. I gave him free rein and bent forward, pressing my body low against the horse's neck. The pinto took off at a gallop. I almost lost the reins of the mare when she pulled back, but then both horses galloped alongside the big gelding.

I heard shouts from the direction of the bunkhouse, but didn't slow down to investigate. Then the loud crack of rifle fire made me worry they might have hit one of the horses, but all three animals kept on going. I had seen the rifle one of the men tried to hide and recognized it for what it was. Most of those primitive hunting rifles in civilian hands were not that accurate and nearly useless.

I left the yard behind me. I knew they'd be following me, but before they were organized enough I'd be out of their line of sight. The land here was not quite flat. Gently rolling hills provided some cover from distant preying eyes. Besides, it was getting dark, and we had a good chance to escape without being seen. We had spent a little over two hours coming here with the wagon and we had not been in a great hurry. On horseback, traveling at a steady trot, it shouldn't take more than ninety minutes to reach the town, but I had no intentions heading straight for the town.

It didn't take me long to catch up with Cassia. She heard the drumming of my horses' hoofs and turned to look back. She stopped the wagon to wait for me.

"Can that *Raesca* of yours find its way back home without you?" I asked.

She nodded.

"Then let it go and get on the brown mare." I spoke with urgency. We didn't have much time to lose. She understood what I planned. *Good girl.* She jumped off the wagon, walked up to the *Raesca* and whispered something into its ear, and then she slapped it on its rump. The little animal hissed and took off. The girl mounted the chestnut and untied the strip of leather that tethered it to the black mare. I took the reins of the mare and followed the wagon for a short time, and then I left the road and headed for the mountains to the south.

It was quite dark now, and when I looked in the direction of the Woodfield Ranch, I saw the glow of moving torches. Cassia must have seen it too because she spurred her horse to move faster, away from the danger she knew was all too real.

When we came this way in the afternoon, I had marked the surrounding area. A stretch of low mountains not far from here cut into this part of the desert. We could hide in one of the caves that I knew would be there. Even if our pursuers should somehow try to follow us, they'd have a hard time finding us in the dark. If they did, well, I would deal with them then. Even weaponless I would not be a helpless victim.

We slowed down. It was too dark for our horses to travel safely without endangering themselves. A horse with a broken leg wouldn't do us any good. Besides, I had paid too much for them to let that happen.

One of the moons began to climb into the sky, providing us with enough light to let us see where we were going. Soon the relatively flat land became dotted with rocks that grew larger as we neared the mountains. Then high cliffs suddenly surrounded us. I dismounted and led my gelding into one of the crevices that separated two giant slabs of rock. My eyes adjusted to night vision. I had no problem seeing, unlike our mounts and Cassia, but they followed me blindly, literally.

When I found the opening into the rock I'd been seeking, I peered cautiously inside and listened for any telltale sounds, but I heard nothing. Sometimes small and sometimes large animals made these caves their home, and they wouldn't be too eager to invite us.

"Are you sure it's safe in here?" Cassia asked with a small voice.

"It's safe," I assured her.

"How can you know? Anything could hide in this darkness."

"Don't worry, Cassia. We'll be quite safe. Anything hiding in here would have made its presence known by now, believe me."

The horses snorted, but otherwise they stayed calm. I stroked my gelding's muzzle and spoke soothingly. He nuzzled my hand. I've always had a good rapport with animals. I was pleased to discover I hadn't lost my touch.

"I can't see anything," Cassia complained. "This darkness scares me."

I reached for her. She gave a little squeal when I touched her shoulder. "It's me," I pulled her close. She trembled in my arms.

Stroking her hair, I calmed her. "Come," I said softly, "sit down here. I'll get us a blanket."

I was glad they had tied blankets behind the saddles, as I had asked them to do. I took all three blankets off the horses and spread a couple of them on the floor. Cassia sighed when she slid on top of them. I lay down beside her and pulled the third blanket over us. "Better?" I asked.

She nodded, snuggling closer. "I'm cold," she said.

We lay silent for a while. I felt her heart pounding in her chest. My eyes had adjusted completely to the darkness, and I studied the inside of the cave. It was large enough to keep the horses at a safe distance. They stood facing the entranceway. A diffused light filtered through the narrow opening. We should be safe in here until morning.

Cherryh would be wondering. I needed to contact him, telling him we were safe and to be on standby, in case I required him to come to our rescue in the morning. I didn't think Mr. Woodfield would give up too easily. He'd comb the countryside for us, especially now that he knew I had seen through his plan. He couldn't let us live. Cassia would talk. It wouldn't be good for future business dealings.

I could be wrong. Obviously, Cassia already knew about his dealings. She had tried to warn me.

"Are you cold?" Cassia asked me.

"Not really." I felt actually quite comfortable. I found it cool and a little damp inside the cave, but not cold.

"I am," she said, shivering. Her hand went to my chest. "You know it is much warmer when two people are naked. " Her voice sounded husky. She began unbuttoning my shirt, and then she undid my belt and pulled on my pants. "Take them off," she whispered.

She took off her own pants and opened her blouse, while I slipped out of my pants. Her hand found my already reacting organ. Giggling, she curled her warm fingers around it, stroked it gently. It didn't take long for me to become hard and aching. Sliding on top of me, she pressed her soft breasts into my chest. My hard mast found a place between her thighs, but she kept her legs closed.

"Not yet," she whispered haughtily and rubbed her slit against my pole. I could feel her slippery lips molding around the head of my mast, and, moaning, I grabbed her solid buttocks. She laughed and began rotating her lower body. Her breath came fast, and her buttocks quivered in my hands.

"Now!" she gasped, opening her legs. Lifting up, she impaled herself on my pole, took it deep into her. A little mewling sound escaped her lips as she bucked on top of me. Sitting up, she shook off the blanket and went wild.

With my night vision, I could see her clearly and watched her ample breasts bobbing up and down as she rode me with wild abandon. I don't know if she would have thrown away her inhibitions so easily had she known I could see her this plainly. Some women prefer to make love in the dark. I like the light. I need to see the woman I am with, need to see her body, need to watch her face as she experiences her orgasms.

I pushed up against her every time she came down to engulf me completely. Her velvety sheath milked me fiercely, and it felt good to be inside her. So much for my resolution to stay celibate.

I pulled her down and held her tight. Then I turned us over. Her legs opened wider, and I began to push into her with forceful deep thrusts.

"Don't give me a baby, please," she whispered breathlessly.

"I won't," I said, my voice hoarse from my heavy breathing, my heart beating faster. I could have regulated it, but I found that it also dampened the height of my orgasms. I let the burning embers inside flare up and concentrated on the pleasure starting to wash through my body. When it hit, I pulled Cassia to me, held her in a tight grip and erupted inside her sucking pussy.

She cried out and quivered in my embrace, her inner muscles almost strangling my gushing organ. When it was over, she relaxed but then she struggled suddenly.

"What is it?" I asked, still enjoying the aftermath of our simultaneous orgasms.

"You came inside me!" she gasped.

"I know I did," I said calmly.

"But you promised!" She became almost hysterical now. "I can't have a baby. Not without a father!"

I laughed. "And you won't." I stroked her cheek. "I am not capable of impregnating a woman. It is a medical condition."

"Are you diseased?" She tried to sit up.

How could I explain it to her? Nothing like that existed on Redsky. They had given me an inhibitor. Just a simple injection…and reversible. Any time I felt like starting a family, I could get the antidote.

"No disease," I said. "Low sperm count. Almost non-existent."

She relaxed in my arms. "Does that mean you can never be a father?" she asked.

"Pretty much," I said.

"That is sad." She kissed me gently and wiggled her bottom. "You are still hard."

"I know," I said and began to move slowly in and out of her.

She gasped and moved her hips. "It doesn't seem to hamper you ability to satisfy a woman."

I smiled. "No, it doesn't. It actually enhances my ability to make a woman happy. The knowledge of not becoming pregnant when coupling adds to the pleasure a woman experiences."

I pulled out of her and told her to kneel on the blankets. She hesitated but then complied. Pushing up her buttocks, she spread her legs a little and let me mount her from the rear. She reached back between her legs and grabbed my searching penis. Guiding it into her dripping pussy, she sheathed me with a loud moan. Then she began rotating her hips while I hammered away between her fleshy buttocks. Clamping my hands around her flaring hips, I steadied her movement and pushed deep into her repeatedly.

Her fingers dug into the blanket, her pussy-walls gripped me tightly as she doused my hard rod with warm liquid. "What are you doing to me?" she moaned. "No man has ever made me feel this way." She bucked like a wild mustang and sobbed uncontrollably.

I sensed another climax gathering and let it build then I gripped her hips and held her tight, filling her with my discharge. My shouts of pleasure joined her whimpering cries.

Then her legs gave away, and she collapsed under me. I fell on top of her and lay on her soft buttocks, my hands still clamped around her hips.

She stirred and wiggled her bottom. "You're getting heavy," she said softly and giggled. "Are you still hard?"

Reluctantly, I pulled out of her warm sheath and chuckled. "I could still go on for a long time."

"I am a little sore." She turned around. "But you can lie in my arms, if you want to."

I got the discarded blanket and covered our nude bodies. She snuggled against me, warm and yielding. I felt content to lie in her cradling arms.

When her breathing steadied and I knew she was asleep, I slipped out from under the blanket, put on my clothes and went outside. A soft wind had come up, cooling the air. Looking up into the sky, I noticed that the stars had disappeared behind a cover of clouds. It looked like it might rain, but I doubted it. This was the dry season. Rain would be unusual.

I activated my transmitter. It took a moment before I got an answer.

"Yes, Major?"

"Cherryh," I said. "I ran into a bit of trouble trying to buy our transportation. I'll explain everything when I get back. I'm safe for now. So is Cassia. We're spending the night in a cave in the mountains. Stay alert. I might need you in the morning."

"I will. I have a fix on you. I won't have any problems finding you."

"If need be, bribe someone to lend you a horse. Steal it, if necessary. I might need you in a hurry."

"Why don't you come home now?"

"I would, but it is a dark night and I don't want to take a chance injuring the horses."

"All right, Major. Keep in touch."

I knew I could depend on Cherryh. I didn't think I would need him, but he had the weapons. I hadn't packed any. His weapons were disguised as harmless devices. Anyone accidentally discovering them wouldn't recognize them as such. Just a precaution.

I went back into the cave. The horses seemed calm. I could smell their droppings, but that could not be avoided. They snorted when I passed them and shuffled, but otherwise didn't move. I touched the gelding's muzzle and nostrils and stroked him gently. He nodded his head up and down. Then I crawled back under the covers with Cassia and spooned myself around her. She moaned slightly in her sleep, but didn't wake up. I smiled smugly. I guess I did wear her out.

Chapter Four

I awoke with a start. Light streamed in through the cave opening. Something besides the light caressing my face had roused me from my sleep. I strained my ears and heard voices in the distance and the clatter of hoofs on hard rock. It seems our friends had not given up their search.

Cassia stirred beside me and opened her eyes. Sitting up, she shivered and yawned. "Is it morning?" she asked.

I nodded and put a finger against my lips. "Get dressed," I whispered.

She gave me a bewildered look, only now noticing her surroundings. "I had a nice dream," she said. "I dreamed I was running through a field of flowers. It was raining gently. You were in my dream, chasing me. I ran away, but then I let you catch me, and..." She blushed. "It was wonderful," she said with a faraway voice.

I smiled and touched her face. "I'm sure it was, but now you better get dressed."

I heard a shout outside, closer this time. We didn't have much time before they'd stumble across this cave. I didn't want to be caught inside. They could wait for us to come out and pick us up as we emerged.

She put her hand to her lips. "It's them, isn't it?"

I nodded, getting up. I rolled up the blanket, threw it across the gelding's back. Cassia dressed hurriedly and rolled up of the other two blankets. I stroked the gelding's flanks. He seemed fidgety. The chestnut and the black mare were stomping their feet, eager to leave the confines of the cave. The horses were probably hungry and thirsty. I opened one of the saddlebags and, as expected, found it filled with oats. A good horseman always carried some food for his horse, especially when traveling across a desolate terrain. I grabbed a handful and fed the gelding and then the other two.

"You stay here," I told Cassia. "Let me scout out the area first."

She nodded. I could see she was scared. "Be careful," she whispered.

I stuck my head out of the opening and looked left and right. The narrow cleft between the two flat rocks seemed clear. Warily, I moved to the right exit, the one we had entered the night before. Straining my ears, I could hear the neighing of a horse. It seemed farther away. Maybe they were moving on.

I relaxed and turned to get Cassia and the horses.

"Hold it right there!" a harsh voice called out. It came from above me.

When I looked up, I saw the upper body of a man leaning over the edge of the rock and the barrel of a rifle aiming at me.

Even my super strength and the ability to jump higher than an ordinary man didn't help me here. I lifted my hands above my head. "I paid for the horses," I called.

He laughed. "Apparently not enough. Now...if you have any weapons take them out slowly and throw them away from you."

"I don't carry any weapons. I'm a peaceful man." I wondered why he hadn't shot me yet. Looking at a rock the size of my fist, I had an idea. Casually, I took a couple of steps and started to crouch. If I could get that rock, it would make a good missile. The sound of clacking hoofs close by stopped my movement. Then things happened very quickly.

When I saw the shadow of a man entering the narrow fissure, my body went automatically into combat mode. I moved to intercept the intruder, grabbed him and held him over my head. He screamed only once when the bullet from above hit him and dropped his rifle. Before the shooter could put another bullet into the chamber, I had dropped his wounded companion, raced out of the crevice and was climbing up the steep slope to the top of the giant rock.

I hoped that the rifle I took from the man I had overcome was loaded. The sniper would be baffled for a while, wondering what happened to me, hopefully long enough to give me time to surprise him.

He was lying on his belly, searching the crevice below for me, when I stepped up to him. Ramming the barrel of my rifle into his back, I said, "Put your weapon beside you, very carefully."

He froze, and then he obeyed my order. I kicked his rifle to the side and told him to turn around. He lay on his back, staring up at me.

"I only did what I was told," he said, fear screaming from his eyes.

"Relax," I said, "I'm not a murderer. I don't shoot unarmed men. Not like you."

"My rifle discharged accidentally. You surprised me when you moved." He gave me a calculating look. "I've never seen anyone move so fast. Who are you?"

"Just a man who's fighting for his life. Where are your other friends? How many of you are after me?"

"Just Miguel and me. The others had to get back to work. Mr. Woodfield figured the two of us should be enough to…" he hesitated.

"To kill us," I finished for him.

He nodded.

"So why didn't you shoot me right away when you spotted me?"

"I couldn't do it. I'm not a cold-blooded murderer. I've never killed anyone."

"Lucky for you I'm also a peaceful man." I stared at him. "What do you suggest I do with you now?"

He gave me a hopeful grin. "Let me go. I'll tell Mr. Woodfield we couldn't find you. He'll give up the search."

"How are you going to explain your companion's injury?"

"We'll say it was an accident."

I nodded. "All right. I'll go as far as giving you back your rifle, without ammunition. I'm not taking any chances."

"Thank you." He seemed to breathe easier. "I won't forget this." He rose, dusted off his clothing and held out his hand. "I am Marcel."

I smiled, but didn't shake his hand. "I wish I could say 'I'm happy to meet you, Marcel.'"

He shrugged. "I understand."

I made him empty his pockets and took all his bullets. Then I emptied the chamber and magazine of his rifle and handed it to him. "I'm going to keep Miguel's rifle," I said. "I will need some insurance."

Unfortunately, when we got back down to check his companion, we found Miguel dead. It would complicate matters, but not for me. I waited until Marcel had tied Miguel onto his horse and watched him ride away.

Cassia was anxiously waiting for me. She gave a little cry when I entered the cave then she fell into my arms and hugged me. "I was so afraid," she sobbed. "I heard a shot. What happened?"

"Everything's fine, for now. Let's get out of here."

We led the horses out of the crevice, mounted them and took off in the direction of the town. I didn't believe for one minute that Mr. Woodfield would believe Marcel's story. He'd send his men after us again, to finish what Marcel and Miguel couldn't accomplish.

Activating my built-in transmitter, I told Cherryh not to worry. We were on our way, but I knew he'd worry anyway. We spurred our steeds to travel at a slow trot, and we made it back to the town in under an hour. As expected, Cherryh was anxious to find out what happened.

Not only Cherryh had worried. The old man Tetrus had been beside himself when the wagon and the *Raesca* showed up without his daughter the night before. He gave me an angry look when we rode in, but he calmed down when I handed him another small Sun-Crystal.

"I will have a word with Woodfield when he comes into town," he promised.

"He'll just deny everything," I said. "Better leave things alone." I turned to Cassia. "The chestnut is yours, Cassia. It's a gift from me."

She squealed happily, put her arms around my neck and kissed me. Her father cleared his throat. Then he walked away, mumbling to himself.

"Can you have someone look after the horses?" I asked Cassia. She nodded. "I'll get Markus. He knows about horses."

"I am hungry," I said to Cherryh. "Have you had breakfast?"

He shook his head. "I wasn't hungry." His eyes took in my appearance. "You look like hell, Major."

Laughing, I clapped his shoulder. "Come on, let's eat." I noticed he was wearing his cleaned clothes. "After that, I'll wash up and put on my own shirt and pants."

Saskia brought our breakfast. She gave Cherrryh a knowing smile and laughed when he slapped her playfully on the rump. She walked away, swinging her hips. If she possessed her sister's passion, Cherryh probably didn't get much sleep last night. At least he'd been more comfortable than I had.

"Fine animals you bought," Cherryh commented, while chewing on a boiled tuber.

"I paid too much for them," I said. "Almost more than I was prepared to pay." I leaned back in my chair. "I grew up on this planet.

I never realized how much criminal activity is a part of our way of life. I have to be more careful from now on."

"The trade-caravan? How difficult will it be to join up with it?"

"I don't expect any problems. Old Tetrus will put in a good word for us. After all, we've primed him for it. If Dragor is as greedy as I expect him to be, he won't question our presence here. We'll just have to take care not to broadcast our apparent wealth too openly."

"I hope he is not too greedy. We'll never make it across the mountains...alive."

I grinned. "I managed to procure a little bit of insurance. I got us a rifle. Displaying it openly may act as deterrent."

"I think I'll rely on my own little arsenal, thank you," Cherryh said.

* * * *

We knew that the caravan had arrived when a half dozen men in dusty clothing, carrying rifles, entered the tavern in the afternoon. One of them stood out from the rest. He was tall, rugged, unshaven, and mean looking. He wore a hat with a large brim. Two oversized revolvers on his broad belt made him even more menacing.

"I think Dragor has just made his grand entrance," I said to Cherryh. We were seated at one of the tables in the corner. With the wall at our backs. One could never be too careful in these places, and I was becoming a bit paranoid.

I saw Dragor talking with Tetrus. They were throwing glances in our direction. Well...I guess introductions were made. If my assumptions were correct the famous caravan master would visit us at our table, and he didn't disappoint me. He tipped his hat to Tetrus and started on his way to our little corner. I watched him casually as he swaggered toward us.

"I hear you want to join my caravan," Dragor said and took a seat across from us. He didn't look behind him. He was confident that his men would guard his back. He gained my immediate respect. Only a powerful man, and a popular one at that, could command the loyalty of his men.

"You heard correctly," I said and pushed a bottle across the table. "Here, have a drink with us."

Looking at the glass in front of him, he said, "Looks like you've been expecting me." He poured from the bottle, held the glass against the light and chuckled. "Seems you only drink the best."

I smiled. "Is there anything else?"

Downing the yellow liquid, he squinted at me with bright blue eyes. His bushy eyebrows pulled together into a frown, creating a deep furrow above his nose. "Tetrus tells me you pay with Sun-Crystals."

I nodded. "You don't accept those as payment?" I asked.

He didn't answer, poured himself another glass. "How many do you have?" The question came unexpected.

"Enough to pay you," I answered.

"Your friend doesn't talk much." He looked directly at Cherryh, who returned his gaze without expression. Only his eyes seemed colder than usual.

"He doesn't trust you," I said.

"Maybe he has good reason." Dragor chuckled. "There are five of us and two of you. I don't see any weapons. What would prevent me from taking all of your Sun-Crystals?"

"This!" Cherryh said. Even I was surprised at the speed events unfolded. He left his seat with fluid movements and stepped behind the caravan master. Before Dragor could react, Cherryh had removed the two pistols and pressed them into Dragor's neck. "You'd be dead right now had I chosen to kill you," Cherryh murmured and put the pistols onto the table in front of the caravan master.

Dragor rubbed his neck, staring at Cherryh, back in his seat. "Handy trick," he muttered. "You must teach it to me. How'd you manage to move so fast?"

"Lots of practice." Cherryh smiled for the first time, but his smile was not encouraging. "It would take more than five men to overcome us. We are no easy targets."

"I'll remember that." Dragor looked thoughtful. "Two Sun-crystals from each of you should be sufficient. Be ready in the morning." He rose and smiled. "I don't rob my customers. It's bad for business." Then he turned and walked back to his men, who had been watching us. They relaxed when he joined them at their tables. Soon they were busy drinking and playing a game of dice balls.

Cassia came out of the kitchen and served them drinks, and then she walked up to us. "Your horses have been fed and watered. Markus even rubbed them down. He's very good with animals." She looked at me. "Maybe you should pay him something. He would make sure they're ready for you in the morning when you leave."

I groped in one of my pockets and gave her some coins. "You're right. It would help us a lot if your friend looked after them."

She hesitated, blushed and bent closer to me. "Can we share a bed tonight?" she whispered into my ear.

I inhaled her fragrance. She smelled good. She had obviously taken a bath and put on some perfume. My loins accepted her invitation eagerly, even though my mind told me not to. I nodded and touched her hand. "Sure, if you so wish."

She planted a kiss on my cheek and left.

Cherryh had been watching. He grinned when I looked at him and lifted his glass. "To collateral damage, sir."

"Oh, shut up, Cherryh!" I joined him in a drink and sighed, remembering something a friend told me once. *There'd be fewer problems in this world, if it weren't for that little black triangle.*

You are so right, my old friend, so right.

* * * *

Cherryh excused himself with a grin when time came to go to sleep. I had the room to myself. Cassia must have been waiting for Cherryh to leave, because she slipped into my room only a few minutes after he left.

"Your friend is spending the night with my sister," she said and began removing her clothing. Naked, she stood in front of me.

I studied her. I actually saw her naked in the light for the first time. Just the light from an oil lamp, but enough to see her body clearly. She had a nice figure. No fat. Nicely shaped full breasts and a flat stomach. Her buttocks, when she presented them to me, were round and firm, but fleshy enough to make them sexually alluring. I've always been attracted to a woman's buttocks. Sparse pubic hair covered her feminine parts. Another thing I preferred. A cleft hidden behind a thick bush of hair does not have the same effect on me as a shaved pussy or one like Cassia's.

She noticed me staring at the small triangle and blushed. Her hand went down to cover her swollen mound.

"Don't," I said softly. "I need to look at you. I enjoy feasting my eyes on the beautiful body of a woman."

"But I'm not that beautiful," she protested. "Look at me. Look at the lumps on my hips."

"I don't see any," I said and smiled. "Maybe your mirror is lying to you."

She laughed. "You're still dressed. That is not fair." She came up to me and began tugging on my pants. "Take them off. Let me look at you."

It was my turn to laugh. "This is the second time you tell me to take off my pants."

Her full lips formed a pout. "I want to see what I'm letting into my belly," she murmured and opened my belt.

I pulled off my shirt and let her push down my pants. She gasped when she saw me naked. "I knew that you were muscular, but I had no idea you looked like this," she said, her breath catching in her throat. Her hands stroked my chest and my biceps. "Such muscles," she whispered. Her hand slid down my belly, down to my manhood. "Have you grown since last night?" she asked, curling her fingers around my reacting pole. "I don't remember him being so big."

"He looks bigger than he is," I said gently and kissed her. My hands grabbed her buttocks and squeezed them.

"Let me kiss him," she said and sank to her knees in front of me.

When her tongue began licking the head of my engorged organ, she almost made me explode. She opened her lips and slipped them over the shiny tip, and then very slowly she swallowed the whole length. Her fingers dug into my buttocks, as she slowly moved her head back and forth. Before I came inside her mouth, she released me and rose to her feet.

Smiling, she lay on the bed, spreading her legs. "Now you do me," she said.

I knelt between her open thighs, bent over her exposed slit. Spreading the thick lips, I rubbed the pink cleft and put a finger into the opening. She moaned. "Use your tongue," she cried out softly.

She had applied perfume to herself, and I inhaled the sweet heady scent of her femininity. Putting a tongue into her moist slit, I licked her gently, pushed my tongue deep into her. She squirmed and lifted her hips. "Yes…yes…that's good. Oh…that is so good…" she sobbed and grabbed my head between her hands. "By the Great Mother of the Desert, never stop doing this to me…"

I finally did, because I was aching so badly for her that I couldn't stand it much longer. Moving on top of her, I thrust my hard organ into her hot, sopping wet love-channel. She let out a suppressed cry and moved against me like a wild animal. "Fill me up!" she sobbed, trying to strangle the intruder in her belly with muscles gone soft, but still powerful.

I turned her around and let her lie on her belly. She lifted up a little to let me back inside her, and then I pressed my body against her smooth back and pounded away between her beautiful cheeks. She gasped underneath me. Her juices were flowing freely, and she let out a loud sob when she experienced an orgasm.

"Let me be on top." Her voice seemed strangled in this position.

I pulled out and flopped onto my back, my satisfier sticking up high. She climbed on top of me and hovered for a moment. Then she sank into my lap. I watched my mast disappear into the soft floss of her swollen mound. With a deep cry, she sheathed me again, her pussy soft and dripping. The shadows from the light of the oil lamp played hide and seek on her writhing body. She had her face turned up and her breasts strained away from her ribcage, as she pumped untiringly on top of me.

She experienced a number of orgasms before I decided to have my own. I timed it so we would come simultaneously. When I felt her stiffen, I released my own pressure and called out hoarsely as the unbelievable pleasure gripped my shaking body.

She collapsed into my arms when it was over and just lay there, trying to catch her breath.

"You can't be a normal human," she whispered after calming down. Wiggling her hips, she gasped. "You are still stiff inside me."

I grinned and kissed her soft full lips. "I'm far from finished," I said and pushed up against her.

Chapter Five

We left the next morning. Cassia's eyes were large when she watched me ride away. I felt a little guilty, but then I shrugged. She would get over me, especially after she realized the value of the Sun-Crystals I had given her. She could move away from this forsaken place and live in any of the bigger cities if she wanted to, meet plenty of eligible young men who would be eager to bed a rich young lady like her, maybe even marry her. On the other hand, she could decide never to marry, just enjoy life.

The caravan consisted of three sleds and eight smaller wagons. The sleds were of the same type they used in the caravans going north through the deserts, platforms carried on the backs of four beasts of burden. Raescas pulled the wagons. Most of the the riding animals were horses. Only one member of the party rode a *Harsa,* the tough, scaly beasts Aleethy raised on her ranch. The man who rode it kept to himself. He was armed with a fancy rifle, which he carried in front of him for all to see. Seems he didn't trust anyone, especially Dragor and his men. Not that I blamed him.

Our saddlebags were filled with food for us and oats for the horses. Behind the saddles hung Gandor-entrails full of water, meant mostly for the horses. Our own drinking water we carried in gourds hanging from our belts.

We followed the only trail crossing the mountains in this part of the country. Another one crossed about two hundred kilometers south from here, but it was rougher and much harsher. I had secretly hoped that the girls might be in this caravan, but more likely, the slave traders would use the one farther south.

We reached the mountains by noon. The ground had become increasingly more rocky and harder. I noticed a slight incline, but not so steep that it put stress on our animals. The trees became more stunted as we neared the mountains, and finally there weren't any. This was not the most inviting countryside. I could never understand why people would want to live here. We past through one small settlement, or what once had been one, now it was just a collection of abandoned shacks and rotting houses with gaping holes for doors and windows.

We stopped at a small watering hole to water the animals. The water looked brackish and dirty, and we didn't bother to fill our canteens. Bleached bones and skeletons of smaller animals cluttered the grounds around it, evidence that large predators visited it frequently. We hadn't come across any, so far, but most of them roamed the desert at night when the temperature cooled down.

The trails through the mountains had probably been created millions of years ago, when quakes and eruptions still plagued the planet. A series of small craters, the majority closed up by rockslides, and fields of hardened lava provided a relatively smooth surface. By evening, we came upon a deep lake, possibly a crater that had been formed when a large meteorite hit Redsky. The land around it looked quite fertile, with trees and grasses growing along the perimeter of the lake.

We made camp close to the lake, in the protection of a grove of trees. All kinds of garbage littered the area, evidence that all caravans passing through this part of the mountain used this as their rest stop.

We took the saddles off our horses and tethered them to one of the trees. Some of the others let their mounts roam around free. Cherryh and I decided to be on the cautious side. Without our horses, we'd be stranded here.

Feeling grubby and dirty, we removed our clothes and jumped into the lake. Cherryh was the first one, while I stood watch. That might sound paranoid, but we didn't trust any of these fine gentlemen.

I was surprised when the mysterious owner of the *Harsa* strolled up to us while Cherryh was in the water.

"Do you mind if I join your friend in the water?" he asked me.

I shrugged. "Be my guest."

He smiled and began removing some of his outer clothing. He seemed younger than I had thought, even though his hair showed a touch of gray. His skin was even darker than Cherryh's.

"I noticed that you joined the caravan in *Rockslide*," he commented while undressing. He put his fancy rifle on top of his clothing, which he piled up close to the edge of the lake.

"Yes, we did," I said, nodding.

"I've been watching you." He gave me a curious look. "You two keep to yourselves. I assume you're not part of Dragor's group?"

I chuckled. "You assume correctly. And you?"

"I don't trust them," he said, looking around with cautious eyes.

"If it makes you feel any better, neither do we." I kept watching the caravan master's men. They were busy setting up a fire pit. A couple of them gathered dried branches, while another one tried to fix the stakes that held the pole for a large pot to boil water or for making soup, so I assumed.

The other two stood around, caressing their rifles.

Our new friend saw me looking at them. "Are they expecting the camp to be attacked?" he asked me.

I shrugged. "Who knows? Maybe there are large animals around. We'd better be on guard against any eventuality." I smiled. "Any."

"I am Abdul Shakur," he said. "And you?"

"Dan Griffin." I held out a hand. He shook it with a strong grip. I pointed into the water. "That is Cherryh."

"We'll talk later," Shakur said and walked into the water. However, he didn't swim out, just stayed close to shore, watching his clothing and rifle, ready to climb back out on dry land.

Cherryh came out, and I took my turn. I swam away from shore. The water felt cold, but refreshing. My backside hurt. My legs were stiff. The exercise would be good, after sitting for hours in the saddle.

When I looked toward shore, I saw Shakur climbing back on land and drying himself with his hands. I dove into the clear water. As I headed deeper, I could see a swarm of fish dashing away. After surfacing, I lay on my back and stared into the evening sky. I had missed this sky all those years away from home. Blood red, streaked with bluish and white stripes, it didn't look at all like Earth's blue sky. On my travels, I had seen blue ones, green ones, purple ones, and even yellow ones, but none as beautiful and haunting as the one on Redsky.

The sun hovered like a huge fiery red eye above the mountaintops, painting them as red as the sky.

A flock of large birds crossed above me. I recognized them by their long necks, the shape of their wings...*Dust Cranes*. On their way to their breeding grounds in the south.

The water began chilling down my body. Time to get out.

Dragor's men had managed to light the fire. Something boiled inside the pot hanging above the flames. Shakur gave me a hand and pulled me out of the water. It was just a gesture. I didn't really need any help.

"Thanks," I said, shaking myself. "The water is quite cold up here in the mountains."

"The lake is deep," Shakur said. "But it's clean." He watched me get dressed. "I notice you don't carry any weapons, except for that old rifle," he said.

"We are not entirely weaponless," I grinned, patting the knife I had hanging from my belt. A gift from Cassia.

"A knife." He shook his head. "Not much good against a bullet."

"The Isramic people are not walking around armed, the way they do in Newland and other provinces. We don't want to offend anyone," Cherryh said.

"Are you from Isram?" Shakur asked him.

"No, but I am a practitioner of the Mislanic Faith," Cherryh answered.

Shakur looked at me. "And you?"

I shrugged. Might as well start the charade now. "I am a believer also."

Shakur studied us both for a moment, and then he smiled and bowed. "I told you my name, but I never told you who I am. I am the son of Abdul-Hakam." He spoke in the language of Isram.

"The Grand Minister of Isram?" I asked, surprised.

He smiled and nodded. "I see you speak our language."

"I'd expect the son of the Grand Minister to travel in the company of at least a dozen guards," I said.

"I am quite capable of defending myself. I am a faithful servant of Allar, the Lord of War," he said proudly. "A dozen guards would only draw attention to my person. I prefer traveling alone."

I bowed. "May you be safe in the net of the Holy Triangle," I said formally.

He laid two fingers of his right hand against his forehead, and then rolled his hand in front of him. "I wish that for you also," he replied.

Knowing who he was explained why he kept to himself. His faith compelled him to shun *Nonbelievers*. Being the son of the Grand Minister added to that obligation.

"I would ask you to join me in a meal," Shakur said, switching back to the common language of Redsky, "but I'm afraid my provisions are meager."

"Perhaps you can share some of our food," I suggested. "We've been fortunate. Our host in *Rockslide* was quite generous." I smiled, thinking of Cassia. *Generous in more ways than one.*

We chose a spot close to our horses and squatted down under one of the trees. Shakur accepted the food we offered him. "Thank you. Maybe I can repay your hospitality?"

I smiled. "Possibly sooner than you think. We are on our way to Rhandistan. We were hoping to gain an audience with The Grand Minister."

"So you shall." Shakur studied us. "May I ask your reasons for visiting our country? I don't see any trading goods."

"None that are visible," I said and switched back to Isramic. "I represent a group of business people from *Highland.* We are dealing in a diverse selection of merchandise and are now branching into different fields. Right now, we are looking for buyers of high quality slaves. Young females, to be more precise. I was hoping to find interested parties in your country."

Shakur sat silent for a while. "There are many things in my country that I do not approve of and which I would like to change, had I the power to do so. I must tell you that I am not in favor of the slave trade. Unfortunately, many of my countrymen have the false belief that slavery is part of our heritage."

"There are many things we do, even if we don't believe in them," I said.

"Am I to understand that you don't approve of slavery, yet you are a slave trader?"

I lifted my shoulders. "That about sums it up."

He shook his head. "So why are you doing it? You strike me as a man with principles."

"Money." I glanced at Cherryh. "We need to raise a lot of money for what we are planning."

"And what would that be?"

"You tell him, my brother."

Cherryh cleared his throat. "I am not a native of Redsky. My home planet is about one hundred light-years away from here. It would be a good world to live on, were it not for the fact that my people are suffering from persecution."

"By your people, you mean *Believers of Mislan*?" Shakur asked.

Cherryh nodded. "We can't hold high positions in the government. Our businesses are bombed and the citizens terrorized.

So my family decided to emigrate. My brother here told me of Redsky where there is a whole country of Believers."

Shakur looked at me and smiled. "You two are brothers?"

"That is correct," I said.

"You don't look like brothers," Shakur gave us a suspicious look.

"I guess it's the color of my skin that gives me away." I chuckled. "We don't of course have the same parents. I was actually born on Redsky and spent my youth here. My parents were citizens of Terra, and when their contract was up, they moved back to Terra. A year later, they were transferred again...to Cherryh's home world. Unfortunately, soon after they arrived there, they were both killed in a freak accident. Cherryh's parents adopted me, since I didn't have any relatives."

The story flowed across my lips so easily I almost believed it myself. Angel sure had done a terrific job with our programming.

Shakur listened with interest. Now he smiled. "The color of a man's skin does not determine his beliefs, but it betrays his lineage." His expression became solemn. "I will see what I can do to help you with that other matter." He rose. "And now, I think, I will have to take care of my steed."

Cherryh looked at me and said with a grin, "That went smoothly, *my brother*."

I grinned back. "I had no idea we were brothers until you said it."

"Neither did I." He stared after Shakur. "I wonder what else that computer put into our heads," he said thoughtfully.

"I think she has a sense of humor, if that is possible," I said, watching the men who sat around the fire, most of them rough looking individuals. It wasn't hard to guess their business. Weapons, drugs, slaves. I wouldn't have minded looking into their covered wagons to see what they carried. I knew there weren't any slaves. We would have seen evidence of that by now. A couple of older men sat by themselves away from the others, probably the only legitimate merchants of the whole bunch.

"Do you think we should sleep in shifts tonight?" Cherryh asked, following my eyes.

"I don't think there is need for that," I said. "You heard Dragor tell us that he didn't rob his customers. I believe him. We should be quite safe."

"From him, but what about those others?"

"None of them would dare, even if they knew what we carry on our persons. Not in the presence of Dragor's men. No, don't worry, we're safe." If I should be wrong, I trusted my own and Cherryh's built-in sentries to wake us in time. I had no intentions of spending half the night awake.

We stowed the food back into our saddlebags and unrolled the blankets. The nights did get quite cold up here in the mountains and, without the blankets, it would have been a bit uncomfortable. Even now, the temperature had already dropped and I could feel the chill creep into my bones.

"Let's warm up a little by the fire," I said to Cherryh.

The men looked up when we approached. Dragor noticed us and waved us closer. "Don't be shy. Join us for a warm drink." Only now, I saw the small wooden barrel on a low stool beside him. He pointed to it. "Help yourself to a cup of wine. But I'm afraid you'll have to supply your own cups."

"I'll go get them," Cherryh said and walked back to our spot.

I looked into the large pot hanging over the fire. There were chunks of something dark floating in the boiling water. "What's in there?" I asked, sniffing the aroma rising from the pot. It didn't smell too inviting.

Dragor grinned. "Snake-lizard soup. You're welcome to a bowl if you like."

I shook myself. *Snake-Lizard.* You'd have to be pretty desperate to eat that. "No, I don't believe so. We brought our own food."

He let out a rumbling laugh. "Some people think it's a delicacy."

Cherryh had come back with our cups. "I'll have a cup of wine, though," I said, not wanting to insult our host. I skirted the men standing around the fire and filled my cup from the barrel.

The wine wasn't the best quality, but it felt good going down my throat.

"You never told me what business you're in," Dragor said jovially.

"Slaves," I said bluntly. "We're buying and selling slaves."

"I don't see any."

"I don't handle them myself," I said. "I leave that to others more qualified. I just make the deals." I took another mouthful of wine, wondering where these words of mine originated. What had prompted me to say that? *What the hell did you do to me, Angel?*

"Slaves, hmm, interesting. I've never seen you on this route before." Dragor stared at me with curious eyes.

"No, you haven't. That's because my employers are just now expanding their interests."

"Does that mean I might see more of you in the future?"

"If things go well in Isram, that may just possibly be the case."

Dragor lifted his cup. "Then let's drink to the future and mutual business dealings."

Chapter Six

The air was brisk when we moved out the next morning. I had slept well and felt quite rested. So did Cherryh. I guess we both had been in need of the rest. There hadn't been much of it the previous two nights. Cherryh refilled the Gandor-entrails with fresh water from the lake, but the horses would be all right for a while. The temperature wouldn't get as hot during the day as it had been in the desert, and food would be no problem either. There'd be plenty of grasses for them.

Shakur decided to ride with us, and we didn't discourage him. His good will and friendship guaranteed us an audience with the Grand Minister of Isram.

The trees were becoming sparser, but there were plenty of tall and thick shrubs, not exactly encouraging, because they provided cover for predators. Human and animal.

Dragor and two of his men rode in the front and the other three in the rear of the caravan, their rifles in their hands, ready to be fired. I noticed that most of the other members of our group also carried their weapons in the open.

"How real is the danger of being attacked here by anyone?" I asked Shakur.

"Quite real," he said. "Once we're in Isram, we should be safe. This part of the mountains is really no-man's land and frequented by bands of rogues. They're mostly criminals from the indigenous population."

"You have a problem with the native inhabitants?"

"Not anymore. Most of the natives live in areas designated to them, have for the last fifty years, and they are quite happy to live their own lives. The ones who live with humans are usually servants. That is all they are able to do. They're not civilized and not very intelligent. There are, of course, still some wild tribes roaming our country, and once in awhile they do raid the more remote settlements.

Otherwise we have them under control. I know it is not so in Newland and the other provinces in the west."

I didn't comment. It didn't surprise me that he called the indigenous people 'not very intelligent'. That was the popular belief among humans. I knew it was not true. I had spent enough time with the tribes to know that they possessed an intelligence equal to humans. They only lacked education.

The day went by without problems, and by nightfall, we stopped at another campsite. This one didn't have a lake, only a small pond with clear water. Cherryh and I decided to sit with Dragor and his men and shared a cup of wine with them. We even ate from the *Snake-Lizard* soup. Sometimes it is better to be part of a group than not.

At first, Shakur was reluctant to sit with the *Barbarian Infidels*, as he called Dragor and his men in his native language, but then he agreed to have at least a cup of wine. He politely declined the soup. "It reminds me too much of the *Jelcas-tails* I was forced to eat when I was young," he said with a chuckle. They all laughed and with that, they accepted his and our presence.

After three cups from the heady wine, Shakur shed his aloofness and turned out to be a man with many interesting stories to tell, but he never revealed his true identity. As far as everyone was concerned, he was just another traveler, possibly a mercenary looking for a job.

It was late when we rolled ourselves into our blankets. The stars were visible in the clear sky and the temperature already quite cold, this being the highest elevation of the trail. After tonight, we would be descending into lower and warmer regions.

I awoke with the distinctive feeling that something was amiss. Opening my eyes, I didn't move, just lay quiet, listening. Then I heard the faint scraping of an object being pulled across the hard ground. It came from the direction of the fire. Turning my head slowly, I saw shadows moving around the fire pit. The fire had burned down. Only embers glowed inside the ring of stones, small sparks exploded occasionally into the air, illuminating the source of the sound.

Someone was trying to steal the large kettle.

My eyes adjusted to the darkness, and my hearing slipped into enhancement. The intruders were clearly visible now. I could make out the intricate tattoos on their naked arms. The blue and yellow color of their horns identified them as members of the *Dark Lizard* tribe. Fierce warriors feared by many of the other tribes. I wondered what they were doing here in the mountains. They usually roamed the expanse between the Golgat Mountain Ridge and the Black River Ridge, but then I saw the bright yellow of a Yellowhorn and realized that these were renegades, outlaws from different tribes.

I saw at least six, but there could be more hiding in the shadows. The ones I saw moved on silent feet. I wondered what had happened to our sentry. Either dead by the hands of the intruders or fallen asleep at his post.

I shifted slightly, as if turning in my sleep, so I could get a look at the wooded area to my right. My suspicion was confirmed. More were hiding among the thicket. How many I couldn't tell. I also heard the soft snorting of their riding animals.

My rifle lay beside me, loaded and ready, but one bullet wasn't going to make a difference. It would only take care of one of them. I didn't see any rifles in their hands, but that didn't mean they didn't have any. Their comrades in the shrubs might be aiming their weapons right now at our heads. No guarantee they would hit any of us, but not impossible.

I knew that Cherryh was awake. I detected the change in the rhythm of his breathing moments after I awoke. No surprise there, since his body had been altered just like mine, and his senses were as alert as my own.

The indigenous people could see better in the dark than humans, but they didn't have the ability Cherryh and I had. We lay in the darkness of the trees and weren't as visible as some of the others. None of the other members of our caravan seemed to be aware of the trespassers in our midst. The consumption of wine had put them into a stupor, and they were probably dreaming of the hot-blooded women they would find in Isram.

I felt the gentle click in my ear as my built-in speaker came to life.

"Major." Cherryh's voice came as a ghostly whisper. "I'll take care of the ones in the bushes."

Activating my own communicator, I whispered, "All right." I knew that he also had seen the path he could take to surprise the unseen watchers. He moved away without another comment. I watched his dark form crawling close to the ground, shielded by the shrubs that connected our sleeping place with the thicket the intruders used as their hiding place. He disappeared from my view into the protection of the tall shrubs.

I waited for a few minutes, to give Cherryh time. I didn't have to wait too long.

"Perimeter secured." His voice sounded cold, distant, all emotions gone from it. He had done what needed to be done.

My own body shifted into combat-mode. I moved before I even had a chance to plan what I would do. It was almost like watching someone else. I was aware of what I did, but it happened without conscious effort.

I didn't need my rifle. It would only have been a handicap. The first of the interlopers fell without a sound when I grabbed him from behind and broke his neck with a quick twist. As he fell, I grabbed his *kiso* and moved behind the Yellowhorn, who was stalking in front of him. Pulling back his head, I drew the sharp blade across his throat. Gurgling and gushing blood, he joined his companion on the cold ground.

The two who were carrying the kettle must have heard the commotion, because they stopped and looked back. When they saw me, they dropped the kettle and went for their own *kisos.* I was upon them before they could pull the wicket blades out of their sheaths. The first one died when I smashed my fist into his face, pushing the bones of his nose into his brain. Then I killed the other one with one vicious kick to his throat, crushing his windpipe with the heel of my foot.

My incredible reflexes saved me from the thrown *Ginsa-staffs* of the last two, who had been heading toward the spot where Dragor and his men were sleeping. Dropping to the ground, I rolled away and rose again, grabbing one of the barbed weapons, which had clattered harmlessly to the ground behind me. Swinging it in an arc above my head, I advanced toward the two, who stood frozen in surprise.

"What and who are you?" one of them asked. He spoke harshly, but I detected the fear in his voice, as he prepared himself to die.

"I'm a man," I said. "Nobody, really."

"Why did you kill my brothers?"

I chuckled grimly. "You slink into our camp in the cover of darkness, steal our possessions and probably would have killed us all, and you must ask?"

"You humans came to our world and took everything we owned. You build fenced-in areas on land that once belonged to us and put us inside, keeping us prisoner. We are not allowed to roam the forests, mountains and desert freely. We cannot hunt the animals to feed our children. We only take what belongs to us." His voice had risen in defiance. "So, go ahead, kill me, human! My spirit and the spirit of my slain brothers will not rest until all humans have been driven from the world that belongs to us."

"A noble speech," I said mildly, letting the Ginsa-staff fall to the ground. My body dropped out of combat-mode, leaving me still alert, but the coldness was gone. I studied him as he pushed out his chest, the short bristles on his head stiff with defiance. I didn't recognize his clan. His horns were black, the clan-ring in his left ear of an unknown design. Most of the tribes I knew wore their rings in their right ear.

"Who are you?" I asked him. I noticed that he seemed more relaxed now, assuming, correctly, that he might live.

"A nobody, just like you," he said quietly, and then he added, "now."

"He's Dorcas, the former chief of the Blackhorn Tribe." Shakur came walking out of the darkness of the trees. He carried his rifle in his hands. "He's a criminal, wanted for the murder of many of my countrymen."

The tribesman turned. I saw his body stiffen as he watched Shakur coming closer. "Shakur," he said, sneering, and spat onto the ground. "*The Butcher*!"

Shakur walked up to him and pushed the barrel of his rifle into his chest. "Do not call me a butcher! I didn't give the order to kill your family. I was the one who tried to save them, if only you would have given yourself up."

Dorcas spat again. "You were the commanding officer. You did nothing when they cut off my oldest son's head and put it on display. You did nothing when your soldiers raped my wife and my daughters. You just watched."

"I *could* do nothing. It was out of my hands."

"You are the son of the Grand Minister! You could have done something."

"Done what?" said a voice from the ground. Dragor's voice. The noise had finally woken him and the others. I saw him rise. He looked at the dark shapes on the ground. "What in the name of the *Seven Demon-heads* happened here?"

"We had visitors," I said dryly. "They tried to separate us from our possessions. I stopped them, that's all."

He gave me an odd look. "All by yourself?"

"No, I had a little help." I watched Cherryh slowly walking out of the shrubbery, his face passive, but I knew what went on inside his head. Even though he looked big and mean, he didn't approve of wanton killings. Neither of us did, but we did it when it was necessary.

Dragor watched him, too. He looked back at me. "Slave traders, right?" he said, and then he turned to Shakur. "What do you want to do with these two rogues, your Highness?"

Shakur stared up at the moon that had risen above the summit of the mountains. The harsh light illuminated his dark countenance. His long hair framed his face like a shadowy veil. I could not help but think of the *Dark Avenger of the Night*. A legendary figure from Isramic folklore. Also known as *The Butcher*.

"Let them go," he said softly, "there has been enough killing tonight." He gazed at Cherryh and then at me. "More than enough."

Dorcas lifted his hand, looked at me and moved his fingers in the air, and then he bowed toward Shakur. His companion, who hadn't spoken all this time, gave me a long look, and then he said, "You are a worthy adversary. Maybe some day you and I will meet in battle." He put his fist against his heart, and then he touched his horns.

I threw him the Ginsa-staff I was holding in my hand. Then I picked up the other one and threw it to Dorcas, who caught it in the air. He touched the tip of his left horn. Both men turned and walked proudly into the thicket. Moments later, we heard their steeds moving away.

"How many?" I asked Cherryh.

"Three," he answered and looked at the dead bodies. "We can't just leave them lying around."

I nodded. "The vultures will get them either way, but we can move them away from camp into the thick of the underbrush and cover them with branches. It will give their souls time to leave before their bodies get ripped apart by the carrion eaters."

He gave me a strange look. "I thought you didn't believe in souls?"

"I may not, but they do." I gave him a crooked grin. "It never hurts to be on the cautious side, just in case."

Shaking his head, he walked to one of the corpses and began pulling it toward the shrubbery. A couple of Dragor's men joined him in the grisly task, and soon the evidence of the violence that had taken place was gone. Except for the kettle, which lay overturned on the ground.

"You have much explaining to do, my friend," Shakur said to me. "I would be interested to know how you managed to overcome four members of a species that is known to possess strength far greater than any human man can ever hope to achieve. And it seems, with your bare hands."

"I surprised them. They didn't expect any opposition." I smiled. "I am a trained warrior."

"It must truly be a very savage world you and your brother grew up in," he said, studying me with great interest. "You must tell me about it, sometimes."

We found the man who was supposed to guard the camp with his throat cut slumped against the tree he had been sitting under. His rifle lay beside him, untouched.

Dragor searched the dead man's pockets, removed his belongings and stashed them inside the saddlebags of his own horse. He saw me watching him. "He's dead. They're no good to him," he growled. "Besides, he was in my employ. Now I'm a man short." He eyed me shrewdly. "You wouldn't be looking for another job, would you?"

I shook my head and smiled thinly. "Thanks for the offer, but I am happy with the one I have."

He nodded. "If you change your mind...my offer stands. I could use a man of your caliber."

Needless to say, we didn't get much more sleep that night. Most of the men stayed up and talked in hushed tones. So many deaths at once were disconcerting even to men as tough as these. They kept throwing glances in our direction. Any connection we made with them had dissipated. Instead of hailing us as saviors, they feared us, and they would be happy to see us depart when we reached our destination.

"These men don't trust you," Shakur said to us. He sat with his back against one of the trees, his rifle in his hand.

"Do you?" I asked.

He laughed. "As much as you trust me."

Chapter Seven

The temperature became warmer as we neared the border of Isram. A group of armed men, soldiers on big black horses, met us. The animals were a strong breed found only in Isram, ridden mainly by the military. None of them would ever find its way outside the country. Anyone trying to sell one to outsiders would be punished severely.

The lieutenant of the small platoon conferred with Shakur for a while, and then he waved us on.

"Why all the soldiers?" I asked Shakur.

"We've had rumors of an army being trained in Newland and other provinces with the purpose of invading our country. We are preparing for that eventuality."

"I guess your journey was a reconnaissance trip to find out if the rumors are true?"

"In a way."

"And did you find them to be true?"

"I found no evidence to substantiate it," he admitted. "But then appearances can sometimes be misleading."

"Maybe there are forces at work who want to create unrest on Redsky," I said. "It happened on other worlds I've been on."

Shakur rode silently beside me. "Much has changed these last five years. You won't know, because you've never been in our country," he said suddenly. "My father is getting old and tired. He may not be able to hold the position of Grand Minister for much longer. The man who will replace him has already been chosen. He is not like my father, as you will find out."

"Won't you be your father's successor?" I asked.

"The position of Grand Minister is not hereditary. He is chosen by the Council of High Priests. I am not the one."

I detected a tinge of bitterness in his words, and his heartbeat increased when he spoke of the successor. "Who is he?" I kept my voice neutral, made the question rhetorical, even though his answer interested my very much.

"His name is Koldar. He is the Grand Marshall of our armed forces. He is also a High Priest and the Thalmani of the Council of High Priests. He claims to be in touch with the Star-Gods themselves. In addition, he is the brother of my father's wife."

"Your mother?"

"My mother was killed six years ago in a bizarre accident. She fell off her horse while riding alone and broke her neck." He spoke with a low voice. Had I not possessed my enhanced hearing I might have had trouble understanding him. "She was an excellent rider, practically born on a horse. She was found by my father's new wife, who consoled him in his time of grief. My father married her a year after my mother's death."

"You don't approve of the marriage?" I asked.

"I am not my father's keeper. I am just his son."

"Are you the only son?"

"*Now* I am. I had two brothers, both older. They died on separate occasions. One in a fight with a rebellious group of natives and the other one only last year when he got lost at sea in his sailing ship."

"No sisters?" I looked at him and saw his expression change.

"Three," he said, smiling. "Three beautiful sisters. And seven nieces and nephews. I hope you will have a chance to meet them."

"Do you have a wife?"

"Yes, I do. And she is the most beautiful creature you've ever seen. I also have two sons. One of them wants to join the priesthood. The other one…?" He shrugged and chuckled. "Who knows? Perhaps he'll be Grand Minister some day." He looked over at me. "And you? Is there a woman in your life? Any children?"

"I was married once, not anymore. Children? A daughter, but she doesn't know me." I saw no harm in telling him part of the truth, finding it easier than making up a completely new story.

"Too bad," Shakur said. "There is no greater joy than children."

"I'm sure there isn't." It was my turn to become bitter. Time to change the subject. "Shakur, answer me a question. According to the scriptures I was taught, believers of Mislan believe in the Holy Triangle. The father, Allar, who is the God of War, the mother, Evar, Goddess of Peace, and the daughter, Aphrody, the Goddess of Love. You mentioned that Allar rules the heavens now. How long has he ruled on Redsky?"

"Ever since Mohmar, the Prophet, came to Redsky three-hundred years ago. He was the first Grand Minister and the first Thalmani. He united all the believers of Mislan and created the country Isram. Allar will rule for another seven-hundred years. After that, the Holy Mother Evar will rule. We will have peace for a thousand years. By that time, everyone on Redsky will be a Believer...according to the prophecies. But surely you know all this?"

"You forget I was raised in the Faith on another planet, where things are different. The history there is similar, but not exactly the same. We never had a prophet named Mohmar. Where did he come from?"

"He claimed to be the reincarnation of an ancient god and declared himself a Holy Man. They say he was also a great warrior." He gave me an inquiring look. "What was your prophet's name?"

I shrugged. "Many claimed to be prophets. Most of them turned out to be false. It is sometimes not easy to prove if a man speaks the truth or if he lies, especially if he claims to be a messenger of the gods. Who will question him and possibly evoke the wrath of the gods?"

Shakur seemed to ponder that remark in a long period of silence.

The countryside we were traveling through had changed gradually. The land seemed more fertile. Tall grasses grew all around us, with different kinds of flowers. The trees were taller, with thicker trunks and far-reaching branches. We traveled alongside a river that wound its way between gentle hills. To the north, I saw thick forests with straight growing trees. No doubt, it was a lush country on this side of the mountain ridge. No wonder they wanted to protect it against invaders from other, less productive regions. However, the threat was imaginary, not real. I needed to discover the ones responsible.

When night fell, we camped beside the river.

"We'll be safe tonight," Shakur said to us, "and for the rest of the journey. No one would dare attack us here."

A couple of Dragor's men went hunting and shot a wild goat. They cut it into smaller pieces and roasted the chunks of meat over the fire. The meat tasted a little gamy, but it went down easy with a few cups of wine. Spirits were high.

We slept peacefully that night and left the camp early next morning. By afternoon, we reached the outskirts of Rhandistan, the central city of Isram, and the first city built when Isram was founded. Larger and older than Capital City in Newland, it featured older as well as newer buildings. They differed in style from the way they built in the west. The further we traveled into the center of the city, the larger and richer the houses became.

Many people walked on the streets and sidewalks. I didn't see any airsleds, only low wagons pulled by donkey-like animals, and men on horses. Technology was not desirable in Isram. According to the teachings in the Book of Faith, technology corrupted the minds and souls of humanity. The mortal human body was not meant to fly, not without wings. Since humans didn't have wings, obviously we weren't supposed to fly.

The people of Isram did not have the monopoly on that idea. Throughout the colonized planets large groups of people clung to the same belief. Many condemned traveling between the stars, most of them ignoring the fact that at one time or another they had been brought to their new world in a spaceship traveling through space.

"My father will be fascinated talking to you about the world you come from, you and your brother," Shakur said as he rode beside me. "He is a strong believer in the teachings of Mislan, but he is open-minded, realizing that ours is not the only religion in the Universe. He is quite aware that Redsky is just one of many different worlds."

"And you?" I asked him.

"I believe that the Star-Gods rule the Universe. Their names may be different on other worlds, but essentially, they are the same spiritual force everywhere. I also believe in Mohmar, the Prophet, and I believe that his mortal body housed the spirit of one of the lesser gods."

I didn't comment, because I didn't believe in any gods, especially not the ones we created ourselves.

Our caravan traveled slowly down the main road, which was paved with flat stones. Shops, stores and warehouses had replaced the private residences on either side of the road. Our first stop was a large open plaza, surrounded by large depots and storage facilities.

"This is where we must part," Dragor, the caravan master informed us. "I hope you will join us again, when you return to your country." He bowed to Shakur. "It was an honor to have you with us, your Highness."

Shakur returned the bow, chuckling. "Since when did you know my identity?"

Dragor smiled. "Ever since you joined our caravan. I recognized the rifle you're carrying. I sold it to your father many years ago, before he became Grand Minister of Isram. Only a son of Abdul-Hakam would be the owner of that weapon."

"I'll be more careful next time I want to travel incognito." Shakur smiled. "I hope your business dealings in my country are successful." He bowed and turned to ride away. Looking at me, he said, "Unless you have other plans, it may be in your best interest to accompany me to the palace. I will introduce you to my father."

I nodded. "Thank you, your Highness."

We arrived at the palace shortly before nightfall. A wall built from large stones surrounded the palace grounds, but nothing barred the entrance, except for a couple of soldiers who stood guard on either side of the open gate. They stepped in our way when we approached, but when Shakur spoke to them, they bowed and moved aside to let us enter.

"Not much security," I commented.

Shakur chuckled. "I told you when we entered my country, you would be safe. Crime is quite low, because criminals are dealt with harshly. Anyone convicted of murder is executed, without exception. Thiefs are sent to labor camps. Child molesters and wife beaters are castrated and will spend many years doing hard labor in the darkest mines. Many don't survive."

"What if a person is convicted but is innocent?"

Shakur shrugged. "I am not saying it doesn't happen, but we have skilled interrogators who usually get to the truth fairly quickly, and they seldom make mistakes." He smiled. "And if one is innocent, he will be considered a martyr in the eyes of the prophets and will go straight to *Nirvana*, just like a warrior who dies in battle."

He reigned in his steed. I noticed that we had come to what looked like a stable. A couple of young boys came running and bowed. "Welcome home, your Highness," one of them said.

Shakur jumped off the *Harsa* and stepped in front of it, stroking the narrow scaly head. "Now, you behave yourself and don't bite anyone," he murmured in the beast's earflaps. The *Harsa* hissed and showed its long teeth as it poked Shakur on the shoulder. He laughed and gave it a gentle slap.

As ferocious as these beasts looked, they were actually mild tempered and quite easy to handle.

Shakur smiled at the stable boys. "Take good care of our steeds," he told them.

Cherryh and I climbed off our animals and stretched our legs.

"Leave your gear with your horses," Shakur told us. "I will send someone later to get it for you. Now, come, we will get ourselves cleaned up first, take a long bath and have something to eat. You will meet my father in the morning. He is old and doesn't stay up late anymore. Aside from that, he doesn't like to deal with visitors this late in the day."

* * * *

The warm water made me drowsy. With half open eyes, I looked at our host, who sat in the large tub across from me, his eyes closed. "I'm surprised you're not rushing to your wife and sons. Aren't you missing them?" I asked him.

He opened one eye to peer at me. "I miss them very much, but I am too tired to deal with them now." He chuckled. "My wife…she…how should I say…she is quite a passionate woman, like all of the women of Isram, and she expects me to…ah…perform my duty as a husband the moment I set foot into my house. You understand?" He grinned.

I grinned back. "You're a lucky man, your Highness."

"Most lucky, but it can become burdensome, sometimes." He sighed. "Tomorrow will be soon enough. Also, before I can go home I have to meet with my father, the Grand Minister."

"You live on the palace grounds?" I asked.

He shook his head. "No. I live in a smaller palace. It is located on the shores of the lake south of Rhandistan. Once you're finished with my father, maybe you can visit me."

"I'm looking forward to that visit."

Shakur stood up and climbed out of the tub. "Time to retire." He took the large towel one of the silent servant girls handed him. Drying himself, he looked at the girl and then at me. "Fara will show you to your quarters and look after your needs. She is quite good at everything she does." Before he walked away, he winked. "I hope you're not too tired."

Fara gave me a warm smile when I reached for the towel she held in her arm. "Do you want me to dry you?" she asked.

I shook my head. "I think I can manage by myself."

She looked disappointed. "A massage would be nice," I said. "Would that be too much to ask?"

"Oh, not at all. I would be pleased to give you a massage." She had a pretty smile and a fine body, clearly visible under the almost transparent gown she wore. She stepped behind me and hung a robe across my shoulders.

"What about my brother?" I asked.

"He will be taken care of, as well." She gave one of the other girls a sign and pointed at Cherryh, and then she turned to me. "Come, follow me."

I followed her down a corridor. She stopped in front of a door and opened it. "This is your room," she said.

The luxury of the room surprised me. I saw a divan with lots of cushions, a wide bed, a table and two chairs. In one corner stood a chest with drawers and on top of it a washbasin and a pitcher. Beside it lay a thick towel, nicely folded.

A thick carpet covered the floor and a partially opened heavy curtain concealed a large window. I could see the star-speckled sky through the open part.

As soon as the door closed behind us, Fara slipped out of her robe and, naked, she walked toward me. She put her arms around my neck and smiled up at me. "Do you want your massage now or later?"

"What did you have in mind?" I asked, putting my hand on one of her ample buttocks.

Without speaking, she began to remove my robe and let it fall to the floor. Her hands touched my shoulders, my biceps, traveled across my chest, down my belly. "You look very strong," she murmured softly. "Are all your muscles this hard?" She had a mischievous light in her dark eyes.

"Why don't you find out?" I asked, pressing my hard mast into her soft belly.

She giggled and made a low sound in her throat. Then she opened her legs a little and captured my organ between her strong thighs. "It is very hard," she moaned, rubbing back and forth.

I took her buttocks into my hands and lifted her. She pulled up her legs and pushed herself away from my body. My pole twitched between her warm thighs. Wiggling her bottom, she descended slowly and slid her sheath over my organ. She felt tight, but slippery, and she took her time to mold her soft walls around my shaft.

Then she wrapped her long legs around my torso and pressed her voluptuous body against mine. Pulling back her buttocks, she began to move very slowly in front of me.

"I think you'll have to help a little," she whispered.

I used my arms like a swing, to give her greater freedom. It didn't take long before her sex-organ adjusted to the thickness of my pole. Her soft inner muscles pulsed gently as she moved back and forth. When she experienced her first orgasm, she went wild, but she was hampered by our position. I waited until she relaxed, and then I walked with her to the divan and put her onto her back.

"That's better," she moaned, pulled up her legs and hooked her knees behind her shoulders, giving me deep access into her hot belly.

We coupled for a long time, constantly changing positions. When she rode me, she acted like a wild animal, whimpering and moaning so loud I hoped no one would hear us. She came with a long wailing cry and collapsed on top of me, her breasts flattening against my chest. She didn't give me much rest. Slipping off me, she knelt on the floor, her rump up.

I got into position behind her and stroked her lovely buttocks. Moaning, she moved them in my hands and whispered fiercely, "Put it back in."

"You're going to kill me," I said, chuckling.

She cried out softly when I entered her again and rotated her pelvis, milking me with ferocious speed. "And you are killing *me*," she shouted when an orgasm racked her body. I let my own release of built-up pressure take over my body, my shouts of pleasure blending with hers. Finally we relaxed, spent and satisfied.

She turned and took me into her arms. "Now I'm too exhausted to give you a massage," she said. "I've never met anyone with the endurance and hunger you possess. Have you gone without coupling with a woman for a long time?"

"It depends what you define as 'a long time'."

She moved lazily beneath me. "It doesn't matter. Do you want me to stay with you tonight? I could give you that massage in the morning."

"The morning will be fine. As long as it isn't too early. I think I'll need some rest. Especially after the workout you gave me."

She laughed and snuggled against me.

Chapter Eight

Someone stroking my chest awoke me in the morning. I pretended to be asleep, even when a pair of tender hands moved across my belly and ended up between my legs. Gentle fingers stroked my penis, and it soon grew inside those soft fingers.

Strong thighs straddled me. I slid into a welcoming, warm sheath. Opening my eyes a little, I looked at Fara's face as she moved slowly on top of me. She had her face turned up and didn't notice that I watched her. Little moans escaped her full lips and open mouth.

When I felt her warm fluid, I grabbed her gyrating hips and slammed up against her, filling her with my own discharge. She cried out in surprise and dug her fingers into my chest, quivering violently until her orgasm subsided.

She looked at me, her dark eyes large. "This is your wakeup call," she said, smiling. Then she slid off me and walked to the dresser where she picked up the washbasin. Apparently changing her mind, she turned to look at me. "Maybe you'd like to take a bath before breakfast?"

I jumped out of bed and stretched. "I think I would."

She brought my robe and laid it across my shoulders. "Too bad you have other duties to perform today." She spoke with a low voice.

"Why?"

She stepped in front of me. "Because I would like to spend the day with you. You made me feel good last night."

I smiled. "Maybe we can carry on tonight."

She shrugged and bent to pick up her gown from the floor. Slipping into it, she held out a hand. "Come, I'll rub your body."

We didn't go back to the huge tub I had been in the night before. Instead she took me into a tiled room. There was a sunken tub in the middle, already filled with warm, steaming water. A young girl sat beside it, a couple of towels across her bare crossed legs.

"Thank you, Shantia," Fara said to the girl. "Go and get some fresh clothing for our guest."

The girl bowed and walked toward the door, turned before she walked out, gave me one last look and smiled.

It hadn't escaped Fara. She chuckled. "She's still young, but the passion is already flowing in her veins, and she can sense a sexually powerful man." She watched me shrug out of my robe. "I promised you a massage." She spoke with a throaty voice.

"Maybe after my bath," I said. As much as I had enjoyed our encounter, I was anxious to meet with the Grand Minister.

"All right." She made a little face, and I knew that a massage had not been the only thing she would have liked to give me.

I slipped into the warm water. Fara joined me and began to soap my body with gentle hands. Then she rubbed me with a small cloth. Her hands lingered on my shoulders and my biceps, stroked them slowly then she touched my crotch and washed it thoroughly, more thorough then necessary. I didn't mind.

Afterwards, she dried me with a large towel. I could have done all that myself, but I knew she had been told to take care of me. It would have been impolite to refuse her.

We were barely finished, when the door to the bath opened and Shantia walked back in, carrying a bundle in her arms. She put the bundle onto a bench and stood beside it, waiting. Her eyes studied my naked body, but she didn't say anything.

"What are you waiting for?" Fara looked at the girl. "Help our guest get dressed!"

The girl bowed again and opened the bundle. She removed a pair of loose pants and put them on the floor, waiting for me to step into them. I did, and she slowly pulled them up. When she reached my crotch area, she hesitated, licked her lips, but then she finished her task and tied a knot into the rope that kept the pants from slipping back to the floor.

Fara chuckled. "Good girl. I hope you got a good look. Maybe someday you may do more than that."

Shantia blushed and looked away. "I didn't mean to…"

"Of course you didn't." Fara laughed. "Now, go and wait outside until we are finished."

With a low bow, the girl left the room, but not without giving me a smoldering look.

I grinned. That girl was a volcano waiting to erupt, and it wouldn't be long before that would happen.

"She's old enough," Fara said, as if reading my thoughts. "Maybe I'll let you sample her." She smiled. "But for now I want you to give me all your attention."

"What about my meeting with the Grand Minister?"

"You're scheduled for this afternoon. The Grand Minister is a man with many obligations." Her hands were busy with my pants. "Now, let's take these off again."

"What about breakfast?"

She smiled. "Later. It'll taste much better after this."

I groaned when her warm hand closed over my rigid pole and I let her pull me to the bench.

* * * *

After breakfast, Fara took me for walk through the gardens behind the palace. Gravel paths led to patches of blooming flowers and meticulously kept ponds with water so clear you could see the colorful fish swimming below the floating plants and among the rocks. The grounds were clean and the shrubs trimmed into shapes of animals and mythical creatures. We didn't meet anyone, except for the gardeners and workers who kept out of sight when they saw us approaching. It was all very peaceful and quiet.

We made love under one of the huge trees, and then we went and sat at a table on a terrace. A serving girl brought us food and wine.

After we ate, we made love again. At last it was time for me to meet with the Grand Minister.

I felt good and, with regret, I watched Fara walk away. She left me standing in a large chamber filled with statues and antic furniture. Pictures hung on the walls that weren't covered by curtains. I was just about to sit down in one of the ancient chairs, when I heard someone enter the room. Turning, I saw a tall man walking toward me. His loose uniform couldn't hide the muscular frame beneath.

"I am Captain Arran." He lifted his hand in a salute.

I returned the gesture. "Dan Griffin," I said.

He smiled. "I know. Prince Abdul-Shakur told me everything about you."

"I was hoping I would see him again," I said.

"He wanted to hurry home to see his family, but he sends his regards." He moved his hand. "Please follow me. The Grand Minister will see you now."

We entered a wide corridor and walked up a flight of stairs toward a set of huge wooden doors. They opened as we approached, and we stepped through into a large chamber.

A full dozen armed guards stood inside. They saluted when we walked in, and Captain Arran told them to relax. They did, but I could see them watching me. Even though their captain had told them to relax, I sensed their tenseness, saw their fingers close to the trigger of their guns.

When I smiled at them, none of them smiled back, only their black eyes flickered nervously.

"Your soldiers seem well trained," I commented.

Captain Arran nodded. "They are. These are the Grand Minister's personal guards. They are the best." He chuckled. "Of course, all of our soldiers are very good. They have to be. It is part of our religion and heritage."

Walking through another oversized doorway, we entered a large room. My eyes fell on the old man seated in a deeply cushioned chair. His eyes were half-closed. He seemed to be listening to the thrilling song of a small red bird sitting on his shoulder.

When we walked in, he opened his eyes fully and watched us come closer. The bird on his shoulder never stopped singing.

"This is the visitor Dan Griffin, your Excellency," Captain Arran introduced me.

"Ah, yes, Dan Griffin. My son told me about you." The Grand Minister's voice was surprisingly strong. He studied me with eyes that were clear and sharp. "Why did you come?" he asked.

"To trade," I said.

"To sell slaves?" The old man shook his head. "Hardly." He lifted an arm, pointed a finger at me. "You are not a simple trader, Dan Griffin. Who are you?"

"What makes you think I am not who I say I am, your Excellency?"

"My son told me how you killed the invaders of your camp. You are a soldier. Tell me again, why are you here?"

I realized that my little charade was over, and I decided to stop the game. I knew with sudden clarity what I had to do.

"You are correct. I am not a simple trader. I did not come here looking for trading partners. I am Major Griffin. I am in the service of the Terran Spaceforce."

The Grand Minister leaned back in his seat. "The mighty Terran Empire never bothered before with our country. Why would it suddenly take an interest in Isram?"

"Newland feels threatened by the built-up of arms in Isram," I told him bluntly. "We don't want a war on this planet."

"Neither do we, Major," the Grand Minister spoke sharply, "but we will defend our Motherland against an invasion from Newland."

His vehemence surprised me, shocked me a little. "Your Excellency," I said, "surely you don't believe the people of Newland will attack your country? They have their own problems with the indigenous tribes, more than they can handle."

"I have heard differently," the old man said. "There are rumors about great hordes of the *Horned-ones* banding together, and also of much activity at our border and of an increase in the number of soldiers. There is talk of a *Holy War*."

"Somebody is feeding you the right information, but slightly distorted, your Excellency," I said softly.

The Grand Minister looked at me in silence. The small red bird on his shoulder had finally stopped singing, as if sensing the tension in the air. Bending forward a little, the old man smiled. "You know, Major Griffin, I am not sure if I like you. You speak very politely. You use the correct words, and yet...there is insolence in your words that even your politeness cannot mask." He lifted a hand, pointed a bony finger at something behind me. "There are two soldiers with automatic weapons behind you, Major."

"I know," I said.

"Each gun has the capability of firing thirty rounds continuously. Not even a soldier of the Terran Empire can outrun those. And you are unarmed. Your life is in my hands. Yet...you're not afraid."

"Hardly, your Excellency. As you point out, I am a soldier." The poor fools would be dead before they'd manage to fire a single shot. Even they wouldn't be stupid enough to keep their fingers on the triggers. My body had automatically gone into combat-mode when I sensed them moving into position.

I had confidence in my own abilities, but I didn't tell him that.

"You are either a fool or very arrogant, or both. I believe you are neither. Are all Terran soldiers like you?"

"I'm not a Terran, just an agent for the Empire." I smiled lightly. "I would advise against any hostilities toward me and my companion. My superiors would not take it kindly."

"A threat, Major?"

"No, only friendly advice. As friendly as my visit."

The Grand Minister stared at me. Suddenly, his dark face broke into a wide grin. "I've decided to like you, Major Dan Griffin. You are an insolent, arrogant man, but likable." His head turned to look at someone coming into the room through a door to my left.

I couldn't help but stare.

Tall and slim, thick black hair spilling over brown shoulders, she was beautiful. She looked young, but her black eyes spoke of experience beyond her years.

"Major Griffin, meet my wife."

Chapter Nine

Tafima.

That was her name. I couldn't keep my eyes away from her. She appeared soft-spoken, but I sensed a deep burning fire waiting to be kindled.

I wanted her.

Sucking on a Kir-bone, she looked at me from across the table. She put the bone into a plate and wiped her fingers with a small satin cloth. "You haven't told me anything about yourself, Major Griffin," she said, smiling.

"There really is not much to tell, my Lady." I tried to cover my lustful interest in her with a chuckle.

She laughed. "Come, come, Major. You are too modest. Your life in the Service of the Terran Empire must be full of interesting stories."

"They would just bore you."

"Oh, no. I'm very interested. The planets out there must be teeming with strange and alien life forms."

"They are. Some of them quite dangerous." I looked into her black eyes, wishing I could be alone with her. I had always been better telling stories with my body than with my mouth.

A polite cough brought me back to the present, and I looked at the man beside Tafima. He was tall, well built, with a handsome dark face. His eyes and hair were black, like Tafima's.

Koldar, her brother.

"Are you a religious man, Major?" he asked me, his black eyes burning into mine.

"Depends," I answered cautiously. From what I had been told, this man was a fanatic, who hated *Nonbelievers*. Nonbelievers in his religion, that is.

"Depends on what?"

"Well...it depends on how you define a religious man, but I prefer not to discuss religion with strangers."

"Why not? It is an important part of our lives." His voice rose slightly.

I lifted a hand. "On my travels among the planets I have seen too many friendships break up over religious beliefs."

"There is only one *True Religion!*"

He was a fanatic all right, and he needed a damper.

"In Isram, perhaps," I said, putting an edge into my voice, "but not in the rest of the Galaxy."

"I'm told you claim to be a follower of Mislan. Am I to understand that is a lie?"

I smiled. "I'm afraid so, and I apologize for that. We were under the impression that it would be the only way to gain access into Isram. It seems we were given the wrong information. I am not here to criticize your faith and possibly cause friction between Isram and the rest of Redsky. The Empire is only interested in keeping the peace, nothing else. What you believe in is not our business."

He looked at me coldly. I had the distinct feeling he didn't like me. "Maybe it should be. It is clear you have never experienced the power of the Star-Gods. I invite you to come to one of our worship services in the Holy Temple. It will open your eyes."

I nodded. "If time allows, I will follow your invitation." I turned my head as the Grand Minister clapped his hands. "Now, now, Koldar," he called out. "You know we have to be tolerant with the *Nonbelievers*. Not all of them are bad." He smiled at me. "You must forgive him, Major Griffin, but Koldar is a very zealous young man. Not only is he the Grand Marshal of our Armed Forces, he is also the Thalmani of our country." Again, he looked at Koldar. "I will have no more talk about religion!"

Koldar bent his head slightly. "As you wish, Grand Minister." He seemed subdued, but he couldn't hide the glowing of his eyes.

"My brother gets carried away sometimes." Tafima laughed softly. "But he is a devoted worshipper of the Star-Gods, and his followers worship him. He has converted many *Nonbelievers.*"

"I thought you had only one religion in Isram?" I asked.

Koldar opened his mouth, but after glancing at the Grand Minister, he kept silent.

"We do," the old man said, "but not all of them are what you might call *True Believers*. Koldar seems to have attracted a great following, and I'm not certain if I am all that pleased about it." Again, he clapped his hands. "But that is not your concern, Major Griffin.

How about some more wine?" He waved toward one of the serving girls.

"Thank you," I said, when the girl filled my glass. She smiled, but her smile seemed empty and her eyes dead. Only when she refilled Koldar's glass did her eyes light up. She moved as someone would in a trance.

"Thank you, my child," Koldar said. She smiled and walked away.

Tafima saw me watching the girl. "She's just a slave," she said. "A girl from Westland. She's one of my brother's devoted followers. He converted her himself."

"So why doesn't he free her?" I asked, looking at the High Priest.

"She is happy the way she is," he answered.

"No slave is happy, Priest!" I said sharply.

He half-rose, anger clouding his face, but then he sank back, smiling. "You are a very arrogant man, Major Griffin."

The Grand Minister chuckled. "That's what I told him already. First time we agree on something."

"I don't believe in slavery, your Excellency," I said, keeping my voice calm, not an easy thing to do. In my mind, I saw the bound naked bodies of Meadow and Aleethy.

"It is part of our way of living, part of our heritage." The Grand Minister rose and turned to Tafima. "Accompany me into my chambers. I am getting tired."

She took his arm and led him through the door.

"He seems quite devoted to your sister," I remarked, looking at Koldar.

He chuckled, actually smiled. "Not as much as a younger, more vital man would be. The Grand Minister is getting old."

I had a feeling he wanted to say more. He stopped suddenly as if afraid he had already said more than he should. He stood up. "If you will excuse me, Major Griffin, I must get back to my duties." He hesitated. "I think my sister will be back. I suggest you wait for her."

He turned abruptly and walked toward the main doors, his movements smooth, powerful. I knew beyond a doubt, there walked a dangerous man. A man to be watched.

I sat alone at the large table, sipping my wine. I wondered what had happened to Cherryh. I needed to let him know that our cover was blown. We had no more reason to carry on with the elaborate scheme we devised. A shame, actually. I smiled to myself. Somehow, it had been fun pretending to be someone else.

The door opened, and the serving girl came back into the room. She came over to my table, carrying a pitcher. The wine proved quite heady. I could feel the effect of it already, but I let her refill my glass. "Sit down," I told her. "Keep me company."

She smiled her empty smile. "Thank you, but I am not allowed."

She was pretty, quite young still. She wore a loose robe of rough spun material, but it didn't hide the shape of her buttocks when she bent down or the swell of her breasts.

I almost put my hand over her round buttock when I heard the fall of footsteps.

Tafima.

She gave me a friendly smile. "I'm glad you waited, Major. I'd like to invite you to come with me to the temple."

* * * *

Since I was a *Non-believer*, I had to stand in the back, with the other *Nonbelievers*, except there weren't any others. I was the only one. I felt somewhat out of place, standing there alone. Tafima had excused herself. "Just watch." With a smile, she'd then vanished through one of the doors.

The Service impressed me, and so did Koldar.

There were other minor priests and acolytes, but Koldar was obviously in power. He spoke with a strong, resonant voice. He had his followers spellbound, silent at times, then shouting and singing with enthusiastic voices.

One thing I found peculiar. I saw only men.

About half an hour into the Service one of the acolytes brought in four robed and hooded figures. He led them up the steps toward the altar. Then four other acolytes stepped behind the figures and removed their robes.

As I had expected.

Women.

Young and stark naked.

They stood very rigid, moving only when directed. I had no doubts they were drugged.

Koldar lifted his arms, chanting with a loud monotonous voice. One of the priests moved behind him and pulled off his robe.

Koldar stood naked in front of the girls, superbly built, like the statue of a god. I could see why young girls would adore him.

He walked slowly past the four girls and stopped in front of one of them. After looking her over, he bent, picked her up and carried her to the altar, where he laid her down.

The acolytes began chanting, while Koldar moved between the girl's spread legs. Below his flat, muscular belly, he sprouted an enormous erection. Slowly, his hands stroked the girl's body and opened her legs wider.

Then with a quick move, he pushed his erect penis into her.

The girl gave a loud moan as he entered her, and it didn't take long before she began writhing on top of the altar. Koldar moved with slow, deliberate strokes, pushing deep into her quivering belly.

I watched with mixed feelings. Somehow, I had not expected a sex-show, not in the temple.

While Koldar pounded between the girl's spread thighs, the acolytes and the rest of the congregation chanted softly to the rhythmic beating of a drum. After a while, the High Priest increased the speed of his lower body, until he suddenly stopped moving.

The congregation stopped the chant. In the sudden silence, the cries of ecstasy from the girl's lips rang through the temple.

I turned when someone tugged on my arm and found a young girl, her hood thrown back, standing beside me. "Come with me, please," she murmured.

I followed her, puzzled, not knowing what to expect. She led me through a narrow door into a long corridor, through another door into a darkened room. It was not very large. A wall-to-wall curtain covered one of the walls.

In the center of the room stood a narrow bed. The girl led me to it, told me to sit down.

I sensed the presence of someone else. Another girl, her face covered by a golden veil. She carried a tall golden vessel, which she handed to me.

"Drink this, please," the girl who had brought me said.

I tasted it, cautiously. It was wine. Pleasant, somewhat tardy. My guardian system registered minute amounts of a drug, but it detected no dangerous and harmful substances.

Slowly, I emptied the vessel.

The girl, who gave me the wine, stood swaying in front of me. Her hands went to her neck and untied the loose robe. With tantalizing slow movements, she let it slide to the floor, exposing her voluptuous naked body. Then she began a slow, sensuous dance.

Watching her luscious body moving in front of me, I felt my penis rise and an urge to grab her swaying hips. I tried to control the urge, but the heady wine I had consumed and the sight of her made it an almost losing battle.

Soft hands touched my body, and only then did I realize that a third girl had come in. She and the girl who had brought me began undressing me. I also realized that both girls were nude.

When I was naked, they suddenly stepped back. The one who had been dancing in front of me came closer and gently pushed me backward onto the bed. Then she moved to the head of the bed, her hands lightly on my shoulders. Dimly, I noticed that she wore a bracelet around her left wrist.

In the semi-darkness, I saw another naked woman coming into view. She stopped at the foot of the bed.

She was tall, slim, her body voluptuous, her breasts full and round, with dark brown areolae around her thick nipples.

My eyes traveled down her flat belly and studied her thick and fleshy Venus mound, completely hairless and smooth.

A golden mask covered her face. On her head, she wore an elaborate sparkling crown.

"Our High Priestess," the girl behind me whispered into my ear. "She will cleanse your sins."

The High Priestess straddled me. Fascinated and somewhat dazed, I watched my erect penis disappear between the fleshy lips of her sex-organ. A loud moan escaped my lips when I felt the hot tight moistness close over my straining member.

Slowly, she began rotating her lower body. I saw a pair of black eyes watching from behind the golden cold mask.

My hands grabbed her shapely hips, and my fingers dug deep into her firm, yet soft flesh.

As the High Priestess gyrated slowly above me, I gradually became aware of a soft chanting, but I didn't care. Only the soft lovely body I held in my hands and the tight sheath that caressed my hard member mattered.

My head was swimming from the wine and the things I had observed in the temple.

The soft muscles of her sex-organ gripped my pulsing mast in a tight vice, milking, sucking. I climaxed inside her like a hot geyser releasing its pressure after a long built-up.

I thought I'd never stop gushing.

The High Priestess held her position above me for several seconds after I was finally finished then she set me free, still hard.

In a clear moment, I noticed that the curtains had been drawn and behind it, I saw a large room filled with people...women. I wanted to sit up, but the girl who stood by my head held me down, gently but firmly.

From the mass of watching worshippers, women stood up, formed a line. As they did so, they dropped their robes and donned small golden masks. The first of the nude women reached my bed, which, I realized now, was an altar. The young woman accepted a small sip from a vessel the High Priestess held to her lips, and then she straddled me. Her hot sheath swallowed my hard organ. After a few strokes, she lifted off and made room for the next woman.

I didn't count how many women impaled themselves on my erect pole. I didn't have to, because I knew, my built-in computer registered each one. A coded impulse would recall every woman who had intercourse with me that night.

All of them were young, their pussies tight and wet. And hairy. None of them stayed with me long enough to let me really enjoy them. When the last one finished, the girl at the head of the altar moved beside me. I didn't see her upper face behind the golden veil, but her body was exquisitely formed. When she straddled me, I noticed her smooth hairless mound. Slowly, the fleshy lips of her vagina closed over the swollen head of my abused penis.

I tried hard not to go off the moment I entered her. She moaned deeply and rotated her lovely body above mine.

I couldn't hold it for long. With a loud grunt, I shot my load and registered her loud cries as she experienced her own orgasm.

I heard the curtain close.

Holding my slowly shrinking member tightly inside her, the girl leaned forward, and through the veil, she kissed me lightly on the lips. Then she left me.

I closed my eyes, suddenly tired, my head spinning. I listened to her footsteps as she slipped out of the room.

Chapter Ten

Someone called my name, but I refused to open my eyes. Finally, just to stop whoever was shaking my shoulder from doing so I lifted an eyelid.

"Well, well. We are finally awake, Major Griffin."

"Don't you believe it," I croaked, groping for my aching head. It felt like a wild Gandor had kicked me.

I sat up. Looking around, I found myself lying in a wide, soft bed. Through a half-open curtain, bright light flooded a spacious room. Framed paintings adorned one wall and a number of statues were scattered throughout the room.

Tafima stood beside my bed, smiling. She looked stunning in the skintight outfit that covered her curvy body like a second skin. Her smile widened when she noticed me staring. "I don't wear this in public. It is not fitting for a woman to be exposed like this to every man's eyes, but these are my private quarters. We have lots of privacy here."

She snapped her fingers and a girl, who had been standing by the doorway, brought a tray with fresh fruit and a glass of juice. "You must be very hungry this morning." A mischievous smile played across her lips.

Detailed memories of my activities from the night before flooded up into my consciousness, up to the point where I passed out. After that, everything was blank.

"How did I get here?" I asked

She chuckled. "It took two of my strongest bodyguards to carry you. You're a big man, Major." She gave me a long look. "I hear you were initiated into our faith last night."

"That's what you call it?" I growled. "I call it rape."

She laughed. She had a pleasant laugh, happy, pleased. "You were quite fortunate. Not every *Non-believer* gets initiated by the High Priestess. That service is usually performed by a lesser priestess."

"What makes me so special?"

"I don't know. Why don't you tell me?" She laughed cheerfully. "Have something to eat."

"I will...later. Listen, I hope you don't think I am a *Believer* in your faith now."

"Nobody said so. But you have been initiated. It's a beginning."

She turned and walked away. Her buttocks moved beautifully beneath the thin material of her outfit.

I sighed.

How I'd love to get my hands on those fleshy mounds.

Biting into a juicy Mang-seed, I grinned at the slave girl. She wasn't so bad looking either. Actually, she was quite beautiful.

She smiled back. Her eyes were clear, not like the eyes of the girl I had seen the night before. I wondered about that other slave girl. The girl watched me silently while I ate my breakfast. I had the feeling she was studying me. When I looked at her, she smiled.

"I listened to your conversation with the High Priest yesterday," she said suddenly. "I gather you don't approve of slavery?"

"I didn't know you were there."

She chuckled. "I was, but you had only eyes for Lady Tafima."

"Hmm." I made a mental note to keep my eyes under control. "Was it that obvious?"

She shook her head, smiling smugly. "Not really, but I noticed. I am a good observer. I also have a gift for reading people."

"You also have a gift of being careless, girl. What is your name?"

"Lawni." She came closer. "And I am not careless. I know I can trust you."

While she refilled my empty glass from a pitcher, I studied her, intrigued by her forwardness. She wasn't quite as young as she appeared, maybe in her early thirties. She wore a loose shift made from thin, fine cloth. It clung to her, detailing parts of her body sharply. She had a nice figure. Her breasts swung freely inside the shift as she bent down.

My head was quite clear now, and I felt my penis stir underneath the light sheet.

She noticed and laughed throatily. Putting the pitcher down, she removed the tray. With a swift movement, she grabbed the hem of her shift and pulled it over her head.

She wore nothing underneath. I caught my breath. She was beautiful, her body ripe with heavy, solid breasts and wide flaring hips.

Slowly removing the sheet from the bed, she exposed my erection. She straddled me and pushed me onto my back. I watched my stiff penis disappear inside her soft pussy. The thick lips of her love-box slipped over the swollen head and leisurely swallowed my shaft until they touched the root of my aching organ.

I took her large breasts into my hands and rolled her thick, long nipples between my fingers. She moaned softly, closed her eyes and slowly began to rotate her pelvis. The walls of her love channel gripped my penis tightly, caressing the head ever so gently. I fought hard not to explode inside her. I wanted to enjoy the exquisite pleasure she gave me as long as possible.

She seemed to know when I was on the verge of coming, because she stopped gyrating. She lifted off, turned around and presented her lovely posterior to my feasting eyes. She hovered over my erect mast, reached down to take it into her hand and carefully she guided it into her dripping pussy. This time, instead of gyrating, she moved up and down, lifting up until my pole slipped almost out of her. Then she slowly sank back down, sucking it back inside her.

Once in awhile she would emit a low moan and sit quivering in my lap. I could feel the clutching of her pussy walls as she experienced an orgasm. After a few moments, she continued her slow up and down movement.

She kept this up for a long time, until she suddenly stopped moving and sighed. "I'm getting quite tired," she said and freed my penis. Slipping off me, she knelt on the bed, her buttocks up in the air. "Take me from the back," she said with a low voice and looked at me with her dark eyes.

I moved behind her and spread her fleshy cheeks with my hands, exposing the thick lips of her sex-organ. Putting my stiff mast between her soft pussy lips, I slid back inside her. She began bucking beneath me, moaning loudly. I put my hands on her hips to steady her movements. When I felt ready to climax, I laid her onto her back and moved between her spread thighs.

"I like it better this way," I said.

Her eyes were closed when I climaxed inside her clutching channel, and she mewled like a kitten.

"You are quite something," she murmured lazily as I rolled away. "Quite something. Are all Earthmen like you?"

"Not all," I said, half asleep. "Just some."

* * * *

When I awoke, she had gone. My clothes lay neatly folded on a chair beside the bed. Sitting up, I tried to recall my last sexual encounter. That tiny computer chip inside me had stored every little detail in its memory. I had no problem remembering.

Damn it! What had come me again? The way I was going, I'd fuck myself to death in a short time. Even a man with my abilities had his limits. I gave a coded impulse to give my body a systems analysis and wasn't surprised when I discovered that there were foreign substances in minute quantities in my bloodstream and nervous system, but I could not determine when and how they had been administered. A tiny program, which I could not decode, kept that fact from me. I also discovered blank spots in my artificial memory banks. Since I couldn't detect any danger alerts, I didn't worry about it. However, I didn't shrug it off, either.

A knock on the door made me look up to see a slave girl walking in. "You have a visitor," she said.

A man pushed past her.

Cherryh.

"What the hell is going on, Major?"

I shrugged. "I don't know what you mean, Cherryh?"

He looked at me sharply. "Are you all right?"

"Yeah. Why?"

"Well...seeing you still in bed at this hour might make a man think you're sick or something."

I slipped from the bed, gathered my clothes from the chair and began dressing. "I'm fine, Cherryh. Don't always worry. You're beginning to sound like Kelsey." I looked at the girl. "I'd like to talk to this man alone."

She nodded and left. I watched her walk out the door, enjoyed the way her shapely buttocks swayed underneath the flimsy material of the robe she wore. Cherryh was watching me, his eyes narrow. "You look kind of pale, Major," he said.

I waved him off. "It's nothing. I feel fine, maybe just a little hungry, that's all." I saw the bowl of fruit on the table. "You want some fruit, Cherryh?"

"No thanks. I had breakfast." He looked around and grinned. "Fancy quarters you have here."

"These are not my quarters. They belong to Lady Tafima."

"The Grand Minister's wife?" He shook his head. "What did you get yourself into, Major?" The disapproval in his voice was not hard to detect.

"It's not quite as obvious as it looks, Cherryh. There is nothing going on between me and the Lady Tafima."

He raised his eyebrows a fraction. "What am I to think, Major? I find you naked in the bed of the wife of the Grand Minister…"

"That you have, and I don't blame you for drawing the wrong conclusions. Lady Tafima took me to the temple last night to observe the worshippers. There I was…initiated into the Mislan faith."

"Initiated?"

"I don't want to bore you with the details. Things got…how should I say…somewhat hairy." I smiled, but didn't say more. Obviously, he didn't get the pun. "By the way, you can stop pretending you've been persecuted because of your faith and are looking for a place to emigrate to. We've been unmasked."

"I know." He smiled, but without much humor. "I had my own meeting with the Grand Minister."

"When?"

"Early this morning. I was summoned by four armed guards and taken into the presence of Grand Minister Abdul Hakam. He may be old, but he certainly is not feeble. He has a powerful presence. But he seems friendly enough."

I bit into a juicy fruit. "Not bad, you should try some." He was still watching me, his eyes sharp, but with a deep crease between his eyebrows. He worried about something. I knew him too well. I stood up and looked at my reflection in a tall mirror. Those pants were a little baggy, but otherwise I presented an imposing figure. "I notice you've changed your outfit," I said to Cherryh.

He grinned. "I guess they didn't like our shabby clothes. I never got mine back this morning. I was told they didn't survive the wash."

"Just as well, now that our cover has been blown."

We were making small talk, and I knew something bothered him. "How will we proceed from here?" he asked.

"With caution," I said. "As you observed, the Grand Minister may be an old man, projecting an aura of amiability and good will, but we can't let that fool us. He is the Grand Minister and the highest power in this country, yet...I can't shake the feeling that he is not the one who makes decisions in Isram. There are other forces at work, powerful and dangerous forces."

"The church?"

"The religious leaders have a lot of power, but I'm not talking about them."

"Who then?"

"I don't know, and that is what we have to find out."

"Now that they know who we are, it will be extremely difficult to get any information." Cherryh looked thoughtful. "With your permission, Major, I would like to tour the city. Talk to merchants, possibly even a slave trader."

"Good idea. However, it may not be easy to get access to anyone. Remember, you're a *Non-Believer,* not really welcome in this country."

He smiled. "Who says I'm not a *Believer?* I never told anyone otherwise. Tonight I will go and pray in the temple."

"Not in the one on the palace grounds, please." I didn't tell him why. "It might also be a good idea if you could find living quarters outside the palace, go underground, so to speak."

"Then I should be on my way. The sooner the better." He saluted sloppily. Before he walked out the door, he said softly, "Be careful, Major."

The moment he left, the slave girl stepped back into the room. "The Grand Minister would like you to join him for dinner."

I followed her down the corridor, through a series of richly furnished rooms, into a large dining room. It was not the same room we had dined in the night before.

The Grand Minister and his wife Lady Tafima sat at a small table, across from each other.

"Sit down, Major Griffin." The Grand Ministers smiled when he saw me walking in.

I followed his invitation, seating myself on one of the two empty chairs. I noticed the fourth plate. "Expecting someone else?" I asked politely.

The Grand Minister nodded. "Yes, but don't worry. You can go ahead and start eating. We are very casual about that in our private quarters."

Tafima smiled. "I trust you rested well," she asked. Again, I noticed the mischievous way she smiled, and I was quite certain she knew what had happened. She looked stunning in the outfit she wore. Her breasts practically jumped out of her open blouse.

"I have, thank you," I said, trying to still the sudden thumping in my loins. So loud, it made me afraid even her husband could hear it.

"My wife tells me you've been to the temple," the Grand Minister said casually.

"Yes, your Excellency, I have."

"What do you think about Koldar?"

"Well..." I looked at his wife. "He has quite a powerful personality and an overwhelming magnetism."

"So he has," the Grand Minister agreed. He looked at me, his dark eyes expressionless. "Let me be candid with you, Major Griffin. I don't trust him."

I glanced at Tafima, but she didn't show any reaction. The Grand Minister noticed my look and smiled. "My wife knows how I feel about her brother. Koldar is one of the problems in my country. Since he is my wife's brother, I don't want him hurt. I don't believe he is an evil mam. He is just such a fanatic. I have never been to any of his services, but I have heard rumors about new ideas, new rituals he has introduced. Because women are not allowed at the service, Tafima knows nothing about it."

He gave me a thoughtful look. "Tell me, was there anything that struck you as odd?"

How could I tell him? How could I say *Yes, the whole damn service was odd*? How could I tell him that I had taken part in a very unusual ritual? A ritual that was not described in any of the holy books of Mislan.

"Everything looked normal to me, your Excellency. Like I said, Koldar has a powerful and dynamic personality."

He sighed. "Maybe I'm just paranoid. Maybe I'm getting old." He reached for a glass. "Have some wine, Major, and join me in a drink."

When I heard someone step into the room, I looked up.

I stared.

She wore an outfit similar to the one Tafima wore. A green, ankle-long bright dress with a slit up to her hip and a décolleté almost down to her navel.

"Good afternoon, Grand Minister. Good afternoon, Major Griffin," she said, smiling.

Stunned, I looked at Tafima, who gave me a wide smile. Suddenly, she broke out laughing. "Meet my sister Lawni, Major, but I believe you have met."

"We certainly have." Lawni seated herself across from me. "How are you, Major?"

I didn't know if I should be angry or not. "I assume you are not a slave," I said, feeling foolish.

Lawni laughed. "No, but Tafima and I thought it would add more…ah…spice to the situation."

The Grand Minister shrugged, looking first at Lawni, and then at me. "I guess you know each other. Well, well. I seem to miss out on all the excitement these days," he muttered, emptying his glass. "Like I said, I'm getting too old."

I could see the resemblance now. Lawni seemed to be the older one, a little shorter and fuller than Tafima, but just as beautiful.

Looking at them, I wondered how Tafima would perform in bed. Probably just as good, maybe even better. Just thinking about it brought on a painful erection. I finished my meal, making light conversation, but the bulge in my pants just would not go down.

I was hoping for desert.

Chapter Eleven

I should have known better than to drink so much of that heavy wine again, but Tafima and Lawni proved to be such pleasant company, especially after the Grand Minister excused himself. "Urgent business," he murmured.

We retired to chairs that were more comfortable, and I felt good. The alcohol slowly went to my head. I had to watch what I said and did. At one time, when Tafima personally refilled my glass, the sight of her honey-colored free-swinging breasts in front of my face almost made me forget my manners, and I almost reached for them. I controlled my hand, but not my eyes.

"Major," she murmured, smiling wickedly, "It is not polite to stare at a woman's breasts."

I heard Lawni giggle. "He is a wicked man. Watch him, sister."

Tafima laughed. "She is right, Major Griffin. You must learn to control yourself more."

"It is very hard in the company of two beautiful women," I said diplomatically, fighting the urge to tear the dress from her luscious body. "I think I will go for a little walk," I told them. "I am quite restless today."

"Too bad, Major. We were having such a good time." Tafima smiled. "Maybe an herbal bath will sooth your nerves and your body."

"Sounds good to me," I agreed.

Tafima clapped her hands. A slave girl came out of the next room.

"Take our guest to the *Bath-Suite*." She turned back to me. "Enjoy yourself."

The girl led me into another part of the palace. Tafima had not exaggerated when she called the bathroom a *Suite*.. It was huge, with a large sunken tub in the middle. There were cushions and scatter rugs all over the place and comfortable couches and chairs.

The tub was already filled. I looked at the girl, but she made no move to leave. Shrugging, I shed my clothing and sank into the water, finding it just the right temperature, not cold, not too hot.

"I will scrub your back," the girl said matter-of-factly and began to apply soap to my back. I didn't object. Closing my eyes, I enjoyed her gentle hands on my body. It felt so soothing.

She stopped rubbing for a moment. I heard the splashing water as she stepped into the tub with me. Her hands resumed their scrubbing motions, moving over my chest, across my belly, down to my thighs. Somewhat embarrassed I tried to hide my erection, but it was too late.

Something heavenly soft and tight closed over my hard organ and swallowed it to the root. The girl's moans of delight were music in my ears.

What the Hell, I thought. Keeping my eyes tightly shut, I lunged upward and met her thrusts. Reaching around, I grabbed her buttocks and delighted in their firm softness.

The water sloshed over the rim of the tub as we thrashed around inside it. When at last I pulled out of her, I was still hard. When her fingers curled around my penis, I opened my eyes to stare into Tafima's smiling face.

"Surprised, Major Griffin?" She laughed mockingly and stepped out of the tub. Dripping, she looked down at me. I noted her hairless cleft and the thick, fleshy lips of her vagina. When I saw the large dark areolae around the thick nipples of her breasts, I knew.

"You are the High Priestess," I said, my voice sounding somewhat hoarse.

She stayed silent, her eyes looking into mine, her lips smiling. Then she bent and held out a hand. "Come," she whispered.

Like a hare under the hypnotizing gaze of a snake, I climbed out of the water and let her pull me to one of the thick rugs. She lay down, on her back. As her satiny thighs fell open, I sank between them with a moan.

I took her roughly, angry at her for playing games with me. She laughed, writhing beneath me with tantalizing movements.

She stopped laughing after a while, her face contorted by the raging fire I unleashed inside her. She kept the promise I had seen in her dark eyes the first time I laid eyes on her.

She was a strong woman, as skillful with her sex-organ as her sister Lawni. Her moans of ecstasy sounded loud in my ears, and I worried someone might hear. I was dimly aware of someone nearby, probably the slave girl, but I didn't care. My built-in sentries had given no warning.

Somehow, we ended up with her on top of me. She rotated her hips expertly, never losing her grip. When I was on the verge of coming, she suddenly lifted up, turned and took the full length of my penis into her mouth. The feel of her tongue around my bursting shaft made me come almost immediately. She drank my gushing liquid, and even when there seemed nothing left, she kept on mouthing and sucking.

I closed my eyes and relished the gentle flicking of her tongue and the tiny pressure as she sucked on the head.

Finally, she let go and, wiping her mouth, she chuckled. "Lawni was right. You are a rare specimen, Major Griffin. Truly gifted."

Still on her knees, she turned away from me, presenting her round buttocks. Below them, I saw her hairless pussy. Touching her soft buttocks, I rubbed her back and her shoulders. My hands reached around her to take hold of her firm breasts. Kneading the thick nipples, my penis hardened between her spread cheeks.

She pushed backward, her pussy-lips teasing the tip of my swollen organ. Arching her back, she laughed as I tried to enter her again. It seemed she had the ability to contract her openin, making it impossible for me to enter.

I groaned, pushing hard.

"Impatient, Major, aren't you," she stated, laughing, but then she suddenly pushed against me and with a cry, I felt myself sliding into her hot inferno.

For a long time I was aware of nothing but my own grunting and her periodic moans and sighs. When I came, I held her hips and pulled her into my lap. Her thighs opened impossibly wide and again she milked and sucked me completely dry.

She had called *me* gifted. She was more than that.

She was the Love Goddess incarnate.

* * * *

I watched her as she padded across the floor to the tub, marveling at the play of soft muscles, her buttocks, the swing of her hips. As she sank into the water, she called, "Come, join me."

I shook my head. "Maybe later. For now I need some rest."

She laughed and ducked under the water.

I closed my eyes, listening to her splashing. I must have dozed off and dreamed. In my dreams, I remembered Pihra and Sehla and felt the ecstasy of their lovemaking. They had called it *feeding*.

Whatever it had been, it had been wonderful.

I slid into Sehla's slippery soft sex-organ, felt her gentle sucking.

The sound of soft laughter brought me back to find my stiff pole buried inside Lawni's greedily sucking pussy. Squatting above me, she pumped her lower body in a steady rhythm, lifting just high enough for my member to stay inside her tightly gripping sheath.

Our sex-organs were the only connection between our bodies.

I reached up to take her swollen breasts into my hands and sank my fingers into their firm flesh.

Again, she laughed and sat down hard, swallowing my pulsing member as deeply as she could.

"Even when you sleep, you can perform," she said, breathing hard and moaning deeply. "I've been riding you for at least ten minutes."

Beside my head, Tafima chuckled softly. She straddled my face, lowering her pink cleft over my mouth. "Tongue me!" she commanded, and obediently I put my tongue into her slit. Her juices were flowing, and I swallowed them eagerly.

Lawni reached out to touch Tafima's breasts. Their lips touched, glued together.

Suddenly, they both lifted off me. Kissing and hugging, they rolled on the floor, their thighs intertwined and their pussies rubbing against each other.

Intrigued, I watched their glistening bodies. Staring at their honey-colored buttocks and at their moving hairless pussies glued together, I couldn't just watch. Moaning, I lay on top of them, my rigid pole frantically searching until I sank it into a soft opening to the hilt. I didn't know or cared who it was.

While they were kissing and fondling each other, I stroked the back of the woman on top, steadily pumping into her.

I knew I fucked Lawni when I caught a glimpse of Tafima's face below their tangle of black hair. It didn't really matter. I slipped out as Lawni spread her legs wider and as she moved up a bit. A hand grabbed my penis and fed it back in. From the angle of the stroke, I knew I had wound up in Tafima's tight pussy. My hand reached down, and I buried a finger inside Lawni. I felt her muscles tighten around my penetrating finger.

It didn't take long before I climaxed again. Tafima cried out as I pushed hard into her. Before I finished, I pulled out and buried my squirting member in Lawni's eager pussy. She let out a squeal of delight as she received my discharge.

We lay unmoving in a tangle for a long time after that.

* * * *

Tafima was the first one to move. "I'd better get back into my quarters and get ready for the evening meal with my husband." She planted a kiss on my lips and untangled herself. "You have him all to yourself, sister," she said to Lawni as she slipped into her dress.

Lawni turned lazily in my arms. "You heard my sister," she said. Opening her thighs, she pulled me on top of her.

"Don't you ever get enough?" I asked, slipping into her soft sheath.

She moaned and moved against me. "Never, especially with a man like you."

After we exhausted ourselves, Lawni called one of the slave girls and told her to bring us something to eat. We dined, sitting on the floor.

"I'm a little confused," I said, "perhaps you can clear up a few things for me."

Lawni yawned. "What would you like to know?"

"Are you a stout believer in the Mislan faith?"

She gave me a questioning look. "Why do you ask?"

"I am not a *Believer*, but I am well versed in the scriptures. I know probably more about Mislan than many of your countrymen. Last night, in the temple, I was *initiated*. I cannot recall any passages about such initiations anywhere in the Holy Books. Explain that to me."

She smiled. "There is nothing to explain. You may know, or not, that Koldar is in communication with the Star-Gods. They were the ones who told him to bless young virgins with his body. When he joins his body with theirs, the girls, through him, become one with the Star-Gods."

"How about when I coupled with all those young women?" I chuckled. "Was I also joining with the Star-Gods?"

"When your body became one with the High Priestess you were transformed into a Holy Vessel. All those women you entered became one with the Star-Gods, if only for a short moment." She touched my face. "For a while you were a god."

I shook my head. "I have a problem accepting that. After all, your sister Tafima is the High Priestess, and she is far from being *holy*."

"Oh, you poor *Non-Believer*. Why can you not accept it? My brother Koldar is a *Holy Man*. He was chosen by the Star-Gods, and so was Tafima. She has the gift, just like Koldar. That is why she is the High Priestess." She reached out and took my hand into hers. "You must believe these things. There was a reason you came here. Soon you will have an enlightened experience. I can feel it."

"How do you fit into all of this, Lawni? After all, you are the sister to these two holy persons. Do you also claim special talents?" I couldn't help being a little sarcastic.

She laughed. "This is my talent." With that, she rose to her feet, pulled me up and dragged me toward a pile of cushions. We were both still naked and before I came to my senses, we were locked together in a deep embrace, her long legs wrapped around my torso, my hard rod buried inside her clutching organ.

I couldn't argue with her. She did have quite a talent.

me, her soft breasts rubbing my chest. She felt velvety and slippery and let out a soft whimper when she experienced her first orgasms.

I lifted her light body off me and bent her over the rim of the tub. Then I stepped behind her and entered her soft sheath from behind. She pushed back against me, cried out when I began moving with forceful thrusts. Reaching under her, I took her breasts into my hands to protect them from the hard tiles. Her breasts were not large, but solid, yet soft and pliable in my hands.

I didn't wait too long before I climaxed inside her. When I pulled out, she sighed and turned her head to look at me. "I wish we could spend more time doing this." She smiled. "But you have to hurry now and join Lady Tafima. She doesn't like to wait."

She dried me with a large towel, against my protests. "It is my duty," she said, and then she used the same towel to dry herself.

I watched her. She had a fine body, slim and well formed, a pretty face, with a healthy complexion, lighter than most of the citizens of Isram. Her large green eyes and small, straight nose betrayed her racial mixture. I also had the feeling she was older than she appeared.

When she finished drying herself, she slipped back into her clothes. Stepping closer, she lifted up on tiptoes and she kissed me gently. "Thank you, Dan Griffin," she whispered. "Be careful." She looked around, suddenly a haunted expression on her pretty face.

"Be careful of what?" I asked.

She shook her head. "I cannot say more." She grabbed my hand. "Come, I will take you to my mistress."

She accompanied me back to my room and helped me to get dressed. Then she walked ahead of me and took me into the same dining room I had dined with Lady Tafima and the Grand Minister before.

"Ah, Major Griffin," beamed the Grand Minister, "I trust you had a restful night?"

I made a slight bow. "May you be safe in the net of the Holy Triangle, Grand Minister." Then I inclined my head toward his wife, but didn't say anything.

She smiled and waved a hand. "No need to be formal, Major. We are private here, and no one will judge you. Besides, you're not even a *Believer*."

"Just trying to be polite, my Lady," I said, avoiding her eyes, which studied me so openly and with too much familiarity. The last thing I needed was creating animosity between her husband, the Grand Minister, and me.

The old man chuckled. "My wife is right, Major. Relax and have some breakfast."

I sat in one of the empty chairs. "Your sister not joining us?" I asked Tafima.

She shook her head. "I'm afraid not. She had other obligations."

"I'm curious," I said, "what exactly is her function, besides being the obvious, your sister?" I smiled and took a sip from the fruit juice a slave girl had poured for me.

"Lawni is responsible for the palace grounds," Tafima said, "but she has many other duties." Her lips curled into a smile. "She is very talented, don't you think so, Major?"

I didn't get a chance to reply. Someone else strode into the room. I watched the newcomer coming up to our table. "How about me? What talents do I have?"

Tafima laughed. "You have a talent to be nuisance, sister." She looked at me. "I believe you and Fara have also met."

Fara chuckled when she saw the astonished look on my face. "Oh yes, the Major and I have met."

"You still owe me that massage," I said, lost for words at the moment.

"That can be arranged," she said throatily. "After all, I mustn't neglect my duties."

"Which are?"

"I'm responsible for the slaves in the palace and the welfare of the Prime Minister's guests." She took the empty seat and reached for a *Mang-seed*. Looking at me from lowered lashes, she said, "I'm also a lesser priestess in the palace temple."

I looked first at Tafima, then at Fara. "A lesser priestess?" I stared at the golden bracelet on her left wrist, suddenly understanding. "You were there," I murmured.

Tafima gave me a warning glance. "Whatever secrets you and my sister have, we don't need to know," she said casually, but I detected her sudden uneasiness as her heartbeat increased slightly.

The Grand Minister cleared his throat. "What kind of secrets could Major Griffin and your sister have?" he asked.

Fara laughed. "As usual, Tafima is reading more into an innocent situation. I was the one who took care of Major Griffin when he first arrived here. Prince Abdul-Shakur gave me instructions to ensure our guest's comfort. I did." She lowered her lashes demurely, even managed to blush a little. "I just did what I was told to do. Perhaps I was a little more enthusiastic about it than I should have been, but you must admit, the Major is a handsome specimen of a man."

Shaking his head, the Grand Minister chuckled. "That is more information than I needed to know." He glanced at me. "I hope you weren't offended, Major. Our customs are somewhat different from what you are used to."

Smiling, I said. "How can I ever be offended by the attention of a lovely young lady, like Lady Fara?"

The Grand Minister wiped his mouth with a napkin. "Now, if you will excuse me, Major Griffin, I have duties to perform. They may not be as pleasant as the duties of the women," he chuckled, "but as ruler of my country, I don't have much choice. Enjoy the rest of the day."

After he left the room, Tafima sighed. "Thank you, Major."

"For what?"

"For keeping silence. My husband does not know that I am the High Priestess. He would never approve. Neither does he know about the initiation rituals." She sighed again. "He is getting old and clings to the old beliefs. As long as he is the Prime Minister, we have to adhere to the old traditional ways. Once Koldar takes his place, we will implement many changes."

"Changes that are not part of the original Mislan doctrine," I commented.

"The Star-Gods have revealed these things to Koldar in his visions. A time of changes has come, and we must follow the new commandments." Tafima bent forward. "I know you don't believe. Tomorrow morning I am leaving for a journey to the *Place of Miracles*. I want you to accompany me there. There you will find that the Star-Gods do exist. You may even find salvation."

"What makes you think I'm seeking salvation?"

She laughed. "Everyone does, Major, including you. You just don't know it."

"The Grand Minister may not approve if I leave the palace grounds," I said. "I haven't even had a chance yet to discuss politics with him. After all, that is my mission, to establish peace between your country and the rest of Redsky."

"It can wait." Tafima's eyes told me more than her lips. "I promise, Major, you won't regret coming. I can be very grateful." She glanced at Fara and smiled. "You've tasted mine and my sister's passion. That was just the beginning of what you could have." She leaned over and kissed me, her tongue darting briefly against my teeth, like a serpent seeking entrance. "Just the beginning," she murmured. "Think about it."

A hot hand caressed my thigh. Fara smiled at me when Tafima pulled away. She put her hand on my crotch, laughed when she felt the hardness.

"I assume you're also coming?" I said, my voice not too steady.

She nodded and laughed again. "So is Shantea. Remember her? Shantea, the little slave girl? I saw you watching her, and I saw the looks she gave you. I didn't miss the desire in your eyes when you stared at her nubile body. I promised you then that I would let you sample her young body and taste her exploding passion. And so you shall."

She didn't have to convince me. My body already reacted, just thinking of Tafima's and Fara's hot pussies. I didn't need the additional temptation of a slave girl half my age and probably still a virgin.

"All right," I said. "I suppose my talks with the Prime Minister can wait. Maybe finding out more about your religion and your country will give me better understanding and help me in my negotiations."

Cut the crap! a little voice inside me screamed. *Face the truth. All you want is to sink your rod into their hot bellies. What about Meadow, Aleethy, Aika, Ninca and the other girls? How will you ever find them when you're traveling through Isram and doing nothing but giving your prick a workout?*

I shook my head to clear it and sent a coded impulse to get control over my emotions. I was only partially successful. It seemed that communication with my built-in devices had become sluggish, but when I did a system's check, everything came up normal. Maybe it was just me.

I glanced at the two slave girls standing not far away from us, waiting to be summoned. "What about them?" I asked in a low voice. "Aren't you worried they'll talk to others, and things we discuss here will get back to the wrong people?"

"Like my husband?" Tafima laughed. "They won't talk, because they are bound to me and to Fara. We have our ways to keep them loyal." She rose to her feet. "I also have duties to perform," she said.

"My sister will spend the rest of the day with you. Maybe you want a tour of our city. She can show you around."

Fara nodded. "I can be a charming companion," she said and smiled. "I am more than just a great fuck."

She laughed softly. My face must have betrayed me. "Shocked, Major?"

I grinned. "I love it when you use such vulgar language."

"It's only a word," she said. "Now, come. Let me give you the grand tour."

Chapter Thirteen

Fara put her arm into mine as we walked out of the door. We passed through a richly furnished room and stepped into the courtyard.

"Looks like it will be a nice day," she said. Then she gave me a quick inspection. "There is nothing wrong with the way you are dressed, but I will have to change into a more suitable traveling outfit. Why don't you come with me to my quarters and wait there until I'm ready?"

I shrugged. "I have nothing planned. Might as well come with you." *Maybe we can take some time out and enjoy desert after breakfast.* My loins already burned in anticipation.

We had barely walked halfway across the courtyard, when I heard the heavy footsteps of booted feet. Fara stopped and watched the two soldiers coming closer. One of them bowed toward her and said, "We have orders to escort Major Griffin."

"Whose orders?" Fara asked sharply.

"Captain Arran's."

"Where are you taking him?"

"Our orders are to bring him to Captain Arran." He looked at me, ignoring Fara. "Please come with us, Major."

"Do I have a choice?" I asked.

"No. Now, please come."

"Go with them," Fara told me and touched my arm. "I'll send a slave to find out what the Captain wants. Don't worry."

The two soldiers walked silently beside me. I scanned them, but I didn't detect any hostility. My built-in sentries did not trigger any alarms.

The gate we used to leave the palace grounds was different from the one we passed through when I arrived. We marched a short distance down a narrow street, and then we walked through another gate into a different courtyard. Low buildings, clearly barracks, formed a perfect square around the yard.

A group of soldiers was exercising in the middle of the courtyard. My escort marched me to the end of the yard, up some steps into a building with a wide door. Two soldiers with automatic weapons guarded the entrance.

Looking at those weapons, I made a mental adjustment to our perception of Isram. The general population might live in more primitive conditions than the rest of Redsky, but the military didn't adhere to this principle of not using technology. The fact that they shouldn't even have automatic weapons like this also disturbed me.

Inside the building, we walked down a wide corridor and finally stopped in front of an open door. One of the soldiers told me to enter. They stayed behind when I followed his order.

"Ah, Major Griffin." Capain Arran sat behind a large desk covered with stacks of paper. He looked up and smiled. "You're probably wondering why I summoned you here. And maybe you're a little worried?"

"I am." I returned his smile. "Wondering, I mean. As for being worried? Actually, I'm not. You wouldn't want to harm a high-ranking officer of the Terran Empire."

He laughed. "You know, the Grand Minister was right. You are an insolent man. Insolent, arrogant and without fear. I like that."

"You didn't bring me here to tell me that."

"No, I didn't." He pointed to a chair. "Have a seat. Oh, and close the door, please."

When following his request, I noticed that the two soldiers who brought me were still standing in the corridor.

"There is not a great chance that anyone will listen in on our conversation, but I believe in taking no chances." Captain Arran leaned back in his chair and folded his arms across his chest. He chuckled. "This sound ominous, doesn't it?"

"It arouses my curiosity," I admitted.

"What is your opinion regarding Lady Tafima and her sisters?"

I was a little surprised by his bluntness. "I'm not sure what you are getting at," I said cautiously.

"Ever since the Grand Minister's new wife and her consort appeared, things have started to change." He gave me a thoughtful look. "Conditions in Isram are different from the way people live in other countries on Redsky. Because of our beliefs, we have always been persecuted, and when the First Grand Minister founded our country, three hundred years ago, our ancestors were finally able to live according to what they believed. We've always been peaceful, and now, suddenly, there is talk of a Holy War and much unrest among our people. It all began five years ago."

"I get the impression you are insinuating that Lady Tafima is to blame for this."

"I am not insinuating, Major Griffin. It is a fact." His voice had risen slightly, and his eyes seemed to blaze with a sudden fire. "You are aware that her brother Koldar is the Thalmani, the head of the Council of High Priests, which means, he is the second most powerful man in our country. He is also the Grand Marshal, thus controlling the military power in Isram. Soon he will be Grand Minister. Draw your own conclusions."

"I can guess," I said. "Isram might be drawn into a war not everyone wants."

He nodded. "I'm taking a great chance just talking to you, Major. You have the power to have me arrested and possibly executed, because I dare to speak out against the doctrine of the state and against Mislan. And against the wife of the Grand Minister, who is above suspicion." He sighed. "The Grand Minister is supposed to be the highest power in Isram, but he is nothing but a puppet. Lady Tafima is the real power behind him, and she has him wrapped around her finger. To make it worse, Lady Tafima is controlled by her brother, Grand Marhall Koldar."

I studied him while he spoke. He didn't strike me as a fanatic or a rebel. What I had seen and experienced in the temple made me wonder about the state of affairs in Isram. "What do you want from me?" I asked.

"I know that the Empire doesn't usually meddle in the affairs of individual planets, except where there might exist a possible threat to the Terran Empire. Am I correct?"

"You are. That is the policy, normally, but there are circumstances where we might interfere, even if there is no threat."

"Such as?"

I smiled. "You want me to discuss politics? I'm not a politician. I'm a troubleshooter."

He smiled back. "Exactly. You came here to prevent a war. Isn't that correct?"

"I came to talk, not to take military action, if that's what you're implying." I gave him a thoughtful look, not exactly sure how much information I wanted to give him. Or should give him. He was only a minor player, without much power. "The threat of war on Redsky is not the only reason I am here. There are others, but I'm not at liberty to discuss them with anyone." I chuckled. "Politics, you know."

"I thought you weren't a politician?" He lifted a hand to wave off my reply. "I've always hated these military secrets." His expression was somber when he looked at me. "On which side is the Terran Empire?"

"Neither," I replied, and that was the truth.

"That is good." He rose. "I want you to accompany me to meet someone. Maybe you'll be comfortable discussing politics with him."

When we stepped outside, one of the soldiers waited for us with two saddled horses.

I grinned at Captain Arran when I swung into the saddle of one of the animals. "I was supposed to take a tour of your city with someone else."

"I know. With Lady Fara."

"You seem to know a lot."

He didn't smile but nodded. "I'm responsible for palace security. It is my job to know what is going on." He gave me a quick glance. "There are spies all over the palace. Not all of them belong to Lady Tafima. And not all are visible."

"I will heed your warning, Captain," I said, letting my horse fall in beside him.

We rode out of the gate, just the two of us. It surprised me, because I expected at least a couple of soldiers to escort us.

The street was busy with pedestrians and small carts pulled by donkey-like draft animals. I noticed the many dark-clad armed men on horseback. They scrutinized us as we passed by, but none stopped us. Captain Arran must have noticed my curiosity after passing a group of four of these men. "They're the new police force," he said. "An implementation of our Grand Marshall."

He didn't sound overly enthusiastic.

"I suppose you disagree with their presence?"

He snorted. "We have little crime in this city and in the rest of Isram. They are an unnecessary expenditure."

"So why are they here?"

"Who knows?" He shrugged. "Another one of the changes, that's all."

We turned into a narrow side street. The houses on either side looked old and shabby, some of them badly in need of repairs.

"Not the best part of town," I remarked.

"It is quite safe, I assure you," Captain Arran said. "The only thing the people who live here are guilty of is that they are poor. But most of them are honest and hardworking citizens. They are also stout believers in the Faith of Mislan, the old faith."

We entered one of the houses through a wooden door that could have used some paint. The room we stepped into was dark and gloomy looking. The odor of cooking oils and the acrid aroma of tobacco hung strong in the air. The furniture in the room looked old. A low divan with cushions and three large upholstered chairs concluded the décor. I didn't see anyone in the room, but I detected the heartbeat of people behind one of the curtains.

The curtain parted, and a young woman came into the room.

She squealed with delight when she saw Arran and slipped into his embrace. He laughed and untangled himself from her arms.

"My sister Jirina," the Captain explained and pointed at me. "This is Major Dan Griffin from the Terran Empire."

Her eyes were large when she looked at me. "From Terra?" she asked with a breathless voice.

I nodded and smiled at her. "I am quite harmless," I said. "I won't bite you."

She laughed shyly. "I wasn't scared of you." Her voice was soft and low.

"You should have told me you had such a lovely sister," I said to Arran.

"I have two more," he said. "But Jirina is the youngest and the prettiest." He looked at the girl and laughed. "But don't tell Kalila and Layali I said that."

She giggled. "It'll be our little secret, Faruk." She hooked her arm into his. "Come, we are just about to eat."

She had called him *Faruk*, obviously his first name. I catalogued that information automatically into my memory.

We stepped through the curtain into another room on the other side, larger than the one we came from. Daylight streamed through a window in the back. In the center of the room stood a long table and chairs. Most of the chairs were occupied, and I was surprised when I saw two familiar faces.

"Major Griffin, I'm so glad Captain Arran could persuade you to come." Prince Shakur laughed when he saw my surprised face.

"Captain Arran can be quite convincing," I said, looking at Cherryh, who sat beside Prince Shakur. "I see you found yourself a place to stay," I commented.

Cherryh grinned. "I'm glad you're healthy and in good spirits, Major. I was a little worried the last time I saw you."

I saw an older man and a woman sitting on Shakur's other side and assumed they were Arran's parents. Two girls sat in the chairs next to Cherryh. Beside him a young man, who looked remarkable like the Captain. He glanced at me, and then his eyes fastened on Arran. His expression was serious, but his eyes sparkled happily. He rose from his chairs and came to greet us.

"My younger brother Bashir," Captain Arran introduced him. "He's the brain in the family. He was smart enough to stay out of the military."

"I've never liked playing with guns and sabers." Bashir laughed good-naturedly and held out his hand.

I shook it. He had a firm handshake. His dark eyes looked into mine. "I know everything there is about you from your friend Cherryh, Major."

I glanced at Cherryh. "I hope he didn't tell you too much," I said, only half joking.

Captain Arran looked at the older couple. None of them had said anything, but the old woman smiled happily.

"Father, Mother, I want you to welcome our guest, Major Griffin."

The old man inclined his head. "Be welcome inside our humble four walls and accept our hospitality."

I bowed slightly. "And may you be safe in the net of the Holy Triangle."

The old woman clapped her hands. "Come, come, sit and share a meal with us."

Arran and I took the two empty seats. I ended up beside Jirina, his youngest sister. The older two girls got up and went through a door into another room, the kitchen, I assumed. The aroma of cooking food wafted in through the open door.

They came back with plates full of steaming vegetables and warm, fresh baked bread, no meat, but small balls of boiled fish, rolled in dough. We filled our cups with wine from tall pitchers that stood on the table.

Simple fare, but quite tasty.

"Do I have to call you Major?" Jirina asked me.

I chuckled. "You can call me Dan. All my friends do."

"I like *Dan* better than *Major,*" she said, and then she offered me a small tuber from her plate. "Here, eat this. Friends share their food."

I let her put it into my mouth.

"Now you must offer me something," she said and smiled at me. One of her hands casually touched my thigh.

"Wine?" I asked.

She lifted her slim shoulders. "Wine is fine."

I held my glass to her lips. She sipped slowly, her dark eyes looking into mine. I felt her fingers digging into my thigh. Feeling uncomfortable, I looked around the table, but nobody seemed to pay attention to us. Everyone was busy talking and eating.

"How long are you staying?" she asked with a low voice.

I shrugged. "It depends on your brother. We'll most likely have to be back in the palace by nightfall."

"Too bad." She sounded disappointed. "Maybe you can come and visit us again? Maybe stay overnight?" Her eyes locked with mine. "I've never known a man with light skin like yours. I wouldn't mind getting to know you better. Especially now that we are friends."

I laughed. "Maybe I will come again. I can't promise."

After we finished eating, the men moved into the dark room in the front. Jirina came in and lit a couple of oil lamps and, with a long look and a smile at me, she stepped back through the curtain.

Arran's father sat in one of the chairs, puffing on a large pipe. Cherryh took the other one. The Captain and I sat on the divan. Arran's brother Bashir flopped into the third chair, where he sat with his legs drawn up.

"I never really believed your story," Prince Shakur began the conversation.

"What gave us away?" I asked, chuckling a little.

"Everything. The way you carried yourself, the way you moved. Then the incidence with the bandits. Only a trained soldier could have done what you did, and a ruthless slave trader would have never let a man like Dorcas get away alive."

"How is your wife? Your sons?" I asked.

"They are fine. Unfortunately, I haven't had much time to spend with them. How are you enjoying your stay at the palace? I understand you've met my father's wife and her sisters?"

I knew what he hinted at, but I kept my face straight when I answered. "I have. They are charming women."

"I'm sure they are."

"You should have told me that Fara was Lady Tafima's sister."

He smiled grimly. "She wanted to surprise you. It wasn't my idea. Fara can be quite persuasive. Add the fact that she has more power in the palace than I have."

"What exactly is your position in the government?"

"My position?" He sighed and shrugged. "I am Prince Abdul-Shakur, the son of the Grand Minister. That's who I am. A man with a title but few powers."

Captain Arran cleared his throat. "Prince Shakur should have been made Grand Marshall, but the Council of High Priests chose Koldar. He not only controls our military, he also controls the Council of High Priests. In fact, he *is* the Council." Arran couldn't keep the bitterness out of his voice.

"Once Koldar holds the position of Grand Minister, he will command total power. There will be war, Major Griffin, because Koldar is a fanatic. He will plunge us into a *Holy War.* But you must believe us when we say Koldar does not represent the true Mislan Faith." He leaned forward and looked at me sideways. "I know you are not a Believer, but you have studied our scriptures. You are knowledgeable in our Faith. I am told you have been *initiated* in the temple, in Koldar's temple. Did anything you've experienced strike you as unusual?"

"Your father already asked me the same question," I said. "You've never been in the palace temple? Never taken part in the worship ceremonies?"

"I have not. Only followers of Koldar, who have been initiated into the Faith, can go there. They call themselves *The Reborns.* You were not aware of that, were you?"

"No, I wasn't." I looked at Captain Arran. "You know what goes on in there?"

"I do. At least I think I do." He nodded and glanced at the Prince. "I never set foot into the temple, but two of my soldiers are *Reborns.* Not by choice. I needed to find out what is happening in the temple, so I sent two of my trusted men with order to join Koldar's followers. When I questioned them afterwards they told me everything was as it should be. I didn't believe them. They acted strangely, and they seemed changed. I did something that I regret, but it needed to be done."

He wiped his face with one hand. I registered the perspiration on his skin. His voice sounded tight when he spoke. "They were good men. They talked, but not before I destroyed their minds and their bodies. Blind men don't make good soldiers." He wiped his face again. "They spoke of rituals that involved young virgins. They spoke of a High Priestess with a golden mask who initiated them into the faith, of visions where a score of young women coupled with them. There were other things they babbled of, but much didn't make any sense."

Prince Shakur stared at me. "Can you substantiate that, Major Griffin?"

I saw Cherryh watching me from his chair. His face was expressionless, but his eyes were watchful. I knew all of his devices were tuned in to me.

I gave a forced laugh. "I have not been brainwashed, if that's what you are afraid of. I am still in control of all of my faculties. My memory is still intact. Your information is correct, Captain Arran. Everything they told you is true, including their story of the score of young women they coupled with. What you may not know is that Lady Tafima is the High Priestess."

Arran took a deep breath and blew it out noisily. Prince Shakur stiffened beside me. "I can't say it surprises me," he said after a short pause. "After all, her sister Fara is a minor priestess in the temple. I should have known Tafima is also involved."

"Your father, the Grand Minister, should know about that," Arran said.

Prince Shakur shook his head. "There is enough animosity between me and my father. His ears would be deaf to what I tell him. Tafima would only deny everything."

"What if he should find out for himself?" Bashir, who had been listening intensely to our conversation, spoke up.

"My father would never set foot in the temple where Koldar leads the services, because he knows that Koldar has introduced many new things. He does not believe in changes, but he is powerless to do anything about it. The Council of High Priests is much too powerful. And should he insist, his life may even be in danger." Shakur looked at me. "Only representatives of the Terran Empire may have enough influence to persuade the Assembly of Ministers to look into the practices of the church."

"As I told you, there is not much I can do. Unless it could be proved that a threat to the Empire exists, my hands are tied." I wish I could have been more positive, but there really was nothing I could do at this point. Besides, my real mission was to find Meadow and the girls, not meddle with internal politics.

"Just by being here you are already interfering," Captain Arran's father said softly. "Every action carries consequences."

"That is true," I agreed, looking at the old man. "I am not saying that I will do nothing." I smiled. "Officially I won't be able to do anything, but unofficially…" I didn't finish the sentence.

The old man puffed on his pipe, surrounding himself with a cloud of bluish smoke. I didn't find the aroma of the tobacco unpleasant, but in the small room, the smoke did irritate my throat a little. He gave me a gap-toothed smile. "I knew you were not an unreasonable man. Your companion Cherryh spoke highly of you. He is a soldier like you."

"Major Griffin is my superior," Cherryh spoke up for the first time since we moved into this room.

"I assume you're not brothers?" Prince Shakur said.

Cherryh laughed. "Not brothers." He gave me quick glance "Not through blood."

Prince Shakur looked first at him, and then at me. "You are fortunate men, Major Griffin. I sense the bond you two have, a bond of respect, trust and great friendship. It is a rare thing."

"We've been together for a long time," I said.

"I told them about Meadow and the other girls," Cherryh said.

"An unfortunate incident," the older Arran said from inside his cloud of smoke. "Cherryh told me about your dislike of slavery. Many in our country do not condone it either, but most don't think about it. It is a way of life. Some are born into slavery. Some are sold into it. It is not necessarily a bad thing. Many poor people sell their children into slavery to give them a secure and better future."

"Everyone has the right to be free, to choose what they want from life. Nobody should have a master," I said.

He smiled. "Are you free, Major Griffin? I mean, really free?"

"I make my own choices, most of the time."

"Aren't you a servant of the Terran Empire? You are a soldier, a small part of a giant military machine. Your superiors are your masters, Major?"

"Yes, they are, but I'm free to quit anytime I want to. I have that choice. A slave doesn't have that luxury."

Prince Shakur laughed softly. "No one is completely free, Major Griffin. Not you, not Captain Arran. Even though I'm the son of the Grand Minister and seem to have nothing but freedom, even I am not free. I'm a prisoner of my social standing. I'm a prisoner of my faith, more so than you and your companion."

I looked away from Shakur when I heard the rustling of the parting curtain. Jirina, Captain Arran's young sister, walked in. "You men," she said, "always discussing politics. Mother wants to know if you want some wine."

The old man chuckled. "What can be better than a hot-blooded woman and a barrel of wine to still am man's thirst." He laughed when he saw his daughter's disapproving face. "My daughter thinks I'm too old to speak of these things. There is still a lot of fire left in this old body." He winked at me and took a drag from his pipe. His eyes took on a far-away expression. "Things were less complicated when I was young. Not many worries, except for the roaming native tribes perhaps. We traveled freely to our neighboring countries, and there was no talk about cleansing our world of the *Infidels* and *Nonbelievers* or a *Holy War*. Yes, everything was much simpler then."

Captain Arran coughed politely. "My father gets sentimental sometimes. He does not believe in changes." He accepted a mug from his sister, let her fill it from a pitcher she carried on a tray. "Let's drink to a better future, a peaceful one, and understanding and tolerance between people of different cultures."

Jirina smiled at me when she handed me a mug and casually touched my shoulder. I registered the heat her body radiated and had to still my own heartbeat and the slight pulsing of my loins.

Damn it! Something was definitely screwed up with my body, but I had no way of having a diagnosis performed by an outside independent system's analyzer.

"Lady Tafima has invited me to accompany her to a *Place of Miracles*, as she called it." I looked at Prince Shakur. "What do you think? Should I decline her invitation?"

116

"No. By all means, go with her. This may be your chance to find out more about what she and her brother are planning." With a quick glance at Jirina, he smiled lightly. "You seem to have a gift that may be of use to you, but I would advise you to be on constant guard. I do not trust her and her sisters. Neither do I trust Koldar."

Cherryh's eyes were grave when he studied me. "Are you sure you can handle it, Major? Maybe I should come with you."

"I think you worry too much. I don't believe I'm in any real danger. But if I am, I will need you here to back me up." My throat felt raw. The smoke from the pipe was getting to me. Jirina refilled my mug again. The wine was not very strong, but I already had consumed too much of it. I sent an impulse to the little computer inside me, and it began to neutralize the alcohol in my blood.

"We should be on our way," Captain Arran said.

"Too bad you can't stay the night," his sister said to him, but her eyes were on me.

"I have my duty to perform, Jirina," he said. "And I have to get Major Griffin back to the palace. We don't want to arouse any suspicions."

We said our good-byes. I didn't get a chance to talk to Cherryh alone, but it wasn't really necessary, because neither of us had found out much. We were linked through our communicators and could talk to each other if the need arose.

When we arrived back in the palace, Captain Arran had me escorted back to my room. Moments after I entered my room, a young slave girl knocked on my door and asked if I wanted to wash up. She then brought me fresh water and a clean towel.

Later in the evening, Lady Tafima and his Excellency, the Grand Minister, summoned me to have dinner with them.

I slept alone that night.

Chapter Fourteen

The same slave girl, who had awakened me the day before, the same one I coupled with in the tub, came to wake me again. She gave me a bright smile when I opened my eyes. I wasn't surprised to see her. I had registered her coming through the door and recognized the pattern of her footsteps.

"You should feel rested this morning," she said, watching me as I climbed out of bed.

"Why is that?"

"You slept alone," she said, laughing.

"Are there no secrets in this place?" I asked.

She came closer. "Not many," she whispered. "There are watching eyes everywhere."

"Even here in my room?"

She nodded, and then she laughed. "Only mine."

"You never told me your name."

"Jana. I am Jana." She passed me my robe. "Perhaps you should hurry. I let you sleep a little longer, but Lady Tafima is already waiting for you in her private chambers. She will take breakfast in her room this morning."

I washed my face in the small washbasin. Jana handed me a small glass. It held a bluish liquid. "To freshen your breath," she said.

Tafima looked up when I entered her apartment. She was seated at a small round table. Her sister Fara sat opposite her. Both women wore loose pants and high-collared blouses. The table was already decked with bowls of fruit and sweet baked goods. Three glasses filled with fruit juice stood beside the bowls.

"Fara tells me you abandoned her yesterday," Tafima said when I took a seat.

"Not by choice," I said with an apologizing gesture.

"What did Captain Arran want?" Tafima asked casually, but I detected the tension in her voice.

I shrugged. "Talk with me. He's a soldier, like me." I chuckled. "What do soldiers talk about?"

"What *do* they talk about?" Fara asked.

"What else but women and war. Boring, unless you're a soldier."

"He took you out of the palace grounds. Where did you go?" Tafima sipped from her glass and looked at me over the rim. Her eyes seemed as dark as the darkness of space, and just like space, they were speckled with tiny glowing points of light.

"He took me to meet his family." The truth was usually better than making up lies.

"Why would he do that?"

I took a bite out of a bright yellow fruit. "I think it was just an excuse for him to get away to visit his parents."

"Did he ask you anything that you may have found as peculiar?"

"Not really." I looked into her dark eyes. "Why the third degree? Is there a problem?"

Tafima shrugged and gave a somewhat forced laugh. "Maybe we're just paranoid. But Captain Arran is not exactly a friend of my brother's. He is a troublemaker. I wish you would not be friends with him."

I waved her off. "I don't think that is going to happen. His views are different from mine." I grinned. "Perhaps he is jealous of my relationship with two of the most beautiful and passionate women on this side of the Golgat Mountains."

They both smiled, apparently satisfied with my answers. "You've tasted only a little of what we are capable of," Fara said.

"Let's not waste more time chattering." Tafima smiled. "Our ship will leave before noon."

We finished our breakfast. Tafima told one of her slave girls to bring traveling clothing for me. She came back with a pair of tight leggings, black high boots and a loose shirt made from rough cotton-like material. A leather coat that reached down to my knees completed my outfit.

"It is always a little cool on the river," Tafima explained. The women donned leather coats similar to mine.

We left the palace moments later sitting inside a coach pulled by two black geldings.

"Doesn't the Grand Minister care if you're going away like this, in the company of a stranger?" I asked Tafima.

She just smiled. "You are Fara's companion, not mine," she said. "Anyway, my husband is an old man. He doesn't show much interest in me anymore. I'm not pretending that he doesn't know about my affairs. As long as I'm discreet."

"What happened to the little slave girl Shantea?" I asked and grinned. "Didn't you promise me I could sample her delicious body?"

Tafima laughed. "I believe you'll be getting your share of sampling with just the two of us."

Our coach traveled down busy streets. I didn't see too much through the small curtain-covered window in the side of the coach. Through the tiny slit of a window in the back, I saw two guards on horseback following us. There were probably at least a couple of armed guards in front of us.

The journey took over an hour. When we finally arrived at our destination, my backside was a little sore from the bumpy ride, in spite of the soft pillow I had been sitting on.

You just can't beat the comforts of a modern airsled.

From the noise of seabirds and the smell of fish, I knew that we were at a riverfront before we stepped out of the coach. I was right, except that it wasn't a river, but a lake. I should have known, because I knew that Rhandistan was located at the shores of Lake Athana.

Small boats and large ships crowded the harbor, most of them fishing vessels, some, the larger ones, freighters, which traveled down the rivers that emptied themselves into the lake. Several of the towns along the *Long-river* could only be reached by water.

Tafima pointed to one of the larger ships. "There is our transportation."

The vessel she pointed at turned out to be a passenger ship, not a freighter. Not very large, yet large enough to be used as an ocean liner. It had no sails, so I assumed it was steam driven. Only Tafima, Fara, and I boarded the craft. The Captain himself, who bowed deeply when Tafima stepped onto the deck, welcomed us.

"I am honored to have you on board my humble ship," he said. "I apologize for not being on land when you arrived, but my cabin slave did not announce you early enough. I will have him punished for his neglectful behavior."

Tafima shrugged it off gracefully. "No need for that, Captain Garzius. I would rather you don't make too much fuss about our presence here. Has my suite been prepared?"

"Of course. I have two female slaves ready to serve you and two young males at your disposal. They are both fresh and eager to please you."

With a glance at me, Tafima said, "I won't need the male slaves, but I thank you for your considerate thoughts. Now, have someone bring my bags from the coach and then let us get on our way."

"Right away, my Lady." Captain Garzius lifted an arm. From a small group of waiting slaves standing not far behind him, two young men came running. "Get the luggage from that coach," the Captain ordered, "and take it to the Grand Suite." Then he beckoned to one of the female slaves. She rushed closer and standing in front of us, she kept her head low.

"Take our honored guests to the Grand Suite."

The girl nodded and, without lifting her head, she turned away and began walking across the deck toward the lounge. A few other passengers gave us curious looks as we walked into the lounge. We headed toward the back where stairs took us down to the deck below.

Our suite was quite spacious, with two rooms, one with a couch and a low table, the second with two wide beds, plenty of closet space and a small bath cubicle, with a toilet and a washbasin.

"The servant's quarters are just across the hall, my Lady," the slave girl said. "All you have to do is pull on this rope. A bell will ring in my quarters, and I will come."

"What is your name?" Tafima asked.

"Alya, my Lady."

"All right, Alya, bring us some wine." Tafima smiled. "But make sure it is not the usual sour poison Captain Garzius likes to serve his passengers."

The girl bowed. "I will make sure. Anything else?"

"That is all for now. Now, go."

Fara flopped onto the couch. "This is nice. A little cramped, but what can one expect on a ship this size."

"Sister, sister," Tafima laughed. "You can adapt. We've had to do it before."

"I noticed there are only two beds," I said. "Where do I sleep?"

Both women laughed at my question. "We'll find a place for you, Major." Tafima smiled wickedly. "Don't count on getting too much sleep. Fara and I have plans for you."

I gave them a foolish grin. "You'll be wearing me out, my Ladies. There are two of you and only one of me."

"He is right, Tafima," Fara pouted. "What will I do while you keep the Major occupied?"

"We can always call one of the male slaves," Tafima said and removed her long coat. "It is hot in here," she complained. "Where are the slaves with our luggage? Maybe I should have them flogged just to show my displeasure."

Someone knocked on the door. I went to open it. "Your luggage." The two slaves walked in, carrying large bags across their shoulders. The first one looked at me. "Where do you want it?"

"Put the bags into the closets, you fools!" Tafima said with a sharp voice.

"You want us to unpack them, my Lady?" one of them asked.

"Just put them in and then leave."

After the two had left, Alya came back with a large beaker and three cups. Another slave girl walked behind her, carrying a tray with fruit and biscuits.

"Put everything on the table, and then give us same privacy."

The girls followed her orders and left, their heads low.

"I should have brought my own slaves. I don't have to give them detailed instructions every time they do something," Tafima said with a sigh. Joining Fara on the couch, she poured a cup of wine and tasted it. "At least the wine is descent. Not as good as the wine we drink at the palace, but it is passable." She looked at me. "Take off your coat and make yourself comfortable, Major. We'll be on this ship for three days. They can be boring and long." She chuckled. "We have all the time in the world to explore each other. Come, join us for a cup of wine."

Not long after we emptied the beaker of wine, we retired into the bedroom. Both women began to tug on my clothing, and soon I lay on the bed, as naked as a newborn baby. My penis had grown stiff from anticipation. I couldn't wait to sink it into one of the hot pussies, ready and waiting just to be filled.

Tafima joined me on the bed and pulled me on top of her. Her legs opened wide and, with a loud grunt, I entered her. She was wet and began to smash her lower body against mine the moment I slid into her.

A few moments later Fara put her arms around my belly to take hold of the root of my organ. Clinging to me, she moved with me as I hammered between her sister's clutching hot thighs, pressing her breasts and her hairless pussy against my back.

"My turn," Fara whispered into my ear, but loud enough for Tafima to hear.

Tafima began milking me. I felt her warm discharge before she let out a loud cry of pleasure. Then she said with a breathless voice, "I think you should service Fara now."

Fara had slid off me and I pulled out of Tafima. Fara knelt on the bed, her buttocks up and her thighs slightly apart. I moved behind her. Below her round cheeks, the puffy lips of her hairless pussy beckoned, and I shoved my stiff member into the welcoming hot sheath. Tafima took position in front of Fara. Spreading her legs, she pushed her clit into her sister's face. Fara clamped her mouth over Tafima's pussy. Tafima moaned loudly and Fara bucked in front of me, rotating her hips wildly.

After a while, we changed positions. I lay on my back, watched Tafima straddle me, watched her tight slippery canal swallow my thick organ. She moved lazily up and down, her solid breasts hardly moving. Then Fara's luscious body blocked my view as she straddled me in front of Tafima. Her pussy touched my face, and my mouth opened automatically to kiss her hot pussy-lips. I lathered her clit with my tongue, and then I pushed it deep into her.

All three of us came at the same time and even though Fara's thighs against my ears muffled the sounds in the room, I heard their loud cries as the women climaxed.

They got off me and moved together. I watched them as Tafima began fondling Fara. The last bout had tired me out. I closed my eyes, listening to their loud cries as they kept fondling and rubbing each other.

When I opened my eyes, the women were still going at it. Fara was on her back with Tafima moving lazily between her widespread thighs. I listened to Fara's loud moans and looked closer, chuckling to myself.

Now I wasn't good enough anymore.

Below Tafima's belly sprouted a long, extremely thick flesh colored penis, obviously artificial. And she used it skillfully. I don't know what she got out of it, but she moaned as loudly as Fara.

Seeing that thick piece of synthetic flesh moving in and out of Fara's love canal gave me a hard on and I decided to join them again. I mounted Tafima. My stiff organ entered her pussy effortlessly with one stroke. Tafima whipped her pelvis up and down. When she pulled out of Fara and pushed up her buttocks, I entered her dripping pussy, pulled out of her when she pushed the dildo back into Fara.

It was terribly exciting, almost like making love to two women at the same time. When I emptied myself into Tafima, I pushed down hard. Fara's legs went up high, her heels digging into my back. She cried out loudly, almost as if she felt my discharge.

Tafima trembled between us, her buttocks clenching and unclenching, her love canal sucking the juice out of me. Both women's mouths locked in a passionate kiss, while I buried my face in Tafima's thick black mane, smelling its intoxicating fragrance. Tafima moaned, writhing beneath me. Fara's thighs opened and closed, and her hands reached up to touch my head.

Finally, I stopped erupting. We toppled over, still locked together.

Tafima was the first one to stir. My limp organ slipped out of her. She turned, gave me a quick kiss and stood up. I got a glimpse of the artificial penis between her legs. It was certainly large enough to put a normal man to shame. Moreover, it looked so damn realistic. No wonder Fara had carried on like that.

Tafima padded away and disappeared into the little bath cubicle.

I turned toward Fara. She seemed asleep. Taking her beautiful face into my hands, I kissed her gently on the lips. Without opening her eyes, she returned the kiss, gently at first, and then with great passion. Her hand moved down to my penis, grabbed it, and stroked until it grew hard again. Then, with her eyes still closed, she rolled onto her back, pulled me between her opening thighs. Almost whining, she frantically fed me inside her dripping canal.

I didn't climax inside her, but she experienced an orgasm almost immediately. When I felt Tafima's hands on my back, I pulled out of Fara and buried my member inside Tafima's welcoming sheath.

Tafima had removed the artificial piece of flesh, and I bucked between her long, widespread thighs, her hairless pussy receiving my organ with great passion. My mouth closed over her large nipple, sucking it deeply into my mouth.

I became aware of a familiar taste in my mouth and I kept sucking and sucking, until she gently removed my lips, pressing her own against mine. Again, I climaxed, and we frantically clutched against each other, our mouths glued together, her saliva mixing with mine.

Lying on top of me in my arms, Tafima smiled. "No man has ever given me as much satisfaction as you. You are special in many ways. You never seem to tire. Your testicles have a constant supply of spermatic fluid. You are capable of multiple climaxes. Very unusual."

"How about your husband?" I asked. "He is quite old. Is he still sexually active?"

"No," she said. "He is quite useless. It is too bad, rather inconvenient, actually."

"Why did you marry him?"

"Out of necessity. I needed status, and my brother needed protection."

"Why protection?"

She propped herself on her elbows, studying me. "My brother would have never reached the position he has. As it is now, I practically control my husband. Even though he can't give me sexual satisfaction, he loves me. He'd do anything for me, and that is why he tolerates my brother." She smiled. "And soon my brother will not only be the Thalmani, he will also be the Grand Minister."

"I understand," I said. Her revelation should have bothered me, but I didn't really care. In her hand, my penis had swollen again, and when I rolled on top of her, she smiled and willingly opened her legs.

Chapter Fifteen

In the evening, we dined in the first class lounge on deck. Captain Garzius joined us and ordered the food for us.

"How are the accommodations?" he asked.

"A little cramped, Captain," Fara said, "but otherwise adequate."

"I apologize for the inconvenience the small size of your suite may cause you, my Lady, but it the largest suite on my ship." He looked at Tafima. "It's the one you always occupy when traveling on my humble vessel."

Tafima gave him an apologizing smile. "You must forgive my sister. She has been spoiled."

Captain Garzius threw a casual look at Fara. "I don't remember ever seeing you on my ship." He smiled. "And I would remember a beautiful woman like you."

Fara chuckled. "You are a charmer, Captain. I've just only recently moved into the palace grounds so I could be closer to my sister."

"I understand. Where did you live before?"

"On my parents' estate in the southern part of Isram." She laughed cheerfully. "Not exactly the center of civilization, I know, but our family has always been somewhat elusive."

"You must be, because I'm not familiar with that part of our country. But then again, I spend most of my time on the water. This ship is my home." Captain Garzius let his eyes travel down Fara's curvy body. "Maybe some time during our journey you will give me the honor of joining me in a private meal."

"I don't know if I can trust a handsome man like you, Captain Garzius." Fara laughed coyly.

The Captain's rumbling laughter echoed through the lounge. Then for the first time he actually looked directly at me. "You haven't said much so far," he said, "you wouldn't be the husband of this beautiful lady, would you? If you are then I apologize for my rude behavior."

I shook my head. "No, I'm not her husband."

"Then who are you?"

"He is a guest in our palace," Tafima answered for me.

"A guest? To be frank, at first I thought you were Lady Tafima's personal slave. But you don't behave like a slave, so I took you for a possible bodyguard. You certainly have the built for one." He inclined his head a little. "My apologies for ignoring you."

"Apology accepted." I said. "As Lady Tafima already explained, I'm just a guest." I laughed. "Nobody important. Just pretend I'm not here."

"All my guests are important. May I inquire what your name is?"

"It's Dan Griffin." I had the feeling that Tafima didn't want to broadcast my true identity. Therefore, I left out *Major*.

Captain Garzius bowed again. "May you be safe in the net of the Holy Triangle, Sahir Griffin."

"And you also," I replied.

He clapped his hands. "Now let us enjoy some wine and the best food you'll find on any ship sailing the rivers of Isram."

As was the usual custom in Isram, we consumed our meal in relative silence, only commenting when we came across an especially tasty morsel. The fish soup didn't taste bad, and the fish stew contained just enough spices to tantalize the taste buds. Desert consisted of bowls of sweet pudding with chunks of fruit.

"Your chef outdid himself," Lady Tafima said, after we finished. "I might possibly buy him from you."

Captain Garzius laughed good-humouredly. "I'm afraid he is not for sale. He is my brother, aided by his wife. But I will let him know what you said. He will be pleased." He rose. "Now, if you will excuse me, I have my duties to perform. After all, I am the captain of this ship and not completely indispensable."

"Handsome man," Fara sighed as she watched him walk away.

I had to agree. Handsome with a likable personality. He reminded me a little of Prince Shakur.

Looking around the lounge, I noticed that only about half of the tables were occupied, but I knew that there were more passengers. I had seen them board the ship in the harbor. Obviously, the majority of them were taking their meals in the dining room in one of the lower decks.

"Are there many ships like this traveling on the river?" I asked.

"No, the *Seaflower* is the only one of this size, and the most comfortable. Most of the other ships transport more freight than passengers." Tafima looked out of the large window to our right. "It is getting dark outside and soon the ship's engines will stop. We will spend the night anchored close to shore," she said. "I'd like you to keep me company on the promenade deck."

"Where else would I be going?" I asked, jokingly.

She gazed at me for a moment. "Yes, where else?"

"I think I will search out Captain Garzius and take him up on his invitation," Fara said, getting up.

Tafima finished her wine and rose. "Come, Major," she said and hooked her arm into mine. "Let's go for a little walk."

The air smelled fresh outside and cool. We walked slowly across the deck for a while, not talking. It was almost romantic. Leaning against the railing, Tafima looked up into the sky, at the appearing specks of light sprinkled across the darkening sky.

"I've always liked the stars," she said. "You've been in space. You've seen many different worlds. How do you like spending your time on the surface of a planet, Major Griffin?"

I shrugged. "Better than spending it cooped up inside a cylinder, hurtling through the emptiness of cold space, separated from certain death by only a thin layer of metal and plastic."

She gave me a questioning look. "You prefer the safety of a planet to living inside a spaceship?"

"Yes, I do. I was born on a planet. In fact, I was born on Redsky. This is my home."

"You never mentioned that before."

"It wasn't really important."

"So how did you end up as a soldier in the service of the Terran Empire?"

"It is a long story, my Lady. Too sad in a way to bore you with." I put my arms around her and kissed her. Her nearness made my head spin a little and put me in a constant state of arousal.

She laughed softly when she felt my rigid organ pressing against her belly and let her hand travel down to my crotch. When her fingers curled around my penis, only partially successful, hindered by the tight material of my pants, a loud moan escaped my lips involuntarily. "It seems I will have you all to myself tonight," she said huskily, her breath warm on my face. "My sister will most likely spend the night with Captain Garzius."

"I don't mind," I said, feeling my heartbeat increasing from her touch. My hands went around her to grab her buttocks. Pulling her against me, I pressed my hard member tighter against her soft belly. "Let's go below deck right now," I said hoarsely.

She kissed me, and then pushed me away gently. "There'll be plenty of time. We have the whole night. It will be so much more exiting."

In my aroused state, I was still aware of my surroundings, but not as alert as I should have been. The sound of voices made me let go of Tafima. Two older couples strolled by us, throwing curious glances in our direction.

"You'll have to learn to control your urges in public," Tafima chided me with a low voice. "Even though I try to keep a low profile when I'm traveling, some people might recognize me for who I am."

"I'm not usually like this," I murmured, "but you have me bewitched. It is becoming harder and harder for me to keep control over my body when I'm in your presence."

She patted my cheek and smiled. "You flatter me, Major. And I will not disappoint you...later."

It had become quite dark by now. When I looked toward shore, I noticed lights on land. My eyes adjusted to night vision. Changing the focus of my eyes, I saw the shapes of houses.

"We should arrive in the small town of *Jadestone* in a short time," Tafima said. "There we will seek shelter in the harbor. We'll take on new passengers, and some of the ones on board will disembark. But we will stay until morning, before we move out again."

"And what will we do?" I asked.

She laughed softly and pulled me away from the railing. "Let's walk a little."

Dim electric lamps lit up the promenade deck. It seemed Captain Garzius didn't believe in lighting up his ship with primitive oil lamps, a fact I registered when we first entered our suite, but I had not consciously thought about it. There was a lot I didn't seem to realize lately. It didn't really worry me, but it gave me food for thought.

When I looked into one of the windows from the lounge, I saw chandeliers hanging from the ceiling illuminating the tables, which were occupied by diners.

"This is quite a luxuries ship," I commented. "I guess Captain Garzius is a wealthy man."

"He is. His father owned the ship before him. Garzius grew up on it, and when his father died, Garzius inherited it. This is the only home he ever knew."

"You know him well?"

I felt her shake her head. "Not really. However, I've known him now for five years, and we've become acquainted. He loves to talk and I have listened to the story of his life many times." Tafima chuckled. "He can be quite charming, and on some of my trips I searched out his company for lack of other companionship."

"You travel often on his ship?"

"I take periodic trips on this river, yes." We had stopped walking again. She looked up into the sky. "The stars seem so much closer out here on the water," she murmured. "You can almost touch them."

"An optical illusion," I said. In the west, one of the two moons appeared above the distant tops of the Golgat-Mountains. The smaller of the satellites. It just occurred to me that the Stardogs used it to hide their starship. Looking across the darkness of the river, I saw tendrils of white mist rising from its surface as the cooling air touched the warm water. It would be a cold night. A gust of wind pushed the reek from the smokestack in our direction, and the noise of the steam engines sounded suddenly loud in my ears.

Tafima seemed to shiver beside me. "It is getting chilly," she said, putting her arm around my waist. "You want to go inside for a drink?"

"I wouldn't mind."

The lounge was divided into two rooms, one intended for dining, and the other for socializing. We picked one of the small round tables and sat down. One of the slave girls came and asked us if we wanted something to drink. There wasn't much choice, just wine and fruit juice.

"Bring us two glasses of wine," Tafima told the girl.

A little surprised, I watched the girl walk away. She was the first tribe's girl I had seen in Isram. "I didn't know you used members of *Shantra's Children* as slaves," I said.

Tafima gave me an inquiring look. "And why shouldn't we?"

I shrugged. "No reason. The tribes don't usually interact with humans. They prefer to live in their own environment. I didn't think they'd make good slaves."

"Everybody can be made into a slave." Tafima laughed. "No one willingly becomes a slave."

"No one should be made into a slave," I said, possibly a little too harshly, because Tafima stared at me for a moment. "You don't believe in slavery?"

"No." In my mind, I saw Meadow with a ring around her neck and a chain hanging from it.

"It is part of Isram's culture."

"I know. It is practiced all over Redsky, not always openly, but it doesn't make it right."

"Who is to say what is right and what is wrong? Sometimes things just are. We adjust to them and take advantage of them." Tafima smiled. "I was thinking of asking that slave girl to join us in our suite tonight. Would you like that?"

"If she came willingly."

"Slaves have no choice. Everything they do is done willingly. They don't know anything different." She shook her head. "You're an idealist, Major Griffin. We don't live in an ideal universe. You of all people should know that. You are a soldier. Do you always question your superiors? Do you ask them if the decision they made is right or wrong? Do you question their motives?"

"Sometimes I do."

"But you still follow your orders...if you're a good soldier. And I believe you are a good soldier." Her smile mocked me when she looked into my eyes. "I also believe that you won't question your moral beliefs when you sink your rod into that young slave girl's hot and tight love-channel. I hear the females of *Shantra's Children* are exceptionally passionate during their cycle. And that girl is at the peak of her cycle." She laughed. "She will come willingly."

She was right. The girl was in her receptive cycle. The glands below her ears were swollen and yellow, a definite sign. I remembered Blue Petal, Threehorn's sister. Remembered her fervor and the way she made me feel during our wild couplings. Just thinking about her made my blood boil inside my veins and my penis swell between my legs.

Tafima was watching me as if she knew what went on inside me. "You've tasted their passion, have you not?" She chuckled. "I will tell her to join our bed tonight."

* * * *

131

Tafima turned off the light in the bedroom. Only the pale light from the moon shone through the window, illuminating the young female straddling me. She took hold of my rigid pole with both hands. Her vagina tube extended, hung over my penis, and gently touched the head. Very slowly, the girl fed my member inside her and slipped it over my organ like a tight glove, engulfing it completely. Then she hovered above me, unmoving, while her vagina tube slid up and down my shaft.

Her grip was firm, but incredibly soft. She looked like a beautiful statue, only her sexual organ and her glittering yellow eyes seemed alive. Her small breasts stood out sharply, the thick long nipples as rigid as the rest of her shapely body.

It excited me terribly to watch her thick tube sliding up and down my penis. She never lost her grip, even though sometimes the tube contracted so much it just barely engulfed the head. Then it would extend again, swallowing the whole length of my stiff pole.

As I watched, I registered only fleetingly the girl's small penis hidden between the folds of her thick mound, right above the vagina tube.

The female above me suddenly sank down, her sexual tube shrank, and I saw my penis disappear inside her belly. A loud moan beside us made me aware of Tafima, who watched us with large eyes. When I turned my head to look at her, I noticed that her fingers were hidden between her closed legs

The girl began rotating her pelvis, and her face lost that stoic expression.

She was ready to receive my sperm.

Taking her gyrating hips into my hands, I lunged upwards, pushing deep into her. Then I climaxed with tremendous force. Greedily, her strong pulsing vagina tube sucked up my gushing spermatic fluid, while she cried out with a series of high-pitched sounds.

Luckily, I had received my anti-fertility shots, so I didn't worry about fathering a couple of *Gourmas*...half-breeds.

The female collapsed on top of me, her breasts flattening against my chest. We lay motionless for a while. When she finally stirred again, her inner vagina tube began to vibrate gently along the length of my hard organ. The sexual secretions she oozed inside her sex-organ contained a highly stimulating substance and created unbelievable pleasure in a male.

I tried to keep my voice low when a deep moan escaped my lips, but I couldn't contain myself. The pleasure proved too great to keep it bottled up inside me. I put my arms around the young female and turned us around. Now she lay on her back. Her legs opened wide as I began to rock between them. I buried my face between her breasts, licked her soft skin and let my lips wander across the small mountain of her breast to her thick sensitive nipples. Suckling on them, I made her squeal with delight. She bucked beneath me, milked my swollen rod feverishly. Inside her burning vessel, tiny hair-like tendrils caressed the tip of my organ, making me lose control. Coming again, I filled her with my discharge, bathed in the glory of the bliss she gave me, oblivious to my surroundings.

She pushed against me. When I pulled out of her, she rolled away from me, her body rolled up into a ball. I was still hard and rampant with lust. I heard a woman laughing beside me. Then soft hands grabbed me and pulled me from the bed.

"Come." I looked at the kneeling form of Tafima in front of me, her rump up. Between her slightly spread legs I could see the dark swollen lips of her sex-organ beckoning below her brown cheeks. She looked back at me, her eyes partially hidden behind her long black hair, which had fallen forward to cover her face.

I groaned and grabbed her hips, stabbed between her soft cheeks, seeking the entrance to her body. Her hand found me and guided me forward. With a loud shout, I pushed into her dripping organ, moved like a berserker behind her, ramming my hard rod into her with forceful thrusts.

She pushed back against me, holding me in a firm grip. Laughing hysterically, she moved with wild abandon, her soft buttocks grinding into my lap. I reached around her, dug my fingers into her swinging breasts and squeezed them in a tight grip. She cried out, but not from pain.

"Pull out and lie on your back!" she told me after awhile. I did. She sat astride me and took me back into her. Then she rode me for a long time, her body swaying and bucking above me, her hips gyrating violently. When I was almost ready to climax inside her, she stretched out on top of me, pushed her nipples into my mouth. "Drink from my body." She moaned when I fastened my lips on her breast, taking the thick nipple into my mouth. I drank eagerly from her breast. The nectar flowed down my throat, and it tasted sweet.

"That is good." She pushed my face onto her breasts. "Drink deeply," she whispered.

I turned her onto her back. She wrapped her strong long legs around my torso and pressed her heels into my buttocks. Her hips lifted up as she met my thrusts, and when I finally came, we both cried out at the same time. I collapsed into her arms, exhausted, but satisfied.

The slave girl still lay on the bed when we joined her. The bed was wide and provided enough room for the three of us. I lay between them, Tafima on my right, the slave girl curled up on my left. Their bodies touched mine, warm and soft.

I felt at peace. With a sense of happiness, I fell asleep.

* * * *

I awoke to find myself sandwiched between Tafima and the slave girl. Tafima stirred beside me. Opening her eyes, she smiled and yawned. Through the window, I could see daylight outside. When I moved, the slave girl woke up and slipped out of my grasp. "I shouldn't be here," she said and sat up.

"It's all right," Tafima said and looked at me. "I want you to have sex with her...now," she told me.

"Now? Why?" I asked, perplexed.

"Do I need a reason?" She laughed. "But if you must know, I enjoy watching."

"Can't we get cleaned up and have breakfast first?"

"Sure. If you want to. We have all day." She slid out of bed and went to pull the cord that would alert Alya across the hall. Moments later, there came a knock on the door.

"Bring us breakfast," Tafima told her.

Alya looked around, her gaze momentarily on the girl on the bed, but she didn't comment. "I won't be long," she said.

I went into the small bathroom and washed the sleep from my eyes. Then I went back into the bedroom. "What is your name?" I asked the slave girl, who was watching me with her yellow eyes.

"*Dancing Leaf*," she said, "but here I am called *Kiromi*."

"All right, Kiromi, you can freshen up, if you like."

She gave me a grateful look and disappeared into the bath cubicle. Tafima sat naked on the other bed, an amused smile on her beautiful face. "You've coupled with her kind before, haven't you?" she said.

I nodded. "A long time ago. How do you know?"

134

"Their sex-organs are different from human sex-organs. You didn't act surprised when her vagina-tube extended from her belly. You knew what to expect. It didn't turn you off."

"Why should it? She's a woman." I shrugged. "Alien and a little different, yes, but still a woman."

"She has a penis."

"For urinating. And it is so tiny, it's no good for anything else."

"Do you know of the existence of any human woman who has a penis?"

"I've never seen one, but apparently sometimes a human is born with a female and a male sexual organ. These unfortunate beings are called hermaphrodites."

"The universe is a wondrous place, isn't it?"

I studied her, as she sat there on the bed, naked and beautiful. So perfectly formed, almost like a sculpture, and so sensuous and seductive. "It certainly is," I said, suppressing the urge to walk over and throw her onto the bed.

She laughed when she saw my erection. "You want me?" she asked, opening her thighs wider to give me a better view of her genital area.

"You know I do," I said hoarsely.

"Do you think that a woman can control a man by giving or withholding sexual favors?"

"Yes."

"Can a woman be controlled the same way?"

"I suppose so, but I'm not a woman. You tell me?"

She lifted her shoulders. Her tongue played across her full lips. With tantalizing slowness, she closed and opened her thighs. I couldn't stand it any longer, walked over to where she sat and grabbed her roughly. "Why are you asking me all these questions? What is it you want from me?"

She pushed me away. "Right now nothing." Her eyes glanced at the opening bathroom door. "I just want to watch you have sex with that slave girl."

Kiromi looked at me, made a weaving motion in the air with her left hand and said, "I am ready." Then her yellow eyes fastened on Tafima. "With your permission, my Lady."

Tafima clapped her hands and nodded. "It is my wish."

Her hand reached out, and her fingers curled around my erect penis. My whole body tingled when she touched me. I pushed her onto her back, pried open her thighs. She resisted, but even though she was exceptionally strong, she couldn't keep me from forcing myself between her spread legs. I entered her with one powerful thrust and wasn't surprised when I found her wet and slippery. She let out a sharp cry, but then she moved against me with a ferocity that startled me, even though I had suspected that she wanted this. Our lips locked in a deep kiss. She pushed her tongue into my mouth. I swallowed the saliva that trickled down my throat.

We moved thus for a long time. She didn't say anything the whole time, just moaned loudly and cried out when an orgasm raced through her body.

Only dimly aware of my surroundings, I heard the opening of the door, heard someone moving across the carpet with soft footsteps. My implants didn't seem to function properly. I should have been more alert to anything that happened around me, but nothing mattered to me except for the wild, passionate woman writhing beneath me. Even when hands gently touched my body, I didn't react to them, just kept on hammering between Tafima's clutching thighs.

"Leave some of that for me," a voice said softly into my ear. Recognizing Fara, I grunted.

Fara laughed and walked away. She spoke to another person who had entered the room after her.

"Just put it on the table in the other room. We'll call you when you're needed again."

"Yes, my Lady." I was still conscious enough to know it was Alya, the servant girl, with our breakfast.

Shuddering in Tafima's grip, I let my climax take me away and crushed my mouth against hers.

I registered Fara stretching out beside us and pressing her naked warm body against ours. She lifted my head and pulled it toward her breast. My lips fastened on her thick nipple. I sucked on it, swallowing the sweet liquid that flowed from it into my mouth.

"Come to me now," she whispered into my ear.

Tafima released me. I shifted from her into Fara's embrace and entered another hot clutching vessel.

Fara laughed when she began moving against me, churned her hips violently underneath me. It didn't take long for her to experience her first orgasm. I never stopped thrusting.

"He's well trained," I heard her say to Tafima, after she calmed down.

Tafima chuckled. "I think I have him under control. He'll do anything I ask him to." She touched my shoulder. "Major, leave Fara and couple with Kiromi."

Obediently, I disengaged myself from Fara and slipped from the bed.

"You know what to do," Tafima said.

I lay down on the floor, waited for Kiromi to straddle me. Her vagina tube was already extended when she lowered herself into my lap. It slipped easily over my stiff pole. I groaned when the pleasure washed through my body.

Tafima knelt beside me, bent forward and offered her breast. "Here, drink," she said. The sweet liquid ran down my throat, seemed to give me strength and stamina. Fara knelt on her other side, offered me her breast.

In my lap, Kiromi bounced up and down, the soft tight grip of her pulsing sex-tube sending waves and waves of exquisite pleasure into my brain.

I was happy.

Chapter Sixteen

We arrived in the harbor of Rivergate in the early afternoon.

"How do you feel, Major?" Tafima smiled as she slipped into her black leather coat.

I looked down at myself, at the tight leggings and black high boots. It felt strange to be dressed again. "I feel fine."

Fara handed me my own coat.

"How's your memory?"

"My memory?" I wiped my hand across my forehead and looked out of the window at the ships in the harbor. "Have we arrived already? I thought you said it would take us three days to get here."

Tafima and Fara laughed. "I guess time flies when you're occupied," Fara said.

I tried to remember the last three days, but I couldn't recall much, except foggy images of me eating, sleeping, and copulating most of the time. The faces of Tafima, Fara, Kiromi, and even a couple of slave girls, their brown gleaming bodies undulated inside my mind, blended into one big blur. However, nothing showed up in my artificial memory chip, as if someone had erased everything that happened on the ship.

I should have been concerned about that, but it didn't seem to cause any alarm, so I shrugged it off.

When we arrived on the upper deck, I saw many passengers already disembarking the ship, while a small crowd of new travelers waited patiently to board. Quite a number of other ships were moored on either side of us, most of them freighters or large fishing vessels. The river was wide at this point, and when I looked to the south at the large expanse of choppy water, I realized this was the ocean. To be more precise, the *Bay of Songs*.

A strong wind blew from the south, and I felt grateful for the long leather coat. I inhaled deeply and breathed in the moist air, laden with the salt from the ocean, the smell of fish and the reek of oil and smoke.

Two male slaves carried our luggage as we walked across the boarding plank onto shore. Another slave directed us toward a horse-drawn carriage, which waited not far away.

After they stowed away our luggage, we climbed into the carriage.

"Where are we going?" I asked, settling into the comfortable seat.

"To our estate. But we'll stay there only until tonight." Tafima refrained from giving me more information.

The coach began to move across the rough stone covered road. The seats may have been comfortable, but it was still a bumpy ride. Looking through the small window, I noticed that Rivergate was like any other town in Isram, not as large as Rhandistan, but still larger than Old Town in Newland. It bustled with people, many of them living off the fishing industry, the main income for the majority of citizens.

And slavery.

Rivergate was the destination of the caravans that brought the slaves from the west. From here, they were shipped to their final destination, either via the river or by land.

The river split Rivergate in half, making it in reality two cities, the only connection by ferries and ships. A road connected the eastern part of the city to the towns and small cities in the southeast of Isram.

I knew all this from my briefing before we left on this mission. Information I possibly never needed.

As we traveled, my mind seemed to clear a bit, and I felt more alert than I had for the last three days. I wondered what Cherryh did at the moment, and I was tempted to contact him and let him know that I was fine, but it wasn't possible in my present situation. I needed to be alone, away from prying eyes and ears.

Tafima sat across from me. She seemed to be asleep, but I saw that she studied me through eyes narrowed to tiny slits. Her sister, who sat beside me, actually did sleep, her head leaning against my shoulder, her breathing shallow and regular.

"You are a peculiar specimen of a man, Major Griffin," Tafifa said suddenly.

"Why is that?"

"You are strong, physically and mentally, and most likely quite disciplined, yet...you are ruled by your sexual organ." Her teeth shone white in her dark face. "Have I discovered your weakness?"

I chuckled. "Is that what you were trying to discover in me...my weakness?"

"Maybe. Knowing another individual's weakness gives one power over that individual."

"You mean...control?"

"That is correct." She opened her eyes wide and leaned forward. Her dark eyes bored into mine. "Have you discovered my weakness, Major?"

"I wouldn't tell you if I did," I countered, but smiled. "What would be the purpose? You and I are not at war."

She leaned back into her seat. "We're always fighting some battle, don't you know? And we must seek any advantage possible."

"The only battle I'm fighting right now is not to fall asleep," I said, chuckling. "I'm quite tired. I have a feeling it has something to do with the battle I've been fighting these last few days."

Tafima laughed, obviously amused by my remark. "I wouldn't call *copulating* a battle, but we did thrash about quite a bit. I must admit I'm a little tired myself. However, we won't get much sleep for a while. When we get to the estate we'll bathe, have something to eat, and maybe we'll get a chance to rest a little."

"Aren't we staying there overnight?"

"No, our destination lies elsewhere. You'll see."

Our carriage slowed down and made a turn. When I looked out of the window, I saw a gate looming before us. It swung open as we approached, and then we passed into a large courtyard.

"It seems we have arrived," Tafima said.

Fara stirred beside me and sighed. "Why are we stopping? Are we there?" she asked sleepily.

"Apparently we are," I said.

The courtyard looked much smaller than the palace grounds in Rhandistan, but still impressive. When we stepped from the carriage, a couple of slave girls and a large, burly man came running to greet us.

The man bowed and said, "May you be safe in the net of the Holy Triangle, Lady Tafima." Then he looked at Fara, "May you also be safe, my Lady."

"And you, Bashir." Tafima inclined her head and lifted a hand. "We are tired from the long journey. I trust you have prepared a bath and something to eat for me and my companions?"

"I have, my Lady. Please follow me." He turned and began walking toward the main house. It was impressive, adorned with statues and pillars. Carvings in the tall wooden entrance door depicted animals and men and women locked in deep embrace.

We entered a vestibule with a high ceiling. A chandelier illuminated a stairway leading to a second floor, but we walked straight ahead into a large dining room. A table in the center had place settings for five.

"Perhaps you would like to freshen up before dinner?" Bashir asked.

"We would," Tafima said.

Bashir spoke to the two girls with him. "Take the Lady Tafima, the Lady Fara, and the *Sahir* into the bathing suite, and make sure the water is not too hot!"

The girls led us into a tiled room with a large tub sunk into the floor. Steam rose from the water inside the tub. It didn't take long for us to shed our clothes, and soon we slipped into the warm water.

Both of the slave girls undressed and joined us in the water. Then they began to spread soap over our bodies, spending more time than necessary scrubbing my shoulders and chest.

"I think the *Sahir* has enough soap on him," Tafima told them.

The girls giggled and moved behind Tafima and Fara, rubbing soap onto their backs.

"I've missed this comfort," Fara said. "We should tell Captain Garzius to install a tub in our suite on his ship."

Tafima laughed softly and turned around to let the slave girl rub her breasts. Closing her eyes, she moaned as the girl caressed her upper body. I couldn't miss the slave girl's hand moving down Tafima's belly. She opened her eyes and looked at the girl. "Not now," she whispered, throwing me a quick look.

The girl pouted and moved away.

When I looked at Fara, I saw her in a tight embrace with the other girl, kissing her deeply. They broke apart when Tafima said, "I think we're all clean enough. Let's have something to eat."

Three more girls had come into the bathroom while we had been bathing. One of them began drying me with a large towel. The other two toweled off Tafima and Fara.

We put on fresh clothing and went back into the dining room. I was surprised to see the two girls who had been bathing with us join us at the table.

"When can we accompany you to Rhandistan? We're anxious to see the big palace."

Tafima stared at the girl who had spoken. "When you're ready."

"When will that be?"

Tafima shrugged. "As soon as Bashir gives me a favorable report of your progress."

The girl hissed something in a language I didn't understand. Tafima threw her an angry look, a warning, I could easily see.

"Trouble with your slaves?" I asked.

"They're not slaves," she said. "They're students." She smiled. "Students with an attitude." She looked up when a male servant walked into the room. "What is it?"

"Forgive me for disturbing your meal, Lady Tafima, but I was told to give you this message immediately."

"What message?"

"There is a courier at the door. He says that your transportation has been postponed until tomorrow night."

"That's unfortunate. I was looking forward to getting away without any delays." She dismissed the servant with a wave of her hand. "But maybe it's just as well. I *am* a little tired. We shall get a good night's rest in a comfortable bed."

After dinner, a slave girl took me to my room, and I happily discovered that I would spend the night alone. Lying in bed, I activated my communicator, but Cherryh didn't acknowledge my call. I received only static, so I assumed he was out of reach.

I slept well, woke in the morning with a clear head, quite rested. The window of my room faced into the courtyard. Opening the window, I inhaled the fresh air and went through a series of exercises, which I had been neglecting lately.

A number of people moved around in the yard, most of them maintenance crew, probably slaves. They were busy cleaning the grounds and trimming shrubs and trees.

Before I could get dressed, someone knocked on my door and walked in without giving me a chance to call out. One of the girls from the night before. She smiled when she saw me naked. "I was told not to try to get you to have sex with me," she said boldly, "but maybe I'll ignore that request." Coming close, she stroked my chest and let her hand wander down to my genitals. "I wonder how this would feel inside me," she murmured and brushed my lips with hers, her fingers encircling my penis.

When I reacted, she laughed and pulled away. "I better not," she said, regret in her voice. "Come, Lady Tafima is already seated at the table. She gets annoyed if she has to wait too long."

"I'd like to take a moment to wash myself," I said. "Can you take me to the bathroom?"

Naked, I followed her down the hallway. I've never been a shy person.

The girl helped me get dressed. Then she accompanied me to the dining room. Tafima gave me an amused look when I entered. Her sister Fara sat to one side of her, the second girl on the other side. Across from them sat a stranger, a man I hadn't seen before.

He studied me as I walked toward the table.

"I trust you slept well," Tafima said.

"Sorry, I slept in." I took the empty seat beside the stranger.

"You must have been exhausted. I wonder why?" Fara commented with a straight face.

I just smirked. "I'm hungry." I said, checking out the food.

"You must be the Major Lady Tafima told me about," said the stranger beside me.

"Guilty, and who might you be?"

"That's Khabar," Tafima answered. "We have business dealings together."

"What kind of business?" I asked.

Khabar chuckled and reached for a piece of cake. "I deal in all kinds of merchandise." He glanced at me. "I'm told you're a soldier."

I looked at Tafima, not sure how much I could say.

"Major Griffin is in the service of the Terran Empire," Tafima said.

"Interesting." Khabar took a bite from the cake. "You're far from home."

"A little, but three-hundred and twenty-five lightyears isn't that far anymore."

"What's your sudden interest in Redsky?" It seemed like an innocent question, but I had a feeling it wasn't.

I didn't answer. Instead, I asked my own question. "What's yours?"

He laughed. "Is it that obvious?"

"That you're not a native of this planet?" I asked. "Not really. Just a hunch."

"You're right. Redsky is not my home planet. Space is my home. I travel from star system to star system, peddling my merchandise."

"Are you human?"

His laughter seemed genuine, but I detected a hint of uneasiness. "I could ask you the same question. Are you?"

I smiled. "I know I am." I was tempted to add *Sometimes I wonder, though.* With all the devices inside my body and the manipulation of my genes and nervous system, I wasn't always certain anymore.

"Listen to those two," Tafima said, laughing. "It is so typical. Put two male strangers into the same room and first thing they do is go into a dance of *Who's the stronger one, Who's the smarter one,* and in this case *Who is the more human.*"

"Maybe we should find out who's the one with the most stamina. What do you say, sister?" Fara chimed in.

"I get the hint." I turned to Khabar. "I apologize for the insinuation."

He shrugged it off. "Don't worry about it." Looking at Fara, he grinned and said, "You might just get a surprise, my Lady."

Fara laughed gaily and batted her eyelids. "Maybe."

"How was your trip, Khabar?" Tafima asked.

"Boring, as usual," Khabar answered. "Couldn't wait to get here."

Tafima looked at me. "We won't be leaving until tonight. I have some things I need to check out today, so I will leave you in Fara's capable hands. She can show you our beautiful city Rivergate. There is much to see."

Inclining my head, I said, "I think I should enjoy that."

We finished breakfast making small talk. The two young girls didn't say much. They just listened and watched. I had the feeling they were studying me with some curiosity, because their eyes were on me a lot, but I didn't comment on it.

"Come," Fara said to me when we were finished. She turned to the girls, "Would you like to accompany us?"

Each nodded eagerly.

"Then let's get ready. I'm anxious to see the new harbor. I hear it is almost finished." Fara turned to Khabar and smiled at him. "Perhaps we'll get a chance to get together later," she said.

* * * *

Their names were Kirra and Afra. Kirra seemed the more aggressive one. She had demonstrated that already in my room in the morning. Both girls were equally pretty and curious. They watched everything with large eyes, as if seeing the city for the first time.

"I never realized this city was so big," Kirra said, as we traveled down a narrow street. We could hear the clatter of the horses' hoofs on the rough stones the road builders had used for paving. Even though our carriage didn't lack springs, we still suffered a bumpy ride.

"And so old," Afra added, looking out the small window.

"You've never been in the city?" I asked.

"They haven't been here long," Fara explained.

"Where do you come from?" I asked Kirra.

The girl looked at Fara and, hesitating for a moment, she said, "From the island."

"The island?"

"Sahir Griffin hasn't been here that long, either. He doesn't know where the island is," Fara said. She glanced at me. "In fact, he is only a visitor and is ignorant about much pertaining to Isram."

"Even more ignorant than we are?" Kirra asked.

"Enough chatter!" Fara said, her voice a bit too loud in the confines of the carriage.

"Sorry," Kirra murmured, shrinking in her seat. The girl's eyes held mine for a short moment before she dropped her gaze.

I had the feeling she wanted to ask me something, but didn't dare.

The carriage stopped. I heard our driver descend from his seat. A few moments later, the door of the carriage opened. He held out a hand to help Fara down the steps. The girls declined his help and jumped onto the flagstones.

"This is the marketplace," Fara explained when I joined them.

The place was bustling with people, merchants calling out their offered goods and men and women looking for bargains. The aroma of food and spices filled the air, but the smell of raw and fried fish seemed to be the most pungent. Looking around, I noticed that we were close the ocean. There were a number of ships in the harbor, but not as many as I thought there should have been.

Fara saw my inquiring looks. "The harbor just opened a short time ago and, as you can see, there are not many ships using it, but before long this one will be the harbor where the majority of vessels will moor."

"What's wrong with the old harbor?" I asked.

"Nothing, really. This one is just more convenient for the freighters, because the caravans don't have to travel through the whole city to deliver their goods. From here the freighters and passenger ships travel to Solana, Raas and Randar, the larger coastal cities."

"What about the island Kirra mentioned?"

"The island?" Fara paused for a moment. "The island is not on any regular routes. Only certain ships go there."

"What's on the island?"

She shrugged. "It's just a retreat, really. Not used by the general population."

I didn't press the issue, but my curiosity was aroused. They were hiding something on the island. I had no idea which island, since there were three in the Bay of Songs.

"Let's go and buy something to eat from one of the vendors," Fara said.

Afra clapped her hands. "That sounds like fun."

"I'm not really that hungry," Kirra said. Ever since Fara had reprimanded her, she seemed subdued.

"Come on, Kirra." Fara put an arm around the girl's shoulders. "Once you taste the food, I promise you'll like it."

We approached one of the vendors. The man behind the counter looked expectantly at us. "Try the boiled root-grubs with the berry-sauce. It tastes delicious. My wife just finished making it," he suggested.

Fara inspected the pot he uncovered and sniffed the contents. "You wife is a great cook," she commented. "We'll take four bowls." Then she pointed at a basket. "And a few of those baked rolls." She handed him a handful of coins.

The vendor beamed happily. "May you be safe in the net of the Holy Triangle, my Lady. You honor my humble establishment with your generosity."

"I have a weakness for good food," Fara smiled. "I'm just an instrument of the gods. They reward the ones who serve them well. And you certainly serve them well by preparing such delicious food."

We took our bowls and headed for one of the benches under the trees surrounding the market place. I smelled the food, not quite sure what the bowl contained, but it didn't smell repulsive, so I dipped the small curved wooden spoon into the thick broth. It actually tasted quite good. Spicy and hot, with a lingering aftertaste.

"I need something to drink," Afra exclaimed after licking off her spoon.

Fara dropped some coins into my hand. "Go, get us some fruit juice." She laughed when I lifted an eyebrow. "I understand you wanted to learn more of our ways. Here is your chance, Dan Griffin."

Her omission to call me 'Major' made me smile. As if reading my mind, she gave me light slap on the arm. "I think we should suspend the formalities, Dan. After all, we've been lovers more than once. Isn't that what lovers do?"

"Lovers?" I asked softly. "I wasn't aware we were lovers."

She leaned closer, brushed my lips with hers and whispered into my ear, "Would you prefer *we fucked*?"

Her nearness made my loins flutter. I knew this was the wrong place and stepped away from her. "*Lovers* is fine," I murmured, turning away.

When I searched for a vendor, I couldn't help but notice the long covered wagon pulling into the market place. Watching the drivers jump off their seats, I saw them open the back of the wagon. A few moment later a group of young girls climbed out. All of them had bands around their necks. A thick rope attached to rings in the bands connected all of the girls together.

Slaves.

One of the drivers picked up the end of the rope and began walking across the courtyard, his destination one of the ships. The other driver headed for a large building at the edge of the yard.

I took a closer look at the girls, but none of them looked familiar. It would have been a strange coincidence if Meadow had been among them. However, I knew I was on the right track.

I purchased a pitcher of juice and four clay cups from a vendor. I knew I should have haggled over the price, but it wasn't my money, so I just dropped all the coins into his hand. After checking them, he smiled broadly and inclined his head. "May you be..."

I walked away before he could finish. Not polite, I knew, but I was getting tired of hearing it. Couldn't anyone have come up with something shorter? I studied Fara and the girls from a distance, stricken again by their exceptional beauty. All three of them. Tafima possessed the same beauty, and so did the other girls I had seen in the palace. The thought that this might be highly unusual entered my mind for a fleeting moment, but then I dismissed it.

The girls accepted the drink I poured for them with a grateful smile. Fara touched my lips with her finger. "Not a hard chore, wasn't it, Dan?" she asked.

The touch of her finger sent slight shivers through my body. Suddenly I wanted her badly, and I had to fight for control of my body. Deep inside me, tiny warning bells seemed to start chiming, but when I initiated a systems check, everything registered normal.

I guess I was just extremely horny. Nothing to worry about.

We spent the rest of the day sightseeing. When we returned to the palace, the sun began disappearing behind the buildings.

Chapter Seventeen

"We'll be leaving after supper," Tafima announced.

"Is there a reason we have to travel at night?" I asked.

"You'll find out soon," she said, evasively. Then she smiled. "Are you afraid of traveling in the dark?"

"Not really," I said, "but from experience, I find that traveling during daylight hours is usually safer."

"We'll be in the capable hands of Khabar. He'll make sure we're safe."

The four of us, Tafima, Fara, Khabar, and I left shortly after we finished eating. The trip took a little more than two hours. The road we traveled on proved to be rough, just a dirt road, which I wouldn't want to travel after a rain. We left the city after about an hour, and from the sound of the surf, I knew we were close to the ocean.

A clear night and the light from one of the moons made it possible to see the road. Once, when we moved through a dark section of the road, I thought I saw a bright light for a short moment, but I could have been mistaken.

When we finally arrived at our destination, my buttocks were sore, and I was glad to see the end of the journey. We climbed from the carriage. Khabar and I helped the driver carry our luggage. I received a bit of a surprise when I saw the vehicle parked under a large tree, close to shore.

An airsled.

We loaded the luggage into the storage compartment. Then we boarded the sled.

Khabar sank into the driver's seat and took us up, headed for the ocean.

"I told you we'd be safe," Tafima said and chuckled.

"I thought you people frowned upon the use of modern technology. I guess I was wrong," I commented.

"We have no problem with technology." Tafima leaned back into the comfort of her seat and sighed.

Looking out of the window, I could see the dark water below us. Whitecaps on the rolling waves made me glad we weren't traveling in one of the small steamboats. The ocean has never really been a friend of mine. Water was just too powerful and destructive, especially when it teamed up with high winds.

Nobody said much during the trip. Tafima and Fara seemed to be sleeping, and Khabar concentrated on his controls. Since there wasn't anything I could do, I decided to catch up on some sleep myself.

I awoke when I felt the sled descend. A dark mass below us told me that we were traveling across land. It looked liked we had arrived at our destination. The buildings below were low and square. The lights I saw through the airsled window didn't look like oil lamps, but more like lights powered by electricity.

We settled on a large landing pad and when we stepped outside, I saw in the beam of bright floodlights that we stood on flat rock that had been smoothed out with atomic burners.

"Don't worry about the luggage," Tafima told Khabar. "I'll have someone bring it later."

We headed for one of the buildings. Squat and square, all the buildings reminded me of army barracks. Entering through a wide door, we stepped into a long corridor. At the end of the corridor, a door opened into a cubicle, which turned out to be an elevator. As soon as the doors closed behind us, it began to move down.

Tafima smiled at me. "Welcome to the Holy Residence of the gods. Nirvana awaits you, Dan Griffin."

I had the unpleasant feeling I was about to enter the gates of Hell.

The elevator stopped smoothly and the door opened to let us out. Another corridor, and then we stepped into a dimly lit huge cavern-like room. The sight and humming of machines and motors along the walls and on the ceiling confirmed my suspicion that this place had not been created by the citizens of Isram. It felt gloomy and unreal.

We walked across the room and entered another corridor. A door led us into a smaller room. This one obviously living quarters.

"We'll get a good night's rest. Tomorrow I'll show you around," Tafima said. Turning to Khabar, she said, "You said the merchandise will arrive in the morning?"

He nodded. "Yes, apparently."

"Good. Then I'll see you in the morning."

He bowed slightly and left.

Fara sat down on one of the soft-looking narrow beds. "I shall sleep well tonight," she announced.

Tafima looked at me. "Come, follow me, I'll take you to your room."

We walked through a door in the back wall, into another room. A narrow bed and a chair were all the furnishings. "The bathroom is through that door," Tafima said, pointing. "Sleep well."

With that, she closed the door behind her.

The unsettling sensation that I stood in a prison cell crept into my mind, but I pushed it away and shrugging, I headed for the bathroom.

* * * *

I had no idea if it was morning or not when someone shaking my shoulder woke me. Opening my eyes, I looked into the smiling face of Fara.

"Time to get up," she said.

The fact that my built-in sensor did not wake me up when she walked into the room should have disturbed me, but somehow it left me unworried. I crawled out of bed.

"Had a good rest?" Fara asked.

I stretched. "Actually, I did." Looking down at my naked body, I grinned. "Too bad you're already dressed. I feel so good, I might just have taken you back into bed."

She smiled. "All in good time. I want you to save your strength. Now, get washed and dressed and then we'll have some breakfast."

Tafima wasn't there when I walked into their room, only Fara. The two of us sat at a small table, and munching on some fresh fruit, I felt quite happy with the world. Everything seemed peaceful. The dreadful feeling from the night before had vanished.

"What is this place?" I asked.

"We call it *The Place of Miracles*."

"I know what you call it, but what exactly is it?"

She bent forward. Her eyes seemed large when she looked at me. "You're no fool, Dan. You saw the lights when we landed last night. You saw and heard the machinery that powers this facility. I have not doubt you drew your own conclusions."

I nodded. "I know this installation was not built by people on this planet. Who built it?"

"The Star Gods. This is where they reside. This is where they perform miracles. You'll see."

Even though my mind didn't seem to function properly, the truth still dawned on me.

The Star Gods.

I knew I had found the base of our enemies. The ones we called Stardogs. And I was trapped underground with no means to communicate with my team.

Tafima came back shortly after we finished breakfast.

"You finally awoke," she said, smiling. "Ready for a little sightseeing tour?"

"I am."

"Good then let's go."

The large cavern seemed to have lost its gloomy atmosphere. Bright lights illuminated the machines and other equipment in the room. Some of the designs were definitely alien. Letting my eyes wander, I registered everything I saw, although I could only guess at the function of most of it.

We took the elevator again. It took us up, but when we stepped into another large cavern, I knew that we were still underground. This room didn't have a high ceiling, and I didn't see any motors or other high-tech equipment, only rows of narrow beds. The sight took me back to the laboratory in the alien black structure in the Strathon mountains, the Stardog base we destroyed.

Most of the beds were occupied by pregnant women. All of them seemed happy, as evidenced by their laughter and smiling faces.

We walked past them toward a door at the end of the cavern. Before Tafima opened the door, she turned to me and said, "Now you will witness one of the miracles I told you about."

The room we entered was not large. The sterile atmosphere reminded me of a hospital. I saw only a few beds. The women lying on them were silent. Men and women in white coats surrounded one of the beds. I noticed the up-drawn spread legs of the woman on the bed. Between them, a man bent over, his hands busy with some task.

"Watch this," Tafima whispered beside me.

I didn't have to guess what I witnessed. Moments later, I heard the loud protesting cry of a baby that had been forced to leave the warm safety of its mother's womb and trade it for the cold world outside.

Taking a closer look, I expected to see snapping fangs and the ripped belly of a human woman, but I didn't see any of that. Instead, I looked upon a beautiful brown-skinned human child. The mother on the bed wasn't torn up. She just lay there, silent and unmoving.

"Is the mother dead?" I asked.

Tafima laughed. "No, why should she be? She's just sleeping. We prefer to sedate them before they give birth. Sometimes there can be complications, and it is less painful this way. Come, I'll show you the infirmary."

This time crying babies and chattering mothers greeted us. Again, I saw rows of beds. Not all of them occupied. The ones that were, held nursing women who contently cuddled their babies to their breasts.

The next room we entered contained tables and chairs. I knew it was some kind of dining room The aroma of cooking food reminded me of the meager breakfast I had consumed.

Men and women in white coats occupied a few of the tables. We sat down, and when a girl approached our table, Tafima ordered something to eat.

"All of the women seem happy," I commented.

"Why shouldn't they be? They were chosen to bear the sons and daughters of the Star Gods. All of them have earned themselves a special place in Paradise. They are the mothers of a new breed."

"A new breed?"

"Yes. A breed of perfect humans. I'll show you later."

After we finished eating, she took me to another level of the complex. Here we encountered the older children, boys and girls of all ages, some in their teens.

"Here the children are given an education. Once they reach a certain age, they are sent to the mainland where they integrate into our society. They become useful citizens. You've met two of them." She smiled. "Yes, Afra and Kirra." She hooked her arm into mine. "Come, I'll show you the new shipment which arrived last night."

* * * *

The women were young and beautiful, without exception. The collars around their necks proclaimed them slaves. Their eyes looked sullen and without expression.

Khabar removed the ropes, but left the collars in place.

"Not all of the women come freely," Tafima explained. "The collars keep them controlled."

"An electronic impulse transmitted into their brains makes them docile," Khabar explained. "You should understand that terminology, Major Griffin."

"I do," I said grimly.

"The Major doesn't approve of slavery," Tafima said.

Khabar laughed. "Even though it has been part of human history ever since the strong ones preyed on the weaker ones."

"It still doesn't make it right," I growled.

These were the same slave girls I had seen in the harbor. "Are you expecting another shipment of girls?" I asked Tafima.

"We have a steady stream of them coming in from all over Redsky," she said. "Why do you want to know?"

I shrugged. "Just wondering. By the way, all those pregnant women, did they come here freely?"

"Some did, but most are former slaves. When we explained to them what we wished them to do, they chose to be free mothers."

"Without exception?"

"The ones who proved difficult needed to be convinced. With the help of drugs injected into their system," Bhakar said with a wide grin. "It's for their own good."

"You talk too much," Tafima said. "Come, Dan, let me show you our place of worship."

Another cavern, with chandeliers hanging from a high ceiling. Rows of pews surrounded a raised dais, in its center stood three altars. I had seen a similar arrangement in the temple in Rhandistan.

"This is where we worship and where the women collect the holy seeds of the Star Gods," Tafima said with a hushed voice.

I had witnessed that also in the Holy Temple.

"The new slaves will be inducted into the Faith tonight," Tafima said. "And tomorrow night they will receive the holy seeds. It will be quite a spectacle." She turned to me and smiled. "I have plans for you also."

"I can hardly wait," I said.

"Don't be sarcastic, Dan," she scolded. "You will experience nothing but great pleasure, I promise."

We finished eating, and then Tafima took me back to my room.

"Am I a prisoner?" I asked.

She gave me an astonished look. "What gives you that idea?"

"I can't help but feel like a prisoner, stuck here in this room, deep underground."

"You're free to walk around the facilities," she said. "But I'm afraid you won't be able to go back on the surface. There is nothing to see anyway, except bare rock and the ocean." She blew me a kiss before she walked out.

I waited about fifteen minutes, and then I decided to do a little sightseeing of my own. Following a sudden impulse, I walked back into the cavern with the machines. I took my time studying the dials and controls, but I could have saved myself the trouble. I couldn't figure out what they were supposed to do. Yet for some obscure reason I lingered, staring at the equipment.

When I heard the opening of the elevator doors, I turned to see who came out of the elevator and what I saw didn't make me happy.

"Well, look who's here?"

I looked at him coldly. "Inspector McClaren of Spaceport Internal Security. Why am I not surprised?" I turned to the other man. "And, of course, Sergeant Marc Cleaver, the silent partner."

Marc Cleaver grinned. "The hot-shot Major Dan Griffin from the mighty Terran Spaceforce. Even you couldn't prevent your own capture."

"I'm here of my own free will," I said, not even believing it myself.

"Are you, Major?" I couldn't miss the irony in Cleaver's voice. "By the way, we brought a couple of mutual friends."

I cursed when I watched the two men walking out. I didn't know one of them, but the second one was not a stranger.

"Hello, Dan." Niels DePratt stroked his thick mustache when he looked at me. "Don't look so surprised."

"Nothing surprises me," I said, groaning on the inside. "I always knew you were a traitor and a murderer."

"Oh my, now you're hurting my feelings, old friend."

"We were never friends, DePratt. Moreover, I don't believe you have any feelings. I know you are one of the men responsible when the blame was put on me for killing Garth," I said bitterly, blood rushing into my face. *Settle down* an inner voice tried to calm me, but for some reason my body didn't obey. I took a step toward DePratt and lifted a fist.

My fist never found its mark. I felt something smash into my back, right between the shoulder blades. Before I slipped into unconsciousness I recognized what they'd hit me with.

A paralyzing beam.

Chapter Eighteen

Recovering from the effects of a *Paralyzer* is not a pleasant experience. My whole body ached, and it took all of my willpower to open my eyes and raise my head. Somebody dribbled some liquid between my parched lips.

"Take it easy."

I recognized Fara's voice. Her expression actually showed concern when she peered into my face. She put a damp cold cloth on my forehead.

"That feels good," I said, my voice like the croaking of a desert frog. I stared at her. "What happened?"

She chuckled. "You don't remember? You attacked a man, that's what happened."

Memory rushed back, and I felt like an idiot. What had come over me to be so foolish and careless and attack someone obviously not a stranger in this place, someone who had the advantage over me by being protected by his friends. Friends with superior weapons.

Paralyzers were listed as restricted weapons on a Class D planet.

"Why did you attack him?" Fara asked.

"He's an old friend," I said, holding my head, which seemed to hum a little song.

"Why would you attack a friend?" Fara lifted a pretty eyebrow.

"Just a joke. He's not a friend," I said. "Do you have anything I can take for pain?"

"I can probably get you something, but it may take a while."

Sitting up didn't make me feel any better, but I couldn't lie there all day. "Then get it, please."

Looking around, I noticed that I was in my own room. I wondered who had been kind enough to drag me into my own bed.

One question loomed above all others. What the hell were DePratt, McClaren, and Cleaver doing here? Even though my head hurt and thinking gave me a bigger headache yet, I had no trouble figuring that one out.

Slaves!

I wondered if the new shipment had arrived. That would mean Meadow and the other girls were on the premises.

I lay on my back, studying the ceiling, when Fara came back with a tiny pill. I swallowed it and within moments, my pain disappeared.

"Feeling better?" she asked.

I nodded. I did feel better, but also a little uneasy. I should have been able to dampen the pain without taking any medicine. Something definitely did not work properly.

"What time of day is it?" I asked.

"Evening," Fara answered. "You've lost several hours. I'll have one of the girls bring us something to eat. Then we'll take a bath together."

Fara took me to a room not far away from ours. It felt like stepping into an outdoor garden. Tall, thick plants grew everywhere, creating a jungle-like atmosphere. A multitude of colorful flowers filled the air with their scent. We walked down a graveled path until we came to a large pond. A few bathers frolicked already in the water.

Above us hung bright lights, like miniature suns, but not so bright they hurt the eyes when you looked at them.

"Beautiful, isn't it?" Fara exclaimed. "Like being outside."

"Is that a real bird?" I asked when I heard the soft twittering of a songbird.

"It's real."

She stripped off her clothing, laughed and rotated her hips when she saw me looking at her naked body. "Come on, get undressed."

It felt good to slip into the warm water. I swam toward the deeper part of the pond, dove under the surface, and to my surprise, I saw fish swimming around me. A hand touched my leg and moved up to my genitals. I turned around and looked into a woman's smiling face. Even with the distorted view under water, I could see it wasn't Fara. She moved closer, pressed her lips against mine. We surfaced, glued together.

Laughing into my mouth, she put her arms around me and clung to me, her legs wrapped around my torso. Then she opened her arms and leaned back, her legs still keeping me prisoner.

"I'm Simi. I saw you coming with Fara. Are you her new lover?"

"Honestly, I don't know what I am. Possibly a prisoner." I felt my penis rise and lodge between her buttocks.

She smiled, clamped her legs tighter around me. "The way you are now in my embrace?"

I reached for her, pulled her close and kissed her roughly. She moaned and moved in my arms, capturing my solid mast between her thighs. With one swift movement, she lifted up and then down, sheathed my pole easily inside her warm sex-organ.

Her buttocks clenched in my hands as she snapped them back and forth. She cried out, quivered and freed me before I could release my own built-up tension. With swift movements of her legs, she swam away from me.

I looked after her, puzzled and unsatisfied. Suddenly angry, I swam after her, but I never reached her, she was too fast. Instead, another naked body slithered up in front me, blocking my way.

"Didn't take you long to make friends," Fara said, touching my erection under the water.

"She practically raped me," I defended myself and pulled her to me, but she pushed me from her. "Save it," she said, and then she too swam away.

Watching her move away, I looked at the others in the pond and noticed that all of them were women. I didn't see any men. Suddenly I had the feeling they were all watching me out of curious eyes.

Don't get paranoid, I told myself. Turning onto my back, I floated with my eyes closed. I needed to concentrate on my reason for being here. To find Meadow and the others and to rescue them. I didn't have the faintest idea how I would get them out of here when I found them, but I'd deal with that later. My incapability to control my own body began to trouble me. Even more worrisome was the fact that according to my system's analyzing program nothing was wrong.

"Dan Griffin!"

I opened my eyes and looked toward shore. Tafima stood there, naked, a smile on her beautiful face. She seemed lovelier than ever. "Come out, Dan," she called.

I climbed onto the grass.

"I think it is time for a revelation, Dan Griffin," Tafima said. Then she walked up to me. Kissing me, she pushed her tongue into my mouth. I tasted her saliva and swallowed it. Then she pulled my head toward her breast. My mouth fastened on her nipple, and I began sucking on it. Sweet liquid flowed into my mouth and ran down my throat. I felt my penis rising between her warm thighs.

She let go of me and stepped back. When I looked around, I noticed that all of the other women had gathered around us.

"I had a talk with your friend Niels DePratt and Marc Cleaver. They told me a lot about you, much of it already known to me." She lifted one hand, which held a small device. "I know everything about you, Major Griffin. I know about the gadgets inside you body, know what they make you. But what has made you a superman, works now against you. When you entered this base, your system was analyzed and your implants neutralized. Actually, they've been taken over by our computer." She laughed throatily. "But that wasn't really necessary, because you've been drinking from my breasts and swallowed my saliva. I had you already under my control."

The woman who had introduced herself as *Simi*, laughed. "I fed him some of my saliva. Does that mean he's under my control, too?"

"He does whatever we tell him to do," Tafima said.

"Good," I heard Simi say. "Then he will feed me now."

"Not yet," Tafima said. "First I will feed from him." With that, she stepped up to me and kissed me again. Putting her hands behind my head, she pulled me down with her. Her legs opened wide and I fell between them. With a shout, I pushed my hard pole into her softly pulsing sex-organ.

"Faster!" she commanded and I obliged her. "Slow!" and again, I obeyed.

"I know what you are," I said between clenched teeth. "This beautiful body isn't really yours."

She laughed. "You want to know what I really look like?" Her face began to change and then I looked into her red eyes and the wriggling tendrils around her lips.

"I know you've been admiring my body. Do you still find me attractive?"

I didn't answer and never stopped moving. After she changed back, she told me to enter her from the rear. I moved behind her, put my pole between her lovely buttocks and pushed it between her puffy lips.

Suddenly, her whole body began to flow, and I found myself kneeling behind a wolf-like, smooth skinned beast, pushing my member in and out of the hairless vagina below the almost human-like buttocks.

"Now!" she growled. "Empty yourself into me!" I came inside her clutching sex-channel, my involuntary cry blending with her joyous howls. She turned her head, fangs gleaming in the bright light of the miniature suns. "Don't stop. I'm far from being satisfied."

It gave me an eerie feeling to hear a woman's soft voice coming from the fanged snout.

There was nothing I could do. My pelvis moved automatically between her smooth buttocks, my hard shaft entering her fleshy, soft vagina effortlessly. After what seemed a long time, her body changed in my hands. Without letting me slip out, she rotated her body, cradling me between her thighs. Except now they weren't thighs, they looked more like boneless tentacles with finger-like tendrils at the end. She wrapped them around my body, holding me tight.

Her arms changed, too. And her face. The tendrils around her mouth moved as she spoke. "Suck my breasts."

I did as instructed, my lips closing around the extremely long nipple. Sucking on it, I tasted the flowing nectar.

She pulled my body against hers, holding me prisoner in her tight embrace. While I sucked on her breast, I felt the gentle sucking of her vagina on my penis, and I knew she was drawing blood.

"We give, and we take," Tafima said, almost gently.

Then she released me and told me to turn onto my back. Sitting on top of me, she changed back into her human form and smiled at me. "I'm not going to suck you dry," she said. "You're much too valuable a specimen."

I studied her lovely face, her shapely form. Her large breasts jiggled softly as she slowly gyrated above me. She looked so beautiful in human form. Surprisingly, it didn't matter to me anymore what she really looked like. I closed my eyes, determined to enjoy the pleasure she gave me.

The pressure of her body was suddenly gone but only for a short moment, and then I felt the sweet sensation of a warm pussy closing around my penis again. Opening my eyes, I looked into the smiling face of Simi.

"Now I will let you enjoy my body, and I will enjoy yours," she said. "Water is always so restrictive."

I reached for her. She stretched out on top of me, pressing her lovely breasts against my chest. I felt her hard nipples on my skin. Kissing me, she snaked her tongue into my mouth. Her saliva mixed with mine. I swallowed eagerly as she fed me.

She moaned, sucking my penis deep inside her clutching vagina. I gave her what she wanted, squirting my sperm into her and let her drink my blood. I seemed to have slipped into some kind of trance. Simi left me. Another woman took her place. Her upper torso was that of a beautiful, voluptuous woman with the head of a great bird. Below her knees, her legs were scaly, her toes long, with sharp claws. Only the arms and hands were human. From her shoulders sprouted a pair of giant wings. Beating her wings, she floated above me, her human-looking sex-organ slipping over my straining member.

I looked around at the watching women, but what I saw made me doubt my sanity. For some reason the light had dimmed and in the twilight, the red eyes of the watching creatures looked upon us out of pale inhuman faces, tiny tendrils moving softly below narrow nose slits.

Another female straddled me. The lower half of her body looked human, with shapely long legs and thighs, but from her hips upwards, she possessed the body and head of a serpent.

Her sinuous body undulating above me, she hissed through her wide-open jaws, her long forked tongue darting back and forth.

How much time passed, I don't know. When I came to my senses, I was alone, lying in the grass beside the pond. I looked at my limp penis and at the dried blood on it, realizing what had taken place.

Tafima had finally revealed herself, confirming my suspicions. It wasn't hard to come to all of the implicating conclusions. Getting up, I stumbled to the water and slipped into it. My body felt drained and tired.

When I climbed out of the water, I saw someone sitting in front of nearby bushes, watching me out of red eyes.

"If you want to couple with me, I'm afraid your friends have sucked me dry," I said.

The creature rose, came walking toward me on legs that had the wrong angle. As she walked, her body seemed to blur. A pair of breasts pushed out of the ribcage, her hips widened and her legs became slim and well formed. Her face changed into the lovely face of Fara. Smiling, she came close. "Is my true form repulsive to you?" she asked softly.

"No, it isn't, but I told you the truth. I am exhausted."

She put her hand behind my neck and pulled it toward her breast. "Here, drink from my body, it will give you strength."

Like a starving child, I sucked on her nipple and swallowed the sweet liquid flowing from it. She was right. It gave me strength and even made my penis swell. She felt it touch her belly and pulled back. "You want to waste my gift?" she asked. "If you do, I will let you."

I shook my head to clear it. *I am not a male Gandor in heat who only thinks of coupling.*

"No," I said with a hoarse voice and let go of her.

"Maybe we should get dressed," she suggested.

I found my clothing on the ground where I had dropped them earlier. "Take me for another tour of this base," I said.

"Why?"

"I would like to understand your species. I feel disadvantaged, because I know nothing about you. Maybe we can come to some mutual agreement."

She smiled. "If you think of escaping, forget it, Dan. This place is a fortress. Maybe it *would* be a good idea to show you more, just so you understand there is no escape for you. And no one will be coming to rescue you, either."

Back in the cavern with all the motors and machines, she said, with a sweeping gesture, "You've seen this. This is the heart of this base, but not the brain. You only see a small part of what makes this place run."

We walked through a door in one of the sidewalls and entered a long corridor. It let us to another cavern, not as huge as the other one, but still quite impressive. What really sparked my interest was the object at the other end.

A small spaceship. It didn't look like one designed by humans, but I would have recognized it as one, even if Fara wouldn't have pointed it out.

"There is our escape from here," she said.

On one wall, I saw screens and controls. Those really piqued my curiosity. "And what are all those controls?"

"When I told you this base is a fortress, I didn't lie. Even though this planet is living in the past technologically, we are aware of the technology humans possess And we are aware of your military might. This installation is not visible from the sky. We've created a shield over it to keep it hidden from spying eyes. However, should an unfriendly aircraft approach us from above for any reason, we will bring it down with our lasers. This includes missiles or any other object thrown down at us. Same goes for anything uninvited approaching from the sea."

"Looks like you have it under control," I commented, studying the controls and gauges. "Any military personnel on the base?"

"On the upper floors and in the buildings topside." She gave me a scrutinizing look. "As you see, we are quite protected in here. So forget whatever you're planning."

I gave her a tight smile. "I guess I didn't play it very smart. I mean, following you and your sister into the lion's den, as it were."

"Tafima is not my sister."

"I guess Koldar isn't your brother, either?"

She shook her head. "No. Nor is he Tafima's."

"What about Marc Cleaver? I suppose he belongs to your species?"

"He does. How did you know?"

"I didn't. Just a hunch, actually. Let me ask you another question. I know you are shape shifters, but how can you keep the human shape for such a long time? I was under the impression that you had to slip back into your original form once in awhile."

"We do. That is why we have to come here every so often. However, we've been having great success in creating hybrid offspring who can hold their chosen shape forever, if need be. You've seen the young children."

"Do they know what they are?"

She nodded. "Of course they do. They also know that they are superior to the real humans."

"Really?" I couldn't keep the sarcasm out of my voice. "Can they change their shape at will?"

"Yes, they can."

I looked at her. "The two men Mark Cleaver came with. Are they human?"

"They're slave traders, that's all."

"You've been here on Redsky for a long time, haven't you?"

"Over twenty years. It is a perfect planet, suited well to our purpose. Plenty of humans to use for our experiments and far away from the Terran Empire." She sighed. "At least until now. Then you showed up. We know about the base you destroyed, and it gives us reason to worry, I have to admit, but we will deal with it. That's why you're so important to us. Studying you will teach us much about your military capabilities."

163

It seems I had blundered in more ways than one. So much for the secret weapon against the Stardogs I was supposed to represent. But to use Fara's own words, *we will deal with it.*

"Speaking of slave traders, did those men bring some new slaves with them?"

"As a matter of fact, they did. A bunch of extremely nice looking girls. Why the interest?"

It didn't matter if she knew. "They may be friends of mine," I said slowly. "Dear friends."

"I can show them to you."

She took me up to another level. I wondered how many levels the base consisted of. I didn't see any indicators inside or outside the elevator.

We walked down a wide corridor. Doors at regular intervals on both sides seemed to lead into a series of smaller rooms. We entered one such room.

It held narrow bunks. On each bunk sat a girl. I recognized each one of them. I spied Meadow on the second one. The girls all looked up when we entered, but none of them reacted when they saw me.

Walking up to Meadow, I looked into her colorless eyes. They stared at me without recognition. "Meadow," I said softly, "It's me, Dan." When she didn't react, I grabbed her, began shaking her. "Wake up, Meadow. Damn it, wake up." I turned to Fara and shouted, "What did you do to them?"

"Calm down, Dan," Fara said soothingly. "Nobody harmed them. They've been drugged, that's all. They'll soon come out of it, with no ill after effects."

I looked at the third bunk where Aleethy sat, her dark eyes as dull and lifeless as Meadow's. Swallowing back a lump that had suddenly appeared in my throat, I said, "They better be."

Fara chuckled. "I don't think you're in a position to threaten anyone, Dan, but I admire your courage." She held out a hand. "Come, I'll take you back to your room."

I followed her like a trained puppy.

Chapter Nineteen

Studying the ceiling above my bed again, I reviewed the things I had learned, and none of them cheered me up at all. I had found the girls and part of my mission had been successful. Now what? We were prisoners inside a fortress from which escape seemed impossible. When I tried to contact Cherryh, I received nothing, not even static. I could forget about contacting the other members of my team. If I couldn't reach Cherryh, I'd be in trouble.

Closing my eyes, I tried to sleep. Maybe I would come up with an idea in my dreams. Sometimes that happens.

It had never happened to me.

I stood in a meadow full of yellow flowers. The scene looked familiar. I remembered being there before.

"Daniel," said a voice I recognized. When I looked up, I saw her standing not far from me.

"Angel," I said. "I didn't expect to see you again."

She laughed. The semi-transparent material of her robe clung to her shapely body. She came closer, put her hands around me and pulled me closer. Her lips searched mine and, kissing me gently, she stroked my naked back with gentle hands. She tasted like sweet berries, just the way I remembered.

Her lips moved down to my neck. I sobbed into her soft hair, inhaled her soothing fragrance.

"I know you've been put into a difficult situation, Daniel, but I'm here now. Everything will be all right."

"How can it be? I am imprisoned deep underground with no way out," I sobbed.

"There, there," said her soothing voice. "Give me all of your frustration. Let your emotions flow out of you." She pulled me down on top of her, pressed her suddenly naked body against mine. Opening her legs, she took me into her. I shouted with joy, felt

strength flowing through my system as I moved between her welcoming thighs. When I climaxed, all my frustration seemed to flow out of me into her.

She kissed me one last time, and then she was gone. Darkness settled around me, took away the blue sky and the sea of yellow flowers.

I opened my eyes and looked around. Things were the same and yet, something seemed to have changed.

I sat up, flexed my muscles and clenched my fists. I felt strong, refreshed.

I listened for sounds from the next room and knew the room was empty. I couldn't detect any movement outside in the corridor.

"How are you feeling, Major?"

Startled, I looked around, but saw no one.

"What the Hell!" I cursed. "Is that you, Angel? Where are you?"

She laughed. "Inside your head, where else?"

"I don't understand. What happened?"

"It is time to act, Major Griffin," she said, her voice suddenly businesslike. "I just triggered a program I implanted inside you the last time we were connected. It will repair all the damage that has been done to you. I was always with you, watching, but I couldn't reveal myself. Did you really think we would send you into the camp of the enemy without giving you some protection?"

"Why wasn't I told?"

"This was the only way. I have studied the base through your eyes and analyzed most of the things you've seen. First thing we have to do is neutralize the lasers and collapse the camouflage web they've created over the base. Now, go. Most of them are sleeping now. You'll be able to move around unobserved."

I rose from my bed, amazed at the vigor I felt. Finding the cavern with all the controls proved easy. It was located one floor above mine. The voice of Angel told me how to operate the elevator. The cavern with the machines lay in semi-darkness. I found the door into the corridor, which led to the control room.

When I got there, I was surprised to find a guard walking around.

"Take him out, Major!" Angel said with a level voice. "No mercy. Don't be fooled by the apparent good will of the alien women. They will kill you without mercy if they think it's necessary. Your life depends on your actions."

He stood near the spaceship, a rifle hanging casually from his shoulder.

Stealthily creeping up on him, I reached him before he saw me. I broke his neck with one chop and let him slide to the ground. Then I pulled him away from the middle of the room and hid his body behind one of the large motors.

Scanning the room, I found no one else nearby.

"Follow my instructions," Angel's voice told me. I began pushing buttons and pulling levers.

"We have to be careful not to alert anyone, especially the sentries on the surface. I don't know how many there are," Angel's voice seemed calm, but I sensed the urgency she tried to hide.

"The camouflage web is gone," she said. "Now, the lasers."

I worked as fast as I could. When she said, "Done," I allowed myself a small sigh of relief.

"Don't relax yet," Angel warned. "Your team is on its way, but let me warn you. Even though you are back to normal, you are still vulnerable. I can only do so much for you."

"I have to get Meadow and the girls," I said, racing back to the elevator. The floor on which the girls were kept was two levels up.

When I entered the room, I noticed immediately that two girls were missing. Meadow was one of them.

"Dan," one of the girls cried out.

"Aleethy," I said, rushed to her side and took her into my arms. "Are you all right?"

"Where are we?" She clung to me for a moment, and then she looked around. "I don't remember how I got here."

"I'll explain later. Where is Meadow?"

"They took her away. I don't know where she is."

Damn! Then I remembered my communicator. I triggered Meadow's code. She answered instantly. *"Dan? I'm in trouble. Help me."*

"Do you know where you are?"

"I saw a large cavern that looked like a place of worship."

"Keep you comm open so I can trace you."

Racing down the corridors, I followed the electronic trail. I knew she was two floors down. So far, I had been lucky, finding the elevator always available when I needed it, and my luck seemed to hold out.

When I dashed through the cavern with all the machinery, I cursed silently. Damn it! Had I known they'd take Meadow to this floor, I could have saved some time. They must have brought her down with another elevator.

"Meadow?" I whispered.

"Dan, hurry!"

I knew I was close. Unfortunately, I also knew what lay between the place they kept her and me.

The chandeliers in the *Place of Worship* lit up the scene on the raised dais around the three altars. I didn't see many worshippers. The number seventeen popped into my head. The tiny computer inside me counted faster than my conscious mind. Changing the focus of my eyes, I took a closer look and saw that eight of the worshipper lay on their backs, their legs open.

Recognizing the slaves Tafima had shown me, I could guess the reason for that. They were waiting to be initiated into the Faith by the Acolytes, while the High Priest gave his final blessing on one of the altars.

With the attention of everyone on the High Priest and his new initiate, I reckoned it was time to sneak by. However, things never go as smoothly as expected. They spotted me as I boldly walked down th aisle. Maybe I should have been nude, like everyone else. I might have had a chance.

On the second altar, a couple writhed in deep embrace. At first, I thought it was a man and a woman. I could clearly see the long penis entering the vagina of the woman at the bottom, but then I saw the breasts of the person on top.

As I stood, puzzled by what I witnessed, the woman on top looked up. When her eyes met mine, I recognized the face.

Simi.

She stopped moving between the other woman's spread thighs and slid off the altar.

"Dan?" she said. "What are you doing here?"

I stared at the half-erect penis below her belly and realized it wasn't artificial. Simi smiled at me and opened her arms. I stared at her lovely shaped breasts. The penis between her legs began to shrink, disappeared into her belly, leaving a hairless cleft.

They're shape shifters, Dan. They can take on any form they chose. A male sex-organ is just another appendix, Angel's voice said inside my head. Then she warned me. *Don't let her touch you! You're not immune to the drug she will feed you. This program wasn't designed for another assault on your system.*

"I couldn't sleep," I said. "I figured a walk might do me good."

Simi smiled. "I know just what you need to help you sleep." She stepped off the dais, came closer and pressed her nude body against mine. Then she lifted up and kissed me. Her tongue fed sweet saliva into my mouth. "Come, make love to me." She put her hand on my crotch.

I could have pushed her away, but I saw the others watching us, with the exception of the girls on the floor, who were still waiting for the Acolytes to initiate them.

Dan, an armed guard at two o'clock. Angel's voice alerted me, but I had already seen him.

"Making love?" I said. "You mean *fuck!*"

"You talk so crudely," she pouted. Her hands began to undo my pants. When her fingers curled around my penis, I couldn't help but let out a little moan. "Tafima said she had you under control," she said. "Now, take off your clothes!"

I pushed down my pants and stepped out of them. Then I took off my shirt. "Can't we just talk?"

"Talk? What do you want to talk about?" She gave me a questioning look.

"Mutual understanding between our species."

She laughed. "Mutual understanding?"

"That's right. Trade. Exchange of information. Peace."

"Why would we want to trade? We already take what we want."

"What is that?"

"Humans."

"You mean slaves!" I said harshly.

"Not just as slaves. We've discovered that humans make perfect breeders and feeders."

I laughed bitterly. "Is that all we are to you? Breeders and feeders?"

"Yes. You see we've known about humans for a long time, even before you discovered space travel. We are an old race, Major Griffin, much older than humanity. Our race is much superior to yours."

"How is it we've never ran into each other?"

She smiled. I looked at her lovely breasts and her perfect shape. She was so beautiful. I found it hard to imagine that this was not her real form. "Oh, we have," she said. "You just never knew."

"We know now," I said. "We've learned a lot about you."

"So you have, at least you think you have. There is much you don't know about us and will never know. For one thing, we are always hungry, Dan Griffin. For your blood and for your sperm. And human males are so eager to please and plunge their organs into our tubes." She laughed, her body undulating. "Aren't you, Dan?"

Don't let her kiss you again, Angel warned me. *I couldn't neutralize all the substance you had in your system. It won't take much to bring you under her control again.*

I noticed that the guard began to show an interest. He held his rifle casually in his hands, but his eyes were alert.

"Now let us stop this chatter, and let me feed." She pulled me down on top of her, capturing my stiff mast between her thighs. She let them fall open and moaning loudly, I slid into her creamy orifice. Moving furiously between her spread thighs, I was determined to bring this to a quick finish. She cried out as she experienced an orgasm and pulled my head toward her breast. My mouth opened instinctively, and I drank eagerly from her long nipple, registering the flow of liquid entering my body.

When I climaxed inside her at the same time, she didn't suck only my sperm out of me. My built-in computer measured the amount of blood the tiny needle-like tendrils inside her sex-organ drew from my penis, not enough to worry about, since it was less than would be lost through a nosebleed.

Then she sank her fangs into my jugular and, moaning, she fed.

When she was done, I pulled out of her. "I am exhausted," I said. "I think I need to rest."

"You humans," she said, contempt clearly in her voice. "You always prove that we are the superior species." She licked her lips and pointed. "Back there are some rooms you can rest in."

I didn't even bother to put on my pants, just stumbled in the direction she pointed. I pushed open the door to the room my tracker had indicated as the one that held Meadow.

On a narrow bunk in the middle of the room lay a naked woman, on her back. Her arms and legs were tied to the bunk, her legs raised and spread. Between them moved a grotesque looking being.

A vaguely human-shaped body, with long legs and arms. Between the long, almost bony fingers, which it clamped around the woman's hips, stretched thin webbing. Below the red eyes, tiny tendrils moved around thick lips.

The woman turned her head and looked at me.

"Meadow," I croaked and walked into the room.

Her eyes widened when she saw me. "Daniel!" she cried out. "Get this ugly thing off me."

I stared at the thing moving between Meadow's thighs. The human-like penis moved in and out of Meadow's vagina with a forceful and steady rhythm. Definitely a male, since this was the creature's natural state. A male Stardog.

With every stroke, it hissed loudly.

"Come on, Dan, what are you waiting for?" Meadow screamed.

Angry and confused, I watched as the creature copulated with the woman I loved, at the same time fascinated by the precise movements of its lower body. Up and down. Up and down. Then it stopped moving. A shudder ran through the muscular body.

"Dan Griffin!" Someone shouted. "This fucking thing just climaxed inside me."

I shook my head to clear it. If I could only think clearly. Everything seemed so hazy, so confusing. I took one step and flung the ugly creature off Meadow. It fell against the wall and lay there unmoving.

I looked at Meadow. So lovely and so inviting with her smooth thighs spread open.

Below the thick thatch of hair, her love channel beckoned.

I lay between her inviting thighs and entered her soft vagina.

"Oh Meadow," I moaned and pushed deep into her.

She cried out.

My head was swimming. Crying, I held her lovely body, crushing my chest against her soft breasts.

Meadow screamed something, but the words just wouldn't penetrate. It didn't matter. Nothing would stop me from making love to my sweet, sweet Meadow.

"Meadow, oh, Meadow," I whispered, stroking her lovely face as she stared at me. I looked into her strange colorless eyes, so large and so beautiful. I gave in to the need to climax and poured all my love into her with my gushing seed.

After climaxing, I became suddenly aware of her loud sobs.

"My God, Dan, what have they done to you?"

"I love you, Meadow. I love you so much," I cried and began moving again.

She smiled. "I love you, too, Daniel. But, please, untie me. We'll have much more fun together."

I nodded and pulled out of her. Meadow, my Meadow, always so logical. How could I not love her?

The straps proved easy to untie, and when they were off, I tried to push Meadow back onto the bunk.

She shoved me hard and made me fall backwards. My head hit the wall, and it hurt. "Why are you hurting me, Meadow?" I wailed, feeling the tears streaming down my face.

She looked at me. Then she bent down beside me and held my head between her beautiful breasts. As I searched for her nipple, she rocked back and forth and made soothing sounds. "Oh, Daniel, what happened to you?"

I found her nipple and sucked on it, but no nectar flowed from it. Again, she pushed me away, but gently this time. "We have to get out of here first. Then we can make love again," she said with a choking voice.

"Yes," I said. "Let's do that."

I could hardly wait.

* * * *

I had enough sense left in me to check on the male Stardog before we left the room. He was still unconscious. I searched his body for a pulse and found one at the base of the neck. His heart beat regularly. At least I hadn't killed him.

I wanted to ask Angel for advice on what to do next, but she stayed silent when I spoke to her.

Meadow opened the door carefully. "There are people out there," she whispered, "but we don't have to go past them. I know another way out."

She slipped out of the door. I followed her, keeping an eye on the group in the temple, especially the guard. His eyes were on the girls on the floor. As soon as we were out of sight, we hurried down a wide corridor.

"We'll have to go through this door," Meadow said. "I hope I remembered the right one."

The moment we walked into the room, I knew Meadow had chosen the wrong door. One of the two creatures standing in front of a counter turned as we entered and glared at us out of red eyes. Then it came walking toward us. As I stared at it, something happened to the body. A ripple went through it, the angle of the legs changed. Breasts pushed out the thin material of the gown covering her flat chest.

I looked upon Fara's lovely form.

"Dan Griffin." She smiled. "You shouldn't be here."

Just looking at her made my head spin and my loins pound. "I know," I stammered, "but Meadow said we should get out so we could make love again."

"Oh, really. She said that." Fara smiled, "If you want to make love with someone, do it with me." She let her gown fall to the floor and opened her arms. I looked eagerly at her large, beautiful breasts with the long nipples. So perfect and inviting. I longed to suck on them, quench my thirst.

"No, Dan!" Meadow screamed, but I had already moved into Fara's arms.

We sank to the floor. Her legs opened. I plunged into her pulsing vagina. My mouth fastened on one of her nipples, and the heavenly nectar flowed into my mouth.

Someone tore at me from the back.

"Get off her, Griffin!"

I recognized Meadow's voice. What made her so angry?

"That thing is not human," she screamed.

Oh Meadow, dear Meadow. Neither are you.

"Don't listen to her," Fara whispered. Her hot tight vagina gently sucked on my penis.

An almost unbearable pleasure flooded through my body. I roared as she drank my semen. I grabbed her buttocks and pulled her against me, declaring my pleasure with loud shouts.

When I pulled out of Fara and looked up, I saw Meadow lying on the floor, Tafima standing beside her, a weapon in her hand. She smiled at me. "Don't worry, Dan. I only stunned her."

She came closer. "How about feeding me?" She presented her lovely buttocks and, eagerly, I mounted her from behind, holding her soft hips as I watched my pole vanish inside her hairless cleft.

I heard a commotion. Fara hissed something. I looked up and saw someone in a shiny uniform standing in the open doorway. Fara moved toward the figure. And then something terrible happened. The metal man carried a huge weapon in his hands. He lifted it and aimed it at Fara. A loud noise and a lightening flash and Fara fell, to lie motionless on the floor.

I kept plunging in and out of Tafima, who struggled to get away from me, but I held her tightly. She hissed and turned her face toward me. I almost let go of her when I stared at her red eyes. I couldn't pull out, not yet. My climax was so close.

She screamed and hissed, her body rippling and changing form. But her vagina stayed soft and tight, and I flooded her with my sperm. Even though she struggled in my grip, I felt her sucking on my spurting member.

Then I sank on top of her, still holding her to me.

"What the hell is going on here?" A man's hard voice spoke close to my ear. "Major Griffin, can you hear me?"

I recognized that voice. My friend Kelsey. He had finally come. Why was he shouting at me?

I rose and looked at him. He had opened the front of his visor, and his face looked grim. "Nothing is going on here, Kelsey, except we are making love." I gazed at the still form of Fara. "You spoiled it now," I said accusingly.

Tafima stirred and managed to squirm out from under me. Somehow, her face had changed, and she stared with red eyes at Kelsey. The tendrils around her mouth moved like tiny serpents.

"Since when do you enjoy coupling with alien creatures, Major?" Kelsey asked.

The lines of Tafima's body smoothed out. Her face changed back into the lovely face I had come to love. She smiled at Kelsey and moved her lower body suggestively. "Come, Kelsey," she said, opening her arms. "There is no need for violence. Take off your armor, and I will give you great pleasure. The same pleasure I gave your friend Dan."

Kelsey stepped back, snapping down the visor of his helmet. "I'll be damned," he cursed. "Another shape shifter." He leveled his weapon at Tafima. "Stay as you are. One wrong move and you will join your companion. Except this time I will shoot to kill."

Tafima turned to me. "You tell him, Dan, how much you enjoy coupling with me. Tell him."

Poor Tafima. Kelsey has never liked women. I shook my head. "It's no use, Tafima. Kelsey has no need for a woman."

"Never mind, Major," Kelsey snapped. "I sure as hell don't have to explain myself to a Stardog." He looked thoughtfully at Tafima. "What have you done to Major Griffin? Why is he behaving so strangely?"

She chuckled and reached for me.

Kelsey raised his weapon. "Stay put or I'll burn you right now!"

"I think not." Tafima smiled. "Because if you do, your Major is also dead."

"How?"

When she laughed throatily, I felt my penis rise. Touching her breast, I pulled her close.

"You see," Tafima said. "He is completely addicted to me. Every time he put his sexual organ into mine, he absorbed some of my secretions. And I fed him through my mouth and breasts to make him my love-slave forever." She rubbed her buttocks against me, rolling my hard pole between her soft cheeks.

Then she bent forward and spread her legs. With a moan, I slid my aching member into her creamy pussy.

"Bitch!" Kelsey cursed. "I should kill you for this!"

She laughed and moved her pelvis in a gyrating motion. "You should try this, Kelsey. I guarantee you will love it. Right, Dan?"

I grunted and held her wide hips, while I moved in and out of her tight slit. I didn't care about Kelsey, not at this moment. All I wanted to do was fuck…fuck…fuck.

Even though the hot yielding pulsating flesh in front of me held my conscious mind ensnared, I did register when Meadow stirred on the floor and sat up. I heard her call out when she became aware of Kelsey. "Am I glad to see you, Kelsey." Then she looked at me and moaned. "My God! Is he still going at it?" Her voice rose. "Can't you stop this, Kelsey?"

Kelsey shook his head. "I don't know how, Meadow. He seems completely controlled. We have to get him out of here and put him on the Med-doc…"

The rest of what he said was drowned out as I reached my climax. Tafima bucked and milked my spurting member, the soft walls of her vagina squeezing with just the right pressure, rippling over my penis at just the perfect speed. The gentle sucking of her blood-drawing tendrils masked by the pleasure I experienced.

As I slowly relaxed, I heard Meadow's voice. "This is obscene, Kelsey. I can't bear to watch it any longer. He is totally out of his mind, obsessed with sex, and this bitch seems to enjoy it as much as he does."

Tafima laughed, her sex-organ still sucking on my penis. "Of course I enjoy it. He doesn't only satisfy my sexual hunger, which I admit is great, he also stills my craving for food."

"Food?" Meadow echoed.

"Blood," Tafima replied. "I drink his blood."

Meadow cursed, reached for Kelsey's weapon and aimed it at Tafima.

Chapter Twenty

The bulky body of Killic blocked the doorway.

"Everything under control, Sergeant?" Kelsey asked.

Killic had his visor open. Even in my befuddled state, I could see the concern in his blue eyes. "Are you all right, Major?" he asked me.

"Don't bother asking him, Killic," Meadow said. "He'll tell you everything is fine." She gave Tafima's unconscious body a kick. "Bitch!" she cursed.

"I *am* fine," I said. "Maybe just a little confused and tired." I grinned and winked. "I've been busy."

"You see," Meadow said.

"Did you bring it?" Kelsey asked.

"I did." Killic walked up to me and pressed something cool into my neck. "Give it a moment, Major," he said. "The D.I.D.A. said it should work."

Something happened. I experienced a moment of disorientation, and then the fog that enveloped my mind lifted. I became aware of my body's systems.

Welcome back, Major Griffin. Angel's voice sounded clearer than ever.

Looking around, I saw the still bodies of Tafima and Fara on the floor. I registered their steadily beating pulse and knew they were alive. Killic and Kelsey watched me silently. Meadow held her breath beside me, an anxious look on her drawn face.

I grinned at them. "*Now* I'm fine. Glad to see you, men." Looking for my clothing, I found them where I had carelessly dropped them onto the floor. "I think I'd like to get dressed now," I said and glanced at Meadow's naked body. "You should, too, even though I don't mind looking at that luscious form of yours."

Meadow sighed and smiled. "Yes, he's back to normal." Then she picked up one of the discarded gowns. "A little flimsy," she commented, "but this will have to do."

177

When we walked into the temple area, I saw a couple of uniformed soldiers guarding the group of naked women and the Acolytes. The guard lay motionless on the floor. I didn't detect any life signs and knew he was dead. His body had reverted to his original form.

"I see you brought reinforcement," I commented.

"We did," Killic said. "The new team of Special Forces on Redsky. We figured it might do the new recruits some good getting first hand experience in the war against the Stardogs. And we needed the manpower."

I walked over to the guard and picked up his weapon. "Has the base been secured?" I asked.

"Not yet," Kelsey answered. "There are many levels here and many pockets of resistance. The upper two levels are secure."

"The control room and the spaceship?"

"Secure. No one leaves without our permission," Killic growled.

"Did you have problems getting in?"

"Very few. We took them by surprise. We were close by when we received the orders to proceed." Killic spoke with a brisk voice, his body still in combat mode.

"Have you found Ninca?" I asked him.

"Yes, along with the other girls," he said. "They're safe."

"Good."

We took the elevator up to the next level, the one with the laboratories and pregnant women. A number of armed soldiers walked between the beds, a precaution I agreed with, even though I knew we didn't face any danger from these women. They seemed confused and upset. Some were crying. Some just sat silently watching us as we walked past.

"These are still humans," I said to my men, "but the young ones in the other rooms aren't."

"Stardogs?" Kelsey asked.

I shook my head. "Hybrids. We have to figure out what to do with them."

"Purge all of them?" He asked with a cold and detached voice.

"Can't do that," I told him. "They are partially human."

"What about the Stardogs?"

"The ones who don't resist, we'll let them live. For now."

I knew I had a tough decision to make, one that wouldn't make me many friends and would create much criticism. But whatever I decided, it would be my decision and I would have to live with it. Right now was not the time to think about it.

* * * *

Looking down at the alien still body of what once had been Marc Cleaver, I turned to McClaren. "You must have known his true identity."

He shrugged. "So what?"

I walked up to him and stared into his eyes. "You're a human, for heaven's sake, MacClaren. What did you think they were up to?"

"I saw a business opportunity and took it. Like I told you once, I am underpaid and overworked." He grinned. I felt like smashing my fist into his smooth face.

"Aren't we all." I looked at Niels DePratt who returned my look with a defiant expression. "And what is your excuse for being involved in this, *old friend*?"

"I thought you said we weren't friends?" He smiled sourly. "You seem to have all the cards in your hand, *Major* Dan Griffin, with the powers of the Mighty Empire backing you up. I liked you better when you were just plain Dan Griffin. We should have killed you after we put the knife to Garth and smashed in the skull of your native friend Threehorn. We could have saved a lot of trouble."

It took a moment to register what he had said. "You killed Garth?"

He laughed. "Not me, but a mutual friend did. Garth was in the way, and so were you. However, I enjoyed killing that loudmouth Threehorn. He and his big plans!" He spat. "Those savages should all be wiped off the face of Redsky. You think you signed a treaty with Callawhan? Stop fooling yourself, Griffin. The natives will never stick to the agreements." He sneered. "My friends and I will see to it."

It was my turn to sneer. "I'm afraid you'll be out of the picture for a long time. I will personally make sure that you end up on a prison planet that is worse than the hell you had in mind for me."

"You'll never be able to prove that I had anything to do with Garth's murder. And nobody gives a damn about that savage Threehorn."

"I do," I said. "He was my friend. You forget one thing. Right now, I am the ultimate authority on Redsky. My word is law. I am judge and jury. In front of my men as witnesses, I charge you, Lieutenant Niels DePratt, with the murder of Garth Oshinsky and sentence you to life in prison. You will be shipped to a prison planet of my choice."

"You can't do that, Griffin!" he shouted. "You crazy bastard. I should have killed you when I had the chance."

"I guess you should have," I said coldly.

"I didn't act alone. There were two others, who are just as guilty. In fact, I wasn't the one who pushed the knife into Garth's heart." He gave me a calculating look. "What if I tell you who the others were?"

I had to laugh. "DePratt," I said, "I already know who they are. Besides, you will tell us what we are still missing as soon as we hook you up to our computer. You will spill every little detail of what happened that day, things even you don't remember."

"I protest. I am the son of the Prime Minister. You can't treat me like this. I demand a lawyer and a legitimate judge. You have no right to connect me to any computer without my lawyer's or my consent. I know my rights."

"The only rights you have are the ones I allow you. You're lucky I don't have you court-martialed and executed right here. Now, shut up, DePratt, I have things to do." I turned to Kelsey, who had said nothing. He didn't have to. His cold eyes said enough. "Take these two into custody. If they try to escape, shoot them."

"Will do, Major," Kelsey smiled grimly and addressed the two soldiers with us. "You heard the Major. Take them up into the skimmer and keep them under guard at all times."

Both men saluted and proceeded to put handcuffs on DePratt and McClaren. Then they led them away.

I sighed and glanced at Kelsey. "Maybe I *should* have shot him. His father, Prime Minister Sir Chales, will do his best to save his son."

"You're not a cold-blooded murderer, sir," Kelsey said, "even though that would be the best solution."

Looking after the two soldiers, I said, "I noticed they're carrying lasers."

"It was my call," Kelsey admitted, "but the D.I.D.A. approved it."

"The D.I.D.A.," I said, smiling. In my mind, I saw a beautiful woman, not the shimmering wall and blinking lights Kelsey probably thought of when he spoke of the Digital Intelligence Data Analyzer. "She seems to make all the decisions lately."

I'm just doing what I was designed for. Her voice startled and surprised me. I looked at Kelsey and realized then that she had spoken inside my head. Before I could make a comment, she said, *No need to speak aloud. Just think what you want to say, Major. I'm connected to your nervous system and will be able to receive your thoughts.*

I'm not going to ask how you're doing this, Angel, but I'm not happy about it. I said in my mind. *Can you read my thoughts?*

Only the ones you're consciously thinking of, but I am aware of everything you say and see. This was the only way, Daniel. Just remember, only I receive this information, and I decide what others will be able to access. Also, remember, I'm just a machine.

I'm not convinced of that, I replied, not sure if I liked having my privacy violated like this. Her silvery laughter inside my head didn't help matters. She withdrew, but I knew she was still there, inside my head, watching and evaluating everything I said and did. I vowed to have a good talk with her and Professor Goldblat when I got back to headquarters.

The arrival of Killic and a number of black-clad soldiers carrying lasers interrupted my thoughts.

"We're in control of the base, Major," Killic reported.

"Good," I said. "Now I want to have a look at that spaceship."

* * * *

We discovered a number of alien skimmers in one of the upper caverns, larger and more sophisticated than any of the skimmers used on Redsky. I decided to add them to our small fleet.

Until a decision could be made what to do with the hybrids, they would stay at the alien base, under the watchful eyes of a selected team of our newly recruited Special Forces.

We assembled all of the surviving Stardogs in one of the meeting rooms. Most of them were scientists and lab technicians. I was surprised though by the large number of guards and soldiers, even though half of them had been killed when our forces stormed their base.

"What are you planning to do with us?"

I looked at Tafima, glad to see her and Fara among the survivors. Some of the Stardogs reverted to their original form, finding no need to carry on with the masquerade, but Tafima kept her human appearance. She looked as beautiful and bewitching as the first day I laid eyes on her. I found it difficult to think of her as anything but human.

"We will let you live," I assured her. "We are not ruthless killers. Our mission here is to initiate good will between our species, not start a war. You will be allowed to leave this planet and join your people in your Mothership." I smiled when I saw her startled expression. "Oh, yes, we know about the ship hidden on one of the moons."

She chuckled and gave me a calculating look. "You act so confident, Major Griffin. What makes you think we won't attack and destroy your spaceport in Newland once we're safely back on our ship? We could do that. We do have superior weapons."

"So do we." I said, smiling grimly. "Be warned. Don't judge the Terran Empire by the conditions you found on this planet. You may discover a grave error."

"I admit, we underestimated your abilities, but let me give you a warning also. Because of our own overconfidence, you managed to surprise us. It won't happen again."

She came close and looked into my eyes. "We may not be of the same species, but I did feel a certain attraction toward you, Dan Griffin. Neither one of us can help being what nor who we are. We might be monsters in your eyes. We're not. Just different."

When she lifted up to kiss me, Meadow, who stood beside me, put a hand between us. "Touch him, and you won't have to worry about ever being surprised again, bitch!" she hissed, anger clouding her voice.

Tafima laughed and stared at Meadow. "You may look almost human, but you're as alien to him as I am. So fuck him as long as you can, until he tires of you and drops you for a real human woman, bitch."

I had to give Meadow credit for controlling her hot temper. A catfight between two women, alien or not, was the last thing I needed now. It would have been good for entertainment, though.

"Watch your tongue," was all Meadow said, her voice almost a growl.

"Please, join your fellow prisoners," I said to Tafima.

Smiling wickedly, she walked back to her place among the others.

I turned to Kelsey. "Has their ship been swept for weapons?"

"Yes, sir. We disabled all their weapons systems."

"Good. Let them board. The sooner they're gone, the happier I'll be." Looking at their large number, I knew they'd be packed like sardines, but their ship did have the capacity to take them all in one trip. "Tomorrow I want to take one of our newly inherited skimmers and pay a visit to the Grand Minister of Isram."

* * * *

Grand Minister Abdul Hakam was not the happiest man on Redsky when I told him that his lovely wife Tafima didn't belong to the human race.

"I still can't believe she fooled me for five years," he said, shaking his head. "How is that possible?"

"The Stardogs have perfected the art of mimicking other species. It is part of their survival."

"And you're saying these Stardogs had a base on one of the islands in the Bay of Songs?"

"For at least twenty years."

"What made them choose Isram?"

"Not only Isram, Grand Minister," I assured him. "We've eradicated another of their bases in the mountains of Dangar and discovered one deep in the jungles of the unexplored territories west of Ariba."

Hakam put his hands over his face. "It is partly my fault. I should never have allowed Koldar to become the Grand Marshal of Isram's military forces. I should have investigated the activities in the Royal Temple. I never even knew that my own wife was the High Priestess." He looked deep into my eyes. "I was a fool, Major Griffin. Her exceptional beauty and her manipulative skills blinded me." He sighed. "Getting old makes a man complacent. Maybe I made a mistake not insisting my son be the one to be the next Grand Minister."

"It is never too late, your Excellency."

"Thank you, Major Griffin, for delivering my country and my people from the evil that held us in its grip and preventing a devastating conflict with the rest of Redsky. How can we ever redeem ourselves?"

"You already have, your Excellency, by allowing me into your home and letting me be the instrument of your redemption. By the way, where is Koldar? And what happened to Lawni, Tafima's sister?"

"They both disappeared." The old man chuckled. "The rumors are already surfacing. This morning several of Koldar's followers reported that he told them Allar called him home. Then he sprouted a pair of wings right in front of them and left the temple through an open window. They're already proclaiming him a god."

"God Koldar." I grinned. "It does have a nice ring to it."

He looked at me gravely. "I don't see the humor in this, Major Griffin. That creature has done a lot of damage to our faith by introducing new doctrines and ceremonies. There is nothing in our Holy Books about hating others of a different faith and nothing about cleansing this planet of the *Unbelievers*. The true followers of Mislan practice love between each other, but they don't have sexual orgies in the temple. They don't introduce virgins into the faith through the actual joining of bodies on an altar. Our clergy abstain from sex, alcohol and drugs."

"My apologies, your Excellency." I bowed my head. "I didn't mean to offend you or your faith. I'm not a member of any religious group and I don't believe in any gods, especially the man-made ones."

"You must feel very lonely and lost sometimes, Major." His old eyes twinkled. "Who do you talk to when you feel despair or when you're seeking answers?"

I laughed. "I'm talking to an entity I call Angel."

"An angel? Do you ever get answers?"

"All the time." I laughed again. "I'm working on getting this angel out of my mind actually."

He looked at me, not comprehending, but I didn't elaborate. He wouldn't understand the technology anyway. Besides, he had enough worries. No need to tell him that one of my men was busy installing tiny spy-devices in his palace and in the temple.

A new god had arrived. In this case, a goddess, and her name was Dida.

D.I.D.A.

Digital Intelligence Data Analyzer.

All-knowing and all-seeing.

Her laughter suddenly rang through my head.

I'm not a goddess, Dan. I'm only an angel.

Chapter Twenty-one

Sometimes it is difficult to understand the way fate works. Ten years can seem like a long time, but finding myself sitting in the seat usually occupied by a judge, took my memory back to a time when I sat on the other side.

Looking over the people on the benches before me, I found it ironic that Mayor Castor Margin sat in the same spot I occupied ten years ago.

It seemed like just yesterday.

It was also refreshing to see a courtroom without lawyers and legal advocates.

As if reading my mind, Margin called out, "Where is my attorney? I want my attorney present. You have no right to treat me this way. I am a respected citizen of Newland, and I'm also the mayor of Old Town."

"I want to talk to my father, the Prime Minister," Niels DePratt chimed in.

"I also didn't get a chance to talk to my legal council. Have you forgotten that I am a senator, Griffin?"

I looked at him coldly. "You will address me as Major Griffin, Senator Clarke. To answer your question, you will all get a chance to talk to your legal council. After the trial."

"That is totally unacceptable," Clarke yelled. "I know my rights. This is not the way it is done. I haven't even been told what the charges are."

"Neither have I," a man sitting beside him spoke up.

I looked at the man. He was big and overweight, with a round, red face. The small goatee looked out of place on his fat chin. I didn't know him personally, but I had his file in front of me. It was impressive.

I shrugged mentally. Might as well start with him. "Would you please state your name, sir?"

He drew himself erect. "I am Enrico Sanchez."

"What do you do for a living, sir?"

"I am in the import and export business."

"And what do you import and export?"

"Exotic spices, health foods and medicines."

"How about slaves?"

"I don't deal in slaves."

I made it a point to look at McClaren who sat not far from him to his right. "My sources say otherwise."

"Your sources are wrong. I'm a legitimate business man." Sanchez noticed me looking at McClaren and turned his head, hissing something under his breath. My enhanced hearing picked it up, of course. *"You're dead, McClaren!"*

I made a show of opening his file, an unnecessary gesture, because I had memorized the contents of each one. "How about assassinations?"

His head came up. He stared at me. "What?"

"Your heard me, Sanchez. I asked you if you dealt in assassinations?"

"Of course not. Besides, you can't prove anything. You're fishing."

Closing the file, I said, "There is no need to waste this court's time playing word games with you or your fancy lawyers. I know who you are, Enrico Sanchez. You are the head of the criminal organization known as *The Winged Serpent*. I am charging you with kidnapping, illegal slave trading, conspiracy to murder, and murder." I looked at him. "Normally I would have you executed within twenty-four hours, but that would be too merciful. You will spend the rest of your life digging for minerals in a dark mine on one of the Empire's prison planets, without parole." I brought my gavel down.

He stared at me, his face white with anger and disbelief. "I know about you, Griffin," he said between clenched teeth. "You're nothing but a thug hiding behind a badge you don't deserve. Too bad you weren't with your parents when I blew your father's brain out and strangled your mother with her own scarf. I think I would have enjoyed squeezing your scrawny neck until your eyes popped."

A cold shiver ran down my back. It took all of my control not to override the damping impulses of my security system that prevented me from drilling a hole between his little pig's eyes.

"Take him away!" I ordered the security men guarding the prisoners, my voice as icy as my brain.

My eyes fell on Slovinsky. He looked back at me, and he must have seen the coldness and fury in my eyes, because he seemed to shrink in his seat.

"Stanislaus Slovinsky, you are a Chief of Police. The citizens of Old Town put their trust in you to protect them from criminals. You, sir, have committed the most heinous crime. You became a criminal, prying on innocent and unsuspecting victims. You may not have directly killed someone, but as a high-ranking member of the organization known as *The Winged Serpent,* you are guilty by association. I sentence you to twenty years, without parole. You will serve your sentence on one of the Empire's prison planets."

"I do not accept that sentence." He had problems formulating his response, stumbling over the words. "You have no proof of anything. This is an illegal court."

"This courtroom has temporarily been declared territory of the Terran Empire. Redsky laws don't apply here," I told him. Then I looked around the courtroom. "Before I carry on with the charges, I will explain the proceedings. New methods of establishing guilt or innocence have eliminated the need for time-consuming investigations and dealing with advocates. The Empire uses sophisticated computers to scan the brain of an accused."

I paused to let it sink in.

"You have been scanned. Anything you remember has been extracted from your mind and recorded. If you've committed a crime, it is in your file." I padded the stack on my desk. "Right here."

"Then you must know I'm not guilty of murder," McClaren said into the silence.

"I know you haven't killed anyone directly, but you are not innocent, Inspector. What makes your crimes worse is the fact that you are a citizen of the Empire in a trusted position. You are supposed to uphold the law, not break it. You must pay the price."

It is no easy thing to be judge and jury, and I did not enjoy what I knew needed to be done. The faces of Lane and her little daughter, my daughter, appeared like ghostly images inside my mind's eye as I looked at the man before me. They would hate me for what I had to do.

"Castor Margin." I spoke without emotion. I could not let personal feelings cloud my ability to think clearly. "You are charged with murder and conspiracy to commit murder…"

Chapter Twenty-two

The huge screen displayed the three-dimensional image of the alien spaceship. Despite its size, the Stardogs had done an excellent job of camouflaging it against the bleak rocky landscape of the moon. As we watched, a smaller craft approached the hidden ship and entered it through an opening that suddenly appeared in the side of the larger vessel.

The image blurred, and then we seemed to be inside the alien spaceship, floating above the shuttle, which had entered the huge ship's belly. A door opened in the shuttle, spilling a great number of aliens into the cargo bay.

Even though I didn't see any human shapes, I knew these were the Stardogs we had expelled from Redsky.

"This was recorded twenty days ago," Professor Goldblat explained. "With the help of our spy-drones, we've been monitoring their activities inside their ship." He smiled. "We've learned a great deal about the habits of the Stardogs in their natural environment. Our engineers are ecstatic and are drooling over their discoveries."

The image on the screen blurred again and changed back to the view of the satellite from space.

"We don't know what they're planning. Obviously, they've decided not to leave." Professor Goldblat looked at us, his eyes fastened on me. "Major Griffin, I must congratulate you on the excellent execution of your mission, but your job on Redsky is done. It is my duty to inform you that as of now you've been relieved of your position. Anything that happens from now on is not your responsibility."

He saluted me and looked at a woman coming through the doorway. Dressed in the black loose uniform of the Empire's ruling elite, she looked like one of the princesses, except I knew she wasn't a princess.

She smiled at me, her eyes locking with mine, as she walked into the room.

"Hello, Major Griffin. Surprised to see me?"

I could do nothing but stare. Even the loose uniform couldn't hide her generous curves, and I questioned her reasons for choosing this appearance.

You'll have to learn to control your thoughts, Daniel. They're wide open to me. Her silent laughter echoed inside my head. *Maybe I just like looking like this.*

"Gentlemen, meet Dida," Professor Goldblat said, beaming.

I heard Killic exhaling beside me. "Dida?" he said. "Are you talking about the Digital Intelligence Data Analyzer?"

I'd never seen the Professor so gleeful. "That's right, Sergeant Killic. Dida, in the flesh, so to speak." He chuckled. "Actually, not really in the flesh, but you'd never know, unless you'd try to touch her." He went over to the woman and made a motion as if touching her shoulder. His hand went right through her body.

"That tickles, Professor," Dida said merrily.

"It tickles!" Professor Goldblat grinned like a kid with a cookie. "She's a hologram, but more sophisticated than anything we've been able to do so far. I'm hoping some day to create an image as solid as a real person. It's really nothing more than compressing a bunch of molecules. I just haven't figured out how to do it."

Dida walked up to me and stood in front of me. Reaching out, she put a finger against my forehead. "Do you feel this, Major?" she asked.

A small shockwave ran through my body. Even this close she looked real.

"Touch me," she said softly.

I pulled my hand back when I felt the resistance of a solid body. "What the hell!"

Leaning forward, she kissed me on the lips. They felt warm and soft. And real.

"It's just a matter of manipulating your implants," she whispered. Her warm breath caressed my face.

I put my arms around her, but she stepped back, right through the circle of my arms.

The tiny computer in my chest dampened the angry impulse rising up inside me. *Why are all the women in my life teasing bitches?* I asked silently. *Even you...and you're a machine.*

Perhaps it's your attitude toward women, Daniel.

She stood beside the Professor, suddenly all business. "As Professor Goldblat told you, Major Griffin, your position has been terminated, and you will not be held responsible for coming events. From now on, I will make all of the decisions and recommendations. After evaluating the situation with the Stardogs, I have decided what must be done, and all the responsibility for possible future repercussions and consequences this action may bring lies with me."

She turned to look at the screen.

"What you are looking at here is a live image of the alien vessel. As you see, the Stardogs ignored our order to leave this system. The Professor told you about our spy-drones aboard their ship. I've recorded and studied their activities for twenty days. I've concluded that the Stardogs are going to attack this base and all of Redsky's military installations within forty-eight hours. Obviously, we cannot allow this to happen. I recommended a pre-emptive strike."

"Meaning what?" I asked, with a sudden feeling of dread.

"We will destroy the Stardog's ship, therefore eliminating the threat it poses to this planet and the Terran Empire."

Meadow, who hadn't said a word until now, asked, "How will you accomplish that task? I don't think our small battle cruiser is capable of attacking them."

Dida smiled. Looking at her made me forget that she was not a real person, but only a projected computer image.

"We did prepare for this eventuality. Back at the Stardog's base on the island, I had a small bomb installed inside the alien space shuttle."

"A small bomb?" I said sharply. "Without my knowledge and without consulting me?"

"You were in no condition to make such decision, Major Griffin." Dida didn't raise her voice, but she sounded suddenly cold and almost metallic. "It is out of your hands."

I lifted my shoulders in resignation, realizing that I had lost my temporary throne. A king no more.

"The detonation of the bomb will open a hole in the side of the large vessel. It will also trigger the explosion of the specially designed spy-drones I've attached to critical components throughout the Mothership. A chain reaction will rip the ship apart in the space of sixty seconds, resulting in the destruction of the alien ship within three minutes and twenty-five seconds."

Only a cold computer mind could talk about this with such efficiency and calculation.

What about the hundreds of living intelligent beings living inside the protective giant metal shell? In my mind's eye, I saw the lovely bodies of Tafima and Fara ripped apart.

They're not human, Daniel. Angel's soft voice said inside my head.

"Damn you!" I cursed loudly. "At least they're flesh and blood, unlike you."

I registered the astonished looks of the others. Meadow put a hand on my arm. "Easy, Dan."

As I stared at the screen in front of me, a huge white hole appeared in the spaceship of the Stardogs, and then a shudder went though the body of the giant vessel. Moments later the world screen lit up as the ship exploded.

Dida had been right. Everything was over in three minutes and twenty-five seconds. Large chunks of debris began settling back onto the satellite's rugged surface, floating like feathers in the low gravity. Smaller pieces might escape into space to travel throughout eternity or until they were captured by the gravity of a planet, just to burn up in its dense atmosphere.

We are not ruthless killers.

No, Tafima, we're not. We just blow up property. Too bad, if you happen to be inside.

I watched Dida as she walked toward me.

"I knew you couldn't do it, Major. That's why I made the decision to relieve you of your post. You're right. You're not a ruthless killer. I am, but I'm only a machine." Before she walked away, she said, "Just remember, they would have had no compunction to destroy us."

I stared after her. She never reached the door. Her body dissolved in front of my eyes.

Good bye, Daniel, she said inside my head.

"Good bye, Angel," I whispered. She knew I would have my implant removed as soon as possible, severing our intimate connection.

Somehow I felt regret over my decision.

Epilogue

Even though my position had been terminated, my assignment on Redsky was still in effect, my services still needed.

Koldar had disappeared. With his ability to change his appearance, he could be anyone and anywhere. We had no knowledge as to how many others of his kind hid among the population of Isram and the rest of Redsky.

In addition, how many hybrids? We had no way to find out.

With the Mothership of the Stardogs gone, much of the threat to Redsky had been eliminated. The surviving Stardogs would be careful and stay undercover.

Our spy-satellites discovered one of their labs hidden deep in the jungles on the other side of the planet. An air strike to destroy it would be ineffective. Like the base on the island, a highly sophisticated detection system and powerful anti-aircraft missiles probably protected it.

Should they try to escape with their space shuttle, which they surely must have hidden somewhere, we could blow them out of space with our battle cruiser. They wouldn't be stupid enough to leave their base. To get to them we had only one recourse, travel across the surface of Redsky.

However, that would have to wait for a while.

Dida created a new branch of Special Services, a new brand of soldiers for Redsky. There were plenty of volunteers, not all of them qualified.

When we came to Redsky, we brought with us a small team of surgeon-technicians, capable of turning a regular soldier into a super-soldier.

None of them would be like the five of us. They would be better. Dida had learned a lot by studying us. She'd make sure none of them would turn out like me.

I turned down her offer to improve my implants and make me more effective.

"Thank you," I told her. "I'd like to keep the little bit of humanity I still have left."

She put Killic in command of the new team, but only until she decided to replace him.

The big blond man grinned at me from across the table. "I love this place, Major," he said, looking around the room. "Reminds me of the tavern I frequented when I was young and immature."

"What makes you think you're mature now?" Cherryh laughed and downed another glass of Whisk. "By the way, how are things going with you and that little girl?"

"You mean Ninca? Fine. I'm planning to propose to her."

"Are you sure that's a wise decision?" I asked. "What if we get orders to leave?"

He gave me a long look. "I've been thinking about that, Major. I'm afraid I won't join you on any new assignments. My position as commander of Special Forces is only temporary, and as soon as I'm relieved of my post, I'm going to resign."

"You're a soldier, man," Cherryh said. "What will you do? What can you do? You don't know anything else."

"I've saved enough money to allow for a comfortable living. And I will get a small pension." He smiled. "I think I deserve that much. Besides, I'm quite handy with fixing things. Shouldn't be difficult to find a job here."

"You can always join the police force," Kelsey suggested, starring into his glass of water.

The man still didn't know how to have fun.

"I'll be sorry to see you leave the team," I said, "but you must know what is best for you."

"What about you, Major?" Cherryh asked.

"Me?" I shrugged. "I guess I'll just wait until I get new orders."

"That's not what I mean." Cherryh waved to the bartender, who came waddling over, that wide grin still frozen in his pudgy round face. "Bring us another bottle, Armand."

The bartender nodded. "Right away, sir." His small eyes locked with mine. I gave him a wink, and he cringed. He still hadn't forgiven me for calling him *Moonface* the first time I visited his place.

"I like him," Cherryh said, watching the fat man shuffle away.

I sighed. "This place isn't the same without old Miguel. I miss him and the old days."

"Speaking of 'the old days', is there a chance you'll be getting together with your wife?" Cherryh asked.

"She isn't my wife anymore. Our marriage has been annulled." I shook my head. "If she had any love left for me, it is gone now. I'm responsible for jailing her husband."

"He is a criminal."

"Not in her eyes. She loved him."

"And what about Aleethy, the other girl?" Killic grinned.

I smiled, remembering the night at her ranch. "I love her, but not like that," I said.

"Why are you bothering the Major with all these questions?" Kelsey said. "We all know he and Meadow are an item." He turned his head and looked at the opening door. "Speaking of the devil…"

Meadow marched in, a sour look on her face. "I hate that damn machine!" she spat.

"You must be talking about Dida," Cherryh said and chuckled. "Have a seat Lieutenant."

Meadow pulled over a chair from one of the other tables and sat down beside me. Then she grabbed the bottle of Whisky and poured a glass. "That bitch can go to hell!"

"She's still talking about Dida."

Meadow's strange colorless eyes flashed angrily. "Shut up, Cherryh!"

"What's the problem?" I asked.

"That…that…thing walking around pretending to be a woman, wants me to leave with the next ship. Apparently, my *talents* are needed elsewhere." She stared at me. "Do you want me to go, Dan?"

"You should know the answer to that one, Meadow. My thoughts have always been open to you. Of course I don't want you to go."

Her hand touched my face. "I needed to hear you say it." She smiled. "I don't ever want to leave you, Daniel."

"Wow!" Killic exclaimed. "I guess you were right, Kelsey."

"Right about what?" Meadow demanded. "Have you been talking about me behind my back?"

"Only good things," Cherryh assured her, grinning. "We wouldn't dare say anything else behind your back."

"That's right," Killic said. "We all know your temper."

"Oh, just be silent, all of you." Meadow looked around the table. "Where is Wu?"

"I sent him and my young driver Anton to Neh-mar."

Meadow searched my face, a question in her eyes. Then she nodded and smiled. "I should have been the one delivering Aika to her aunt in Neh-mar. After all, her father put her under my protection."

"You did make a good-looking *Windsister*," I said, grinning. "Unfortunately, you were a fake. However, Cerbus didn't know that. He put his faith in you."

She sighed. "Funny thing about faith. All those people in Isram. How could they let the Stardogs fool them like that?"

"Fanatics, especially religious ones, are much easier to influence and control than the *Unbelievers*, because they already believe in a higher power and a better life after this one. If someone with charisma and hypnotic powers comes along, shows them miracles, and almost guarantees them a better life, they will follow willingly. However, much of what has been rumored about Isram was just that, rumors. Most of the citizens of Isram don't want to start a Holy War. They want to live in peace like everyone else and practice their faith, which should be their right."

"Nice speech, Dan," Meadow said. "Are you running for office? I hear the job of Chief of Police in Old Town is still available."

I grinned. "Maybe Killic wants it. He's planning to leave the team, get married and settle down on Redsky."

"I know." Meadow looked at the big blond man. "Don't disappoint that sweet little girl, Sergeant. She loves you, you know."

"I know she does."

"Well, here's to Love," Cherryh said, lifting his glass.

"To Love," Kelsey echoed.

"You'll have to learn to drink something stronger than plain water, Kelsey," Killic said. "Come, live a little."

Meadow's hand stole into mine. When I looked at her, she smiled. "And love a little," her lips mouthed.

I squeezed her hand.

It felt good to be among friends.

The End